THAT WASN'T IN THE SCRIPT

D1453874

THAT WASN'T IN THE SCRIPT

SARAH AINSLEE

BOW'S
BOOKSHELF

EBook ISBN: 979-8-88716-016-0

Trade Paperback ISBN: 979-8-88716-014-6

Hardcover ISBN: 979-8-88716-015-3

Cover artwork and design by Amber Liu

Published by Bow's Bookshelf, Inc.

Join our Bow's Bookshelf Reader's Club for new projects, deals, and giveaways. Sign up at Bowsbookshelf.com.

To everyone who still believes in happily ever afters. Regardless of the plot twists.

"The best thing I know is to do exactly what you wish for a while."

—*Roman Holiday* (1953)

CHAPTER 1
JOSIE

I KNEW I wanted to become a screenwriter the day I realized romance is dead. At least the version of romance I'd always envisioned in my head. The kind you would see in old movies that would leave you with that fuzzy, swooning, clutch your pearls, *why can't a guy kiss me the way he's kissing Audrey Hepburn* feeling.

Picture it: A thirteen-year-old, underdeveloped Josie, spending a lazy, rainy Sunday afternoon with her family watching *Dirty Dancing* for the seven-zillionth time. I arise from my cocoon of decorative throw pillows and proudly declare my objective career path to my father and then seven-year-old sister, Prudence.

"Is this because everyone in this movie is unrealistic and perfect?" Pru asks.

"No, but that is an astute observation."

"What's an astute?"

"It means 'that's true' in Josephine," my dad would laugh. "Besides, Johnny Castle is far from perfect."

"Are you talking about *Dirty Dancing*?" My mother, the embodiment of unrealistic and perfect, would ask as she bounded across the living room holding a basket of freshly folded laundry. "I love this movie! I had the biggest crush on Patrick Swayze as a kid!"

"Told you!" Pru boasted with annoying matter-of-fact arrogance.

I tossed myself back onto the spray of pillows behind me and sunk down deep with a groan. "Not the point, guys! Don't you just wish movies about romance were more... romantic? Like Johnny and Baby? Or how they all used to be?"

Pru would roll her eyes in disgust, tossing a handful of cold, cardboard popcorn at my face. "You're such a grandma, Josie. Real love doesn't work like that."

"You're seven. You don't know anything about real love."

She'd proudly push her dark-rimmed glasses up her broad nose. "At least I know Johnny and Baby aren't real."

"Neither is Santa Claus." I'd crudely stick out my tongue as her freckled smug grin melted into unadulterated horror.

"Santa's not real?! Daddy, is she lying?!"

I definitely got grounded for that, but it hardly mattered. From that point on, my future was set. Most girls my age possessed normal aspirations, dreaming of becoming doctors or teachers. I wanted to create stories that gave people hope of finding their own happy endings someday. A story identical to my parents. They had the meet-cute nineties movies were made about. How was I expected not to have high standards?

The scene was set: My mother had been living in Manhattan for all of seventeen hours when she was catching a Q-train to a modeling audition and nearly fell off the platform in her four-inch heels. Enter, my father, standing beside her with his face in a textbook, pulling her into his arms as the oncoming train came to a screeching halt. Dad gave her his number and asked her to call him later to make sure she was alright. A year later, they were married, they got pregnant six seconds after that, and the rest was happily ever after at its finest.

Almost.

"Hey Josie!" Mom calls to me from the bedroom. "Can you come help me with something?"

I toss my half-finished homework onto the floor and swing my legs off the side of my bed. The inconspicuous hissing noise coming from a zipper being pulled open and shut already tells me exactly what my mother needs. I heave a defeated sigh.

Every great story arc has this thing called negative value, a climactic moment of either success or failure that changes the main character's life forever. For our family, it came in stages. The first being when Dad walked in the door from work one night and proudly announced: "We're moving back to New York!"

Dad was a lawyer for a massive immigration firm right outside of Cincinnati. One of his old superiors had recommended him as the head of a new office over in Manhattan. For a man who adored his job more than anyone else on the planet did, it was a massive honor.

He and Mom had gone back and forth on the offer for months and eventually agreed that while the transition would take time, it would be the best decision for all of us. Dad would get to further pursue his passion of helping others, Pru and I would be exposed to culture outside of our three local museums (and the remodeled Taco Bell), and our mother would finally be back in the environment that first ignited her love of art.

"We know this won't be easy," he'd reassure us, "especially for you girls, but I think Brooklyn is going to grow on you. I spent the first twenty-five years of my life there, and I know you'll love it just as much as I did."

Spoiler: I don't.

If you're wondering why I keep referring to my father in

the past tense, allow me to introduce you to the second negative value: pancreatic cancer. Stage four, to be exact.

We'd been living in the city for a couple of weeks when Dad wakes up one morning and mentions he's not feeling like himself. It didn't come as a surprise. He'd been acting off for the last month, complaining of random body aches and bouts of nausea. He chalked it up to the stress of moving and sported his famous mega-watt smile despite the very obvious warning signs. Dad left for work as usual, only to abruptly collapse in his office later that afternoon. He was rushed to the nearest hospital, where an army of tests revealed a tumor that had spread rampantly.

Oh yeah, and there was little that could be done to save him outside of some Hail Mary chemo and a few thousand major miracles.

That was in August. He barely made it past Thanksgiving. Every day since he died felt less and less like a fairy tale and more like a B-list horror movie. Only this was way worse than some low-budget jump scare. He'd been gone for eleven months, and I was starting to believe my heart would never beat the same again.

It's because of the aforementioned career path I've chosen that I'm currently greeted by my dad's contagious smile, welcoming me in the form of a picture sitting on Mom's night-stand. It lies directly next to a stack of unread self-help books and a half-empty bottle of water. His dark eyes meet mine and cause my whole body to ache. And apparently, also my finger?

"Sorry!" Mom cries as I yelp in pain. "Can you move your hand, Jojo?"

I break my focus on the picture and set my throbbing thumb onto my lap. I'm sitting atop a small black suitcase with Mom grunting forcefully as she props one of her bare feet onto the edge of her bed. She yanks at the zipper until it meets the other end of the bag. Her pale fingers slip off the silver D-ring, knocking her backward onto her dresser with a thud and toppling over several bottles of lotion and perfume.

"SHIT!"

"Swear jar! One dollar!" Pru cries from the kitchen, where she's quietly reading an overdue library book on bracelet making.

"Sorry!" Mom flops forward onto the suitcase with a pitiful bleat, running both hands through her mess of golden curls. "I swear, this suitcase was made for people who wear the same two outfits while traveling. I can barely fit three pairs of jeans in this!"

I scrunch my face and nervously itch the nape of my neck, earning my mother's famous Tess Bradford Look of Contempt. She knows how much I hate what she's about to go and do, even if I know that if she doesn't do it, college is out of the question for the foreseeable future.

Remember my mom and dad's great love story? They encountered a few antagonists along the way. Specifically, my mom's parents.

As Pru and I got older and began asking questions about her mysterious side of the family, Mom always made sure to downplay their wealth to keep us from feeling resentful of our modest upbringing. We'd come to find out she had grown up the only child of a plastic surgeon power couple in Washington, DC. She spent every free moment not being educated by her legion of private tutors vacationing abroad in Europe.

Yes, they were *that* wealthy white family.

You can imagine my grandparents' absolute horror when my mom moved to New York straight out of college and announced she was dating Greg Bradford—a liberal immigration advocate drowning in student debt. They gave her an ultimatum: end the relationship or never see another cent of financial support.

Spoiler: I exist.

For close to two decades, Mom and Dad were entirely on their own, and that's how they liked it. Dad moved us to Ohio shortly after I was born to pursue a job opportunity, and being untethered from her parents' overbearing perfectionism gave Mom the freedom to finally pursue her own desires for once.

Enter negative value strike three: Lawyers make money, artists don't, and after Dad died and left us with a sea of medical bills, Mom was suddenly thrown into the workforce for the first time in her adult life. Between her working three jobs and my income at King Kone on weekends, we'd been getting by, but just barely. If we were lucky, everything would be paid off by the time my hypothetical grandkids were dead.

I run my fingers along the worn stitching of Dad's old suitcase, my mom's words from dinner a few nights ago buzzing in my head with all the stillness of an active beehive.

"Girls," she thoughtfully breathed out as I was mid pizza chew, "I've decided to go see my parents next weekend. I'm going to ask them to set their feelings about your dad and I aside and help support you both financially. It's the least they could do after being absent from your lives for the last eighteen years."

Let's just say once I swallowed that bite, I ended up putting fourteen uncharacteristic dollars into the swear jar. After my rage-fueled, expletive-laden tirade ended, Mom leaned over the dinner table and gently rubbed my hand with a wrinkled half-smile. Her bright eyes hung low, accompanied by sleepless bags.

"Josie, I can't ask you to put your dreams aside because of our situation."

I tossed my cold pizza crust onto our dinky old China

covered with chipped flowers, reaching back to pick off a burnt corner.

"I hate this, Mom."

"Me too," she'd sigh, sounding exhausted, "but your future is worth it. And don't forget, they reached out first."

By 'reached out,' she means how they included a phone number in the condolence card they sent right after Dad died. It had a cheesy, pre-written poem on grief and a short-hand-written sentiment underneath: *Call if you need us.*

After all this time, having her turn to my grandparents felt like life cruelly reminding me that Dad was gone, *forever*, and nothing was going to be the same again.

"Grandma tells me that it snowed yesterday!" Mom attempts to lighten the mood in the bedroom as she pulls another dress from inside the suitcase. It's long and raven-colored with delicate lotus patterns. I remembered her wearing it on date nights with Dad. They'd come in late and I'd hear them giggling like teenagers as they'd march upstairs, Dad telling Mom to keep it down before the kids woke up. Seeing it lying crumpled on the bed stung like a fresh paper cut.

I push myself off the suitcase and move towards a pile of rejected clothing. I mindlessly fold a mountain of shirts, placing them neatly into the dresser to make myself feel useful.

"It's not even November," I state. "That sounds miserable."

It takes Mom swapping out two more pairs of pants in exchange for a casual jumper to finally get the suitcase to zip shut without a struggle. She offers me a celebratory high five and slowly wraps me into her thin arms for a hug. She delicately strokes my mess of curls and breathes in deeply.

"This is for you and Pru, you know." Her raspy reminder rattles my bones. "You girls deserve so much more than this."

A lump rises into my throat, my eyes instantly pooling up as I look around at a still half-unpacked bedroom. Tall, brown boxes of Dad's stuff sat in the corner, collecting chalky layers of dust. I blink the tears back tightly as I smoosh my face into her t-shirt and inhale her oppressively sweet vanilla body soap.

"I know."

"Oh god, who's dying now?" Pru's footsteps squeak up to the bedroom door. She tosses her bracelet-making book onto the edge of the bed, her wide eyes looking like saucers behind the lenses of her glasses.

Mom unlocks her arms from around my waist and chuckles. "Nobody, but I *am* going to miss my flight if I'm not out of here in the next twenty minutes."

Pru places her hand on her hips and cocks her head to the side, her long, kinky waves bouncing against her shoulders.

"I was the one telling you to pack after work last night, but *noooo*," she sings. "You just had to help me with my math homework instead."

"It got finished, didn't it?"

"Accomplished and finished are two different things, Mom."

I nearly urge my sister to give Mom a break, but instead, I bite my tongue. Dad was always the homework parent, the one we turned to when our math assignments became impossible. It was a miracle if Mom could manage bills on time, let alone help my sister with where to properly put a decimal.

Mom stuffs the remainder of her things into her tiny handbag. Wallet, lipstick, sunglasses. She rolls the suitcase into the dark, narrow hallway, inspecting her mess of hair in the living room mirror as she passes.

"You have my list of phone numbers, correct?"

Pru and I shoot one another an annoyed glance as we sluggishly follow along, propping ourselves onto the sliver of distressed wood we called a dining room table.

"Yes." I motion to the manifesto lying flat on our refrigerator. "311 for non-emergencies, Mr. Chung upstairs, Grandma Meryl's cell number—barf—"

"Josie," Mom warns with a disapproving look.

I raise an enthusiastic hand in defense. "Kidding!"

"I printed off all my flight info behind it, too." She points. "I get in after nine, but I'll have my ringer on if you need me for any reason. My flight home comes in at—"

"7:02 AM on Thursday," Pru mocks her stern, maternal tone, scrunching her forehead into a hard crease for the full effect. It was scary how much she could emulate our mother.

"Mom." I hold back a laugh. "We're going to be okay. Seriously. It's less than a week."

She nods understandingly. "When do you get off tonight?"

I rack my brain, the details of my weekly shifts at King Kone blurring together. "At nine. I'm closing. Same tomorrow night."

Pru reaches into the cupboard for a bag of potato chips and sneers. "It is bad enough Mom won't be here, now I won't have anyone to trick-or-treat with? It should be a law that nobody works on Halloween."

Mom's face scrunches into that same signature hard crease as she hails an Uber to the airport. "It's not a national holiday, Prudence. Plus, I thought you were going to that block party thing with your friend Destiny and her family tomorrow night."

"I was until they decided to go to Coney Island instead." Pru rolls her eyes. "Who passes up a block party on Halloween for overpriced theme park hot dogs they're inevitably going to throw up?"

"Who wouldn't?" I tease.

"Not everyone plans to be in bed by eight on Halloween," Pru hisses.

"I just said I was working until nine," I correct her, ripping the bag of chips from her hand and sneaking one for myself with a salty crunch.

"Enough!" Mom motions to both of us like a traffic controller. "My ride is two minutes away and I'm anxious enough as it is. Please try not to kill each other."

"No promises," Pru scoffs. Her bare feet slide across the ancient hardwood floor with deafening creaks as she flops onto the side of our couch, pulling her phone out of the back pocket of her jean skirt.

"I probably need to go get ready." I gesture to the closet-sized bathroom my sister and I share. "I work in about thirty minutes."

Before my mother can wrap me in another hug that is sure to leave me a hysteric mess, she tenderly grips my shoulders and looks me square in the eyes.

"Behave yourselves while I'm gone. Please? Positive big sister mode?"

I smirk. "Probably not the best time to tell you I hooked up with some random dude in the alley next door then, huh? It was very intense. You might be a grandmother soon."

"Very funny." Mom deadpans. "I can trust you to stay out of trouble, but will you make sure your sister cleans up after herself, does her homework..."

"Stays away from the random dudes in the alley?"

"I'm more likely to wind up with one of them than you are!" Pru cries over the noise of whatever video she's watching.

She's not wrong. My mother, that is, not Pru. Trouble wasn't even on my radar. Since we'd moved here, I'd had two sole objectives—survive high school, and get back home to Ohio as soon as possible after graduating.

My application for the University of Cincinnati had been sitting on my laptop since the start of the summer. I'd been meticulously writing and rewriting my entrance essay since

January. Each version including why their film program had been my academic dream for years. It was a seamless plan. I'd get into UC, finish high school in May, turn eighteen, then move back and into an apartment with my best friend, Hannah. Once it happened, life would feel normal again. As normal as it could be without Dad anyway.

I just needed to make it through the last few months here, keeping my nose down and certainly not going out of my way to get comfortable like Pru had. She walked in after her first day of sixth grade with four new best friends and a potential crush. She and Mom spent every free evening going into the city and crossing items off their New York bucket list, while I stayed behind and worked on extra credit assignments that would look good on my transcripts.

The both of them loved it here the way Dad hoped they would, but all I wanted was to get the hell out as fast as I could. If Mom's plan to plead for tuition money worked, my seamless plan was more of a reality than it had been in the last year.

Seven more months, I was constantly reminding myself. *You can survive the chaos of New York City for seven more months.* I was beginning to wonder if I'd need it tattooed on my eyelids to make it through the next shift at work.

Mom's phone pings loudly, signaling the arrival of her ride. She pouts as she invitingly swings her arms out wide to the two of us. Pru jumps up from the couch to join us in a deep, warm hug.

"I love you, rats," she mutters, planting wet kisses on both of our foreheads.

The moment feels bittersweet and final. This is the first-time Mom has left the two of us alone since Dad died. Even when he was alive, I could count on one hand the number of times they were ever away from home for more than a night or two. Dad's co-workers used to tease him about how close our family was. They'd say we would all get sick of each other one day. Little did they know we'd never get that chance.

Mom bops the top of Pru's nose, causing her to giggle. "Keep your nose clean, Rat Two." Her pale eyes squint as they meet mine, tapping the apple of one of my plump cheeks in the same playful manner. "Maybe go find a little trouble, Rat One?"

My gaze sinks. I force myself to meet her plea with a solemn smile. "I'll do my best."

Unlikely, I think to myself. *Seven more months, Josephine. You can survive for seven more months.*

CHAPTER 2
ROWAN

MY CAREER IS OVER.

That's all I've been telling myself in the days since the fight happened.

Warm flashbulbs pierce my vision as someone rips the corner of my jacket and shoves me through a small herd of screaming fans at baggage claim. They're all holding different pictures of my face they want signed. My feet are dragged over multiple loading zone tripping hazards before realizing the hand pulling me along belongs to my bodyguard, Alex. He leads the three of us forcefully to our tinted getaway suburban outside, the locks clicking loudly behind us as the driver attempts to speed away.

Growing up, my grandmother had a flip phone—one of those thin, hot pink ones with floral designs on it. I would always know when she got a call that pissed her off because she'd slap the thing shut and you'd hear it shutter two counties away. Now, everyone owns a smartphone, and there's no warning on the other end of a bad phone call. No intimidating cell phone slap. Only a muted *end call* button, followed immediately by...

"GODDAMN IT!"

Aunt Lexi is anxiously bobbing her head, having just finished an extremely long phone call with the executive producers of *Dawn Heights*. Her skinny fingers massage the top of her glossy, blown-out hair. She quit smoking a year ago, but something tells me she's about to start up again.

"Am I fired?" I ask, not brave enough to look up from my muddy Converse.

Furious was an understatement. My typically attentive aunt was slowly being burned alive by an internal inferno. I'd eaten six complimentary peanut butter cups since getting inside the car and she hadn't batted an eye.

"No," she grumbles, "but your ass is on the line."

"I didn't even start it!"

Lexi clenches her fists and releases them mid-air. "You didn't walk away from it either!"

It had been nearly forty-two hours since the incident that potentially derailed my entire acting future. The whole thing is starting to feel like a massive blur. Alex and I got home just before news outlets began reporting on it. The outside of my aunt's gated home in the Hollywood Hills was teeming with paparazzi for hours afterward. Since then, Lexi had been living on her phone, solely communicating with my publicist and trying to put a positive spin on what happened.

In case you missed the memo, I've apparently been canceled.

Aunt Lexi delicately places her hands on her laptop in an elaborate illusion of staying calm. "They're insisting Michael Brewer take an anger management course, and they would like for you to make a formal apology for your behavior. When we meet with them tomorrow, I told them you'd apologize in person as well."

I nearly choke on the mouthful of melted peanut butter gluing my jaw together. "Are you 'ucking 'idding me?!"

"Someone told the cops you were drinking at the party, Rowan," she continues. "Were you?"

Alex's eyes grow wide in light of the claim. He stares me down as he folds his muscular arms across his broad chest. He was there. He never missed anything. Somehow, he'd missed this. I hang my head low, hoping this mess is one big nightmare I'm eventually going to wake up from.

"Because one of the directors gave me a drink. Just one. Like, a single shot."

This isn't helping my case in the slightest, but if the press is going to report on my downfall, the least they can do is be the slightest bit factual about it.

Yes, there was a fight with my co-star at the *Dawn Heights* season three premiere party. Yes, I threw the first punch, and yes, I might've had alcohol in my system, but that's barely the tip of the iceberg. Nobody knows how the fight started or why. Not that I felt comfortable coming clean with any of it to Lexi.

I bite down on my lower lip to keep the series of f-bombs in my head from pouring out. "Michael Brewer apologized, so why am I being asked to? It's not like he wasn't six beers deep when it happened."

"You know why," she snaps. "We're not going to meet with everyone tomorrow to play nice. This meeting has been on the books for weeks. If you want to continue to be part of the show, we need to make things right."

Alex's husky voice finally chimes in. "The guy who provoked the fight is getting a slap on the wrist, but Rowan is somehow coming out of this looking like the bad guy?"

We can both see the inward flames begin to spill out onto my aunt's face, made all the more terrifying by her spider-like lash extensions.

"Because the other guy isn't Rowan Adler!" She loudly argues. "Michael Brewer's contract is on the line for next season too. This is about you though, Rowan. The sooner we bury this, the sooner it goes away."

I push my dark sunglasses further up on my nose, sinking into my seat with an exhausted sigh. I don't sleep well on airplanes, unlike Alex, who is usually dead to the world before the flight attendants finish their safety spiel. Rest hadn't been easy to come by lately, the added concern of flushing my future down the toilet only adds fuel to the sleep deprived fire.

"You look tired." Aunt Lexi observes my deflated body lying lifeless in my seat. She begins feverishly digging through her glossy, snakeskin purse.

"I'm fine, Lexi."

"You need to try and rest when we get in," Alex insists.

"Gee whiz. Thanks, *Dad*. I'll be sure to do that." He ignores my jab, his orange pompadour bouncing sideways against the jerking vehicle.

On the outside, Alex was a three-hundred-pound teddy bear with a splotchy chain of freckles lining his nose and cheeks. Little did anyone know he was trained by Special Ops and could kill you before you had time to wonder if he possibly could. Hiring him was one of the best decisions my aunt had ever made. Mainly because he was one of the few people I'd grown to count on as always having my back, even when I made his life a living hell.

The chaotic energy in the car begins to settle as we roll to a slow stop. I look out the shaded windows to see The Four Seasons towering over the lower Manhattan skyline. Alex and I are enamored by the spectacle while Lexi frantically looks side to side, vigilant of her surroundings. I grab the hood of my dark jacket and raise it over my flat airplane hair, grabbing my faded Lakers hat from my computer bag and pulling it tight over the top to conceal it in place.

This widely exaggerated nightclub fight wasn't the first

time I'd been on thin ice with the producers of *Dawn Heights* in the past several months. The real trouble started when production on season three wrapped, and I impromptu decided to shave my head. Little did I know when I did it, I was needed for reshoots and press photos a week later. Lexi was livid, and the tabloids had a field day, accusing me of having a Britney Spears 2007 level meltdown. I only did it because the bleach they used to keep me platinum was causing my hair to fall out in clumps.

"Not to mention, Britney was actually dealing with mental illness." Alex would defend me—and apparently, Britney. I didn't have the heart to tell Lexi he's the one who helped me shave it.

My hair had grown back enough to style it again for campaigns and photo spreads, but that didn't stop the costume department on the show from bitching about how tacky my character Hunter's wig looked throughout the rest of filming. Part of me felt horrible about it. Classic Rowan acting without thinking, as my grandmother would say. Then there was the other part of me that could care less.

As I exit the car, Lexi practically forms a human barrier to shield me from the non-existent paparazzi. I prolong the moment to breathe deep and take it all in. A small part of me feels like I'm home, even though home was technically another three-hundred miles away in Rochester.

Alex jumps out behind me. His spotted nose bunching in disgust.

"I don't remember the nice part of New York smelling like rectum."

"It's not New York if it doesn't smell like rectum," Lexi scowls. She directs the bellhop coming to greet us on where to take our luggage.

"When did we all become rectum experts?" I tease.

"It happens when our heads are constantly up your ass," Lexi fires back.

I wince. "Ouch."

The inside of the hotel room looks like some pop-up art museum. It's large and acutely minimalist. Bare white wallpaper lies behind dark wooden furniture, expressionist paintings hanging all over the walls. Alex and I share a large double bedroom while Lexi sleeps next door in an adjacent studio loft. Far enough away to give me space, close enough to hover like a helicopter. It's what she'd been good at ever since I was a kid.

I lifelessly flop like a fish onto the uncomfortable velvet couch in the common room. Lexi shouts a startling 'ah-ha!' and finally pulls what she's been digging for out of her massive purse.

"Here!" She tosses a neon orange pill bottle from across the room. It plops onto the lap of my jeans with a soft thud. "Those will help you sleep. Only take half of one, they're intense."

My dry, sunken eyes shoot out of their sockets. "Seriously?!"

"As a heart attack. You look like shit, and you need rest." Leave it to Lexi to offer tough love. She'd been working as a talent agent since before I was old enough to know what 'personal branding' even was. She laid things out straight for people and never cared if she hurt your feelings doing it. It's what made her great at her job, and simultaneously, the worst person to live with.

I shove the pills into the pocket of my jacket with a scoff, feeling the smooth edge of my sunglasses poking out a small hole in the stitching.

"I'm already on anxiety medication," I remind her. "I don't think it's smart to throw in some mystery sleeping drug because you think I'm a toddler who needs to go night-night."

Lexi clenches her jaw, her bright red lipstick forming a

pencil-thin line. That always meant one of two things. Either you were in for an insensitive lashing, or she couldn't think of a comeback and would dramatically exit the room with visible disgust. In this case, it was option two.

"You're welcome," she seethes.

My insides sink to the floor. My aunt could insult you directly to your face and still manage to squeeze an apology out of you as if she deserved it. I jump to my feet and prepare to sincerely thank her when she abruptly slams the sliding doors to her loft. It shakes the walls of our hotel room all the way down to the ground floor.

Alex pulls a plain black shirt out of his suitcase, inspecting it with a smell before ripping off his sweaty airplane shirt and replacing it.

"She cares about you, you know."

"I've endured six years of her caring. Trust me. I get it."

A steady stream of gushing water comes echoing out of Aunt Lexi's loft. I breathe a welcomed sigh of ease. She was notorious for her hour-long showers, sometimes longer depending on her stress levels. I was pretty sure she stood under the running water and screamed the entire time. Effectively, it always calmed her down.

Regardless of how she spent her time in there, and I wasn't too keen on learning, I could always count on it being one uninterrupted hour of freedom a day where she wasn't breathing down my neck about something *Dawn Heights*-related.

The two full beds wrapped in velvety sheets call my name, even if my brain is moving too fast for sleep to even cross my mind as a viable option. My stomach groans in hunger as I fall face-first onto the mattress closest to the window. The fading sun lights the New York skyline in a cascade of soft oranges and pinks. I can't help but smirk into my pillow, wondering what Grandma would think if she saw it. Sunsets were her favorite.

"Are you sure you're okay?" Alex asks for the one-millionth time since the plane landed.

"Yes. I'm just hungry," I half-lie.

"Order room service then."

"I can't. I'm fasting." I add finger quotes around 'fasting.' Those peanut butter cups I inhaled on the drive are hitting my stomach like molten chocolate meteors.

Part of playing Hunter Cade meant being contractually obligated to keep the physique of Hunter Cade, which also meant working out more than I ate on any given day. Ironic considering Hunter Cade isn't athletic. Being the anti-jock is sort of his thing.

"You could always say it's for me!" Alex cheerfully offers. He parks himself on the edge of his bed and stretches his legs out with a loud pop. He wasn't much older than me, mid-twenties at best, but his supportive demeanor automatically made him the closest thing I had to a father figure.

I momentarily tilt to my side with a grateful yet coy grin. "I could always leave this hotel room. Just run away and never look back."

He shifts his eyes to the ceiling. "Ha-ha."

I sink my head, my words going muffled against the comforter. "Wouldn't it be nice? One day without worrying about the press, or cameras, or freaking cheerleaders."

Alex's oversized ears perk up at the mention of cheerleaders. Months ago, a *Dawn Heights* fanfiction circulated on Archive of our Own. It involved a group of Heights High cheerleaders kidnapping my character and locking him away in one of their basements to fulfill all their weird sexual fantasies.

Rumors started swirling that the person who created the fanfic was some fourteen-year-old girl from Florida who was secretly planning on finding and abducting me, using each chapter as some decipherable code on where she'd take me. It was one of the dumbest conspiracy theories I'd ever heard, but it became popular enough to pose a valid concern for Lexi. After that, Alex went from my occasional red-carpet chaperone to my round-the-clock, grown-ass Navy SEAL babysitter.

The silence in the room lingers. Alex's fair eyebrows wiggle in a line across the top of his forehead. He taps his fingers against his torso for a moment before jerking his body off the bed. He leans across the doorframe to be sure Lexi's sliding doors have indeed slammed all the way shut. Everyone in the hotel below us could've told him they had.

"She'll be in there a while, right?" He asks.

I prop myself up on my palms and remove my hat and hood to give my hair a shake. "She usually is."

Alex nods slowly, stroking the orange stubble on his chin. "Would she kill me if I took a power nap?"

"Only if you get caught." I smirk. "She'd probably say something about naps being for the weak."

"Explains the black-market sleeping pills," he snorts. Alex digs through his mammoth leather backpack and pulls out a fuzzy sleeping mask, fanning his face with it. "You're not the only one who hasn't slept much the last few days. Would you mind if I crashed for a bit?"

"Not at all." I shake my head, twisting the bill of my cap as far as I can without snapping it in two. "I'll try and be quiet."

He triple-checks her door a final time before relaxing his gargoyle-sized shoulders and landing on his bed with an impressive thud. If there was anyone on the planet who perpetually had a stick shoved farther up their ass than my aunt, it was Alex. He deserved a break, as short-lived as it may be.

"Go order some food and watch a movie!" He suggests. "One better, maybe get some sleep yourself. You have that meeting tomorrow."

"Not until two," I nudge. "There's plenty of time to not sleep between now and then."

Alex ignores my sarcasm and lowers the sleep mask over his eyes, pulling his AirPods and a tan leather wallet out of his back pocket. He sets the wallet on the nightstand next to some silver alarm-looking device that doubles as a desk lamp. His throaty voice bounces off the walls, his projection skewed by the blasting AirPods.

"ORDER ME FOOD IF YOU GET SOME TOO, OKAY? I'LL TRY NOT TO BE LONGER THAN AN HOUR."

Great. Because if there was one thing I wanted right now, it was to be locked up in a hotel room in Manhattan with two certified guard dogs while I stewed alone in my thoughts. Oh, and I hadn't eaten since yesterday afternoon.

Angst gets the better of me as I unprop my hands and allow myself to fall backward onto the bed. I grab one of the heavy feather pillows off the headboard and place it directly over my face, deeply breathing in the smell of cheap laundry soap and the cologne of whoever slept on this pillow before me. If I wasn't confident Alex was already dead to the world, I'd scream to see how quickly either of them would notice.

They won't notice, I tell myself. They *never* notice.

It starts as a thought. A sinister, careless, trademark Rowan Adler-type thought.

I have a history of reckless decisions (if you haven't picked up on that already.) They date back as far as fifteen-months-old when I went against my grandmother's warning to stay away from her neighbor's evil Pomeranian named Jitsu. I nearly lost a finger. A year later, I didn't listen when she told me not to climb the massive oak tree outside my house to reach the top of our tire swing. I broke both my arms.

The rebellious streak intensified as I got older. In third

grade, my teacher Ms. Carpenter sent home the following statement on my report card: *bright, creative, but defiant.*

"You're not defiant, Rowan." Grandma would go out of her way to encourage me on the drive home as I sulked headlong into a vanilla milkshake. "You're passionate. Passionate people can be wonderful, but they can also be stupid."

'Challenging' was Aunt Lexi's word. She would use it to describe me at least once a day after moving in with her, usually after one of our screaming matches. I'd say something scathing about how I hated living in Los Angeles and didn't need her to take care of me, only to have her follow it up with an offended valley girl hair toss as she'd shout, "you are just like your mother!"

She would know better than anyone. Only, unlike my mother, I didn't abandon my kid and leave my relatives to raise him. In the end, words like *creative* and *defiant* may not have made for A+ report cards, but they sure as hell explained why pretending to live like other people came so naturally to me.

The voice in my head becomes louder, repeating itself once again. *They won't notice.*

I'd basically admitted it to myself already. My aunt would be in the bathroom for another sixty minutes, minimum. That's not even counting her extensive shower follow-up routine, consisting of hundreds of dollars' worth of creams that helped her look forty-five instead of forty-eight.

If I were lucky and she was as pissed off as I know she is, I wouldn't see her again until the morning. Alex would eventually wake up, break out his Nintendo Switch, and game in silence until two in the morning. If I left this hotel room right now, nobody would notice for another hour.

Abruptly, I rip the weighted pillow off my face and slowly rise like a corpse brought back from the dead. My heartbeat starts to thud rapidly. I have no plan for what I'm about to do other than standing to my feet and grabbing my disgusting old Converse to quickly throw them back on. I move around quietly, trying not to stir Alex as his chest moves up and down in a rhythmic breathing pattern.

Out of an abundance of caution, I hover over his lifeless body and flail around obnoxiously, flipping him off repeatedly to see if he'll notice. He doesn't even flinch, and I'd be willing to bet any amount of money he has a Celtic Woman album playing on those earbuds.

I raise my hood up and reach for my computer bag, quietly removing my laptop and several coffee-stained *Dawn Heights* script pages. I spot my sunglasses and dive in to grab them. Suddenly, Alex breaks into a loud snore that jolts me backward a solid foot. I wait for my pulse to come down before pulling the Lakers cap above my hood. I reach back into the bag to mindlessly grab whatever might be rolling around at the bottom, patting at my full jacket pockets as I stare blankly ahead. Sunglasses, a stick of gum, and my bottle of medication. Perfect.

I'm mere moments from freedom when Alex's wallet calls to me from the nightstand like a siren. His disdain for banks was notorious, one of the many conspiracy theories he held to. He once told me he kept his military money hidden in jars all over his house. I asked once what he'd do if his house ever caught fire, and he deadass responded "be poor" without an ounce of hesitation.

It's a horrendous method of financial security, but when it means he is always guaranteed to have a few hundred dollars in his pocket and I can't be caught dead using any of my credit cards, it works out in my favor.

I reach over and quietly unsnap the fold of the buttery wallet, thumbing through a stack of crumpled bills and grabbing whatever I can. I promise myself to pay him back later and pray he doesn't notice in the meantime. Alex unleashes another jet-engine level snore that forces me to pause and rethink exactly what I'm about to do.

Stop overthinking it, my inner voice chants louder and louder. *Go, and go now.*

I bob my head wildly like a dashboard Jesus, mindlessly tugging at my jeans to feel around for my legs as they move toward the door, one foot after the other. Within seconds, I'm standing outside my hotel room and keeping my eyes laser-focused on the ground as I take the elevator down to the main lobby.

I have no clue where I'm going. All I know is, I can't stay here.

CHAPTER 3

JOSIE

MOM SENDS Pru and me at least five updates in the hour since she's left.

In the Uber!

At the airport!

Thru security!

Miss you guys!

About to board the plane!

I nearly expect a series of pointless follow-up messages like 'the plane is accelerating!' or 'they just started passing out drinks!' before I even make it across the street for work.

A job in fast food wasn't my first choice, but when Mom spotted the *Cashier Wanted* sign hanging at King Kone across the street earlier in the summer, it was a no-brainer. The shifts were short, the pay was decent, and it freed up my days to be with Pru while Mom worked. Plus, I couldn't pass up the ninety-second commute, not when the thought of stepping foot onto a subway platform by myself petrified me.

The plan was to quit in August once school started again and my schedule picked up. When things got tight for us, I figured a few more months of late evenings and discounted meals wouldn't hurt, mainly when every extra cent I made that wasn't contributed to bills was being saved for UC.

King Kone wasn't just your run-of-the-mill Dairy Queen knockoff. From what I'd been told, it had become something of a neighborhood institution years ago when Vin Diesel randomly came in to order a chocolate malt and took a bunch of pictures with the shop's sleazy manager, Armani. Since then, they were no longer that one greasy burger shack in Brooklyn that sold decent vanilla soft serve. Now, they were that one greasy burger shack in Brooklyn that sold decent vanilla soft serve and had a bunch of awkward Vin Diesel selfies all over the walls.

Armani soon installed a flat-screen television in the corner of the restaurant to keep the buzz alive after his brush with fame... if you can even call an establishment of King Kone's caliber a 'restaurant.' It aired Vin Diesel movies on loop for ten hours a day, seven days a week. If you had told me I'd be forced to watch *The Fate of the Furious* at least five dozen times in my life, I would've politely asked not to be born at all.

Lately, Armani had been present mostly during day shifts while I was at school, freeing me from his crusty grab hands and meaning whoever worked the front register at night often got control over the TV. Had I not clocked in several minutes late, I'd be the one wielding the power of the remote instead of my co-worker, Indio, already scrolling through our options with sharp focus.

I boorishly pick a stray piece of dryer lint off the front of my faded teal employee shirt, which reads in bold white letters KING KONE: WHERE THE LOYALS ARE ROYALS. Friday nights were filled with the usual suspects. A handful of familiar local students looking for cheap sustenance, stray tourists who had walked themselves into near starvation, and several feral drug addicts who slept in the alleyway across the street. We always made sure they walked away with something to keep them on our good side. Even Indio, who is by all accounts, vying to become Brooklyn's most pretentious art school asshole.

"Nobody likes your geriatric black and white movies, Josie," he once spat as he leaned into the countertop, pressing one palm into the hollow of his cheek. "They're misogynist and sad."

Powerless in tonight's choice of entertainment, his fingers frantically toggle between the left and right buttons as he signs into his Webstream account. Indio is only a year older than I am, but similar to me, has been working here since the summer before his senior year of high school. His plan was practically identical, bank enough money for college and then never look back. The fact that he was still at King Kone and actively into his freshman year at The School of Visual Arts didn't bode well for my future.

"Have you watched that new docuseries with Olivia Rodrigo?" he asks. His shimmery silver eyeliner looks more effortless than anything I've ever attempted in my life.

I shake my head. "I'm not really into her music."

"You might be the only teenage girl on the planet who isn't."

I raise an eyebrow. "Are you stereotyping me?"

"If the shoe fits." He points down at the AP History assignment I'm not-so-secretly brainstorming on a napkin underneath the register. "Do you even have a life that isn't dictated by schoolwork? Or are you going for that whole 'I'm not like other girls' thing?"

Bile rises up in my throat. "That's none of your business."

Indio gently sets the remote on the counter with a sorry frown. "I'm not trying to be a douchebag. I just don't want to see you become me."

I grin playfully, resting my defenses with a tired sigh. "Never going to happen. Your taste in movies is too bad."

"I think you mean TV shows." Indio's face lights up. He picks up the remote and holds it up to the screen for me to see what he's decided on, clicking the aquatic blue splash banner that reads *Dawn Heights: Season Three Now Streaming!*

I groan. "You hate me, don't you?"

"This is what you get for making me watch that depressing Christmas movie with Jimmy Simpson last week."

"It's Jimmy Stewart," I correct, trying to mask my utter disappointment. I'll mentally note how he thinks *It's a Wonderful Life* is a 'borefest' and spare him a rewatch come the holiday season.

"Do you watch *Dawn Heights* at all?" Indio's chipper voice raises an additional billion octaves, his eyes glimmering with excitement. "Not that I expect you to. I'm halfway through season three. I'm obsessed!"

"Didn't it come out last night?"

"Pssh, yes." He waves his hands. "I shirked all my assignments and skipped my morning classes because I stayed up half the night to watch!"

"Yet I'm the weird one working here."

He ignores the comment and hovers over episode fourteen of season three, titled *I Threw a Brick Through a Window.*

I'd never intentionally sat down to watch *Dawn Heights*, but back home before I moved, Hannah had become all-consumed with it. Her interest led me to read a massive magazine spread in a hospital waiting room once. It mentioned how every episode was named after a different U2 song.

That random article was my only real insight into the show, minus its pop-culture phenomenon status. It singlehandedly put Webstream on the map as a streaming service and spawned millions of rabid fans who spent hours theorizing about the characters and memeing pivotally emotional moments.

The series revolves around professional high school sad boy, Hunter Cade. He and his recently divorced mother move to the fictional town of Dawn Heights, Connecticut, where he broods twenty-four seven and catches the eye of the popular yet misunderstood Sophia Singh, dating town hero quarterback and amateur dick, Noah Lawrence. A love triangle ensues between the three, and basically, if you've seen any other teen soap opera from the last three decades, you've seen *Dawn Heights*.

The show became an overnight sensation thanks to the cliffhanger finale of season one. Having unsuccessfully confessed his love to Sophia, Hunter's character jumps in his car and plans on leaving town, only to get hit head-on by a semi and have his vehicle tossed around with the best CGI the production could afford. Hunter is seemingly left to die, aside from having the strength to make one last call to alert his mother. Turns out he gets ghosted while his mom has a vulnerable one-night stand with his English teacher and pseudo mentor.

I snicker to myself as I recall a quote in the article. *"That was a real turning point in the show for me." Rowan Adler (16) confesses. "Hunter is more than some heartthrob. He's a regular teenager like the rest of us, facing real problems."*

Either Rowan Adler's publicist had answered the question for him, or he was devastatingly naïve. Relatability had nothing to do with it. His face is the only reason the show is the sensation it is. He had everything you'd come to expect from your white boy flavor-of-the-month. Greasy, bleached blond hair that blows when there isn't any wind, a body he is more than willing to reveal on camera, and a level of body hair that proves someone taught him to manscape at a young age.

Indio presses play on the episode, leaning so far over the register in focus, I fear he might fall over and break his neck. I dart my eyes to the floor with a puff of my cheeks, reaching below the counter to grab one of the clean towels sitting in a neatly folded pile underneath the employee handwashing sink. I run it under a quick squirt of scalding water.

"I'm going to wipe tables. You've got the register?"

Indio nods, his face still glued to the screen. I peek up to see what's happening as I work my way around the wrapped counter onto the checkered white and green tiles. A series of scenes flash by, quickly recapping the last episode. One of the clips involving Hunter aggressively approaching an older man (the mentor?) and slapping him hard in the face, the clip ending with him shouting, "YOU GOT MY MOTHER PREG-NANT?!" as a single strand of spit trails out of his quivering lip. I'd almost say it was decent acting if it weren't so laughably unbelievable.

At present, three customers are occupying two separate tables on opposite sides of the restaurant. In the front, near the rusting silver door, there's an older couple. Both are sporting gray hair and silently argue over their atlas map of New York that looks four decades outdated. On the other side, there's a guy with a dark hoodie zipped all the way up and a black cap that has a Los Angeles Lakers logo on it. He's hunched over his plate like an overcooked cocktail shrimp, balling the white paper wrapper from his straw between his fingers.

One at a time, I make my way to each empty table, using the damp rag to dust off any residual crumbs and avoiding the fighting couple at all costs. The man vaguely threatens to leave and take the map with him.

"See how well you'll get along without me, Cheryl!" his sticky southern accent barks. I get the feeling she'd somehow be better off.

I'm one table over from Hoodie Boy and casually observe his empty red basket of abolished food. Two wilting discarded tomato slices leak all over the patterned paper underneath and make a small lake next to his sweating cup of ice water.

"Care for me to get your table?" I wave the rag in a flag motion. He nearly jumps up in surprise and smushes the straw wrapper flat underneath his palm.

"I'm sorry?" His voice is still, yet panicked. He reaches down into his pockets rapidly, tugging at them as if he's looking for something. From the side, his profile looks young, late teens, if I had to suspect.

"Your table." I point with a friendly smile. "You have a melting water glass and some tomatoes crying you a river."

He continues to frantically check his pockets and stiffens upright, pointing to the television Indio is enthralled by.

"I'd be crying too if I were being forced to watch this."

An obnoxious chuckle causes my face to go red. "Sadly, I was outvoted."

Hoodie Boy nods, finally locating what he'd been searching for in his pockets: a pair of sunglasses. The lighting in here might be obnoxiously fluorescent yellow, but it's not 'sunglasses indoors when it's dark outside' horrible. He peers up at me for a moment as he quickly throws them onto his square face, granting me a quick peek at his bright green eyes. Something about him seemed vaguely familiar.

"Do you go to Bedford Academy?" I sheepishly ask. "I feel like I've seen you before."

"Uhh, yeah." He clears his voice. "I'm a, umm, senior."

That familiar fuzzy feeling I get whenever I watch Humphrey Bogart washes over me. Leave it to me to find myself attracted to either dead old guys or potential bank robbers who look like they have scoliosis. Our student body wasn't exactly small, but how on earth hadn't I noticed him before?

I lean over and wipe the puddle away from his space, offering a smile as he carelessly tosses the straw wrapper into the basket.

"Can I get you anything else?" I ask. I'm almost certain it comes out sounding like *I anything get else for you?*

"Unless you can convince that guy to turn the TV to anything else." He points to a blank-stared Indio. He hasn't blinked once in the last two minutes.

"I hear Webstream added *Killer Klowns from Outer Space* just in time for Halloween."

He snorts, flashing a brief toothy grin. "Make it happen, and I'll throw in a five-star Yelp review."

I place the sticky, damp towel into one of the pockets of my apron and motion my hands upward like a theater marquee. "Came for the food, stayed for the top-notch entertainment."

"The service isn't horrible either," he says softly.

My heart practically freefalls out of my ass. During the summer, when Pru came during my shifts and practically lived off malted milkshakes, she'd tell me guys were constantly flirting with me. I was either 'too oblivious or too uninterested' to notice. I was starting to think she had a point. Only in this case, there was nothing oblivious or uninterested about it.

The front door of the restaurant swings wide open, followed by the decrepit old chirp of the motion sensor that sounds like a robotic bird slowly suffering a stroke. If my heart had indeed just fallen out of my backside, I'm relatively sure our newest customers had walked in and stepped on it.

"Hey, Crimson Wave!" A deep voice snickers. I don't even need to turn around, instantly knowing who it is. Julian Varma, also known as my own personal Steff McKee.

Here's a fun story: My first day at Bedford Academy came

a day after Dad was admitted to the hospital. As you may imagine, I wasn't in a steady state of mind walking into junior year between his cancer and the move. Determined to make it count academically, I decided to trudge through and attend classes like everything was fine at home, even if it extremely wasn't.

Thanks to my oblivious condition, I walked into Algebra II that morning, utterly unaware that I was due to sport my red badge of honor. It was midway through class when I felt my uterus implode and the internal dread set in. It's not exactly like you can hold molting organs. By the time I'd summoned the courage to raise my hand and ask for a hall pass, the damage had been done. The back of my acid-washed denim looked like something straight out of an episode of *Criminal Minds*.

Gratefully, our teacher took pity on me and allowed me to go to the restroom to amend the situation. As I shamefully walked past the rest of the class, masking the blood with a ruled notebook and failing spectacularly, something small hit my back and bounced against my sweater. Looking down, a small tampon in a pink wrapper sat at my feet, hurled at me directly from the back row by Julian Varma himself.

His greasy forehead shone bright as he stood on his chair and immediately lead the class in a rousing chant of "SHARK WEEK! SHARK WEEK! SHARK WEEK!"

I never told Mom out of fear of her cliché threats to call everyone's parents. Plus, Julian *did* get detention for it. Even so, that proverbial (and literal) blemish on my character had forever marked me as Period Girl to him and just about everyone else at Bedford ever since. If Hoodie Boy had, in fact, gone to our school, there was no way he didn't know who I was unless he was a transfer student or taking profound sympathy on me.

The fighting couple exits the shop and causes the door to whine in agony once more. Julian and his small gang of basketball teammates leap over the tables and park themselves behind the duo's mess of melted milkshake and cold French fries. Two crumpled one-dollar bills sit on the table, flicked to the floor by Julian with a snotty smirk.

"Might want to clean this if you want to actually earn it, Scarlet Witch."

I grit my teeth. How many clever nicknames for menstruation did this guy have? Why did everyone think they were hilarious? And more than anything at this moment, why was I born?

Whipping the disgusting wet rag out of my apron, I plaster a fake smile onto my face and glide over to the table as gracefully as I can, sopping up the table residue and snagging the money off the floor.

"Hey! You work here?"

One of Julian's basketball buddies leans over the table and catches my attention. I recognize him from homeroom—Aaron somethingorother? He's unnaturally tall, clearly the team's center. Small nose, but an otherwise nice face. He's cute in that *I've gone through puberty but I still can't grow facial hair* type of way. Was something in the water tonight that caused my pheromones to act extra potent?

"Uhh, yeah." I nod, collecting the last of the fry crumbs into the palm of my hand and sprinkling them onto the floor. "Since the summer."

"Nice." His teeth are slightly crooked, and somehow make me feel better about my own crowded mess of a smile. Mom always said it made me look adorable, which means nothing from a former teen model who spent three years sporting thousand-dollar invisible braces in junior high.

"I'm Josie." I nervously lick my lips, glancing around to make sure Julian and the others have their faces glued to their phones. The last thing I need is for him to catch on to my awkward flirting. "Are you in homeroom with Mrs. Garcia?"

His smile spreads wider. "Yeah! I'm Aaron Lopez. I thought maybe I recognized you."

From the corner of my eye, I catch Hoodie Boy peek his head around the table to get a glance at what's happening. I wonder if he'd recognized the group the same way I had. It was hard to miss anyone sporting blue and white varsity jackets with PANTHERS printed across the front.

"Hey, Girl Flu!" Julian leans over the table and runs a hand through his slicked-back mop of black hair. "Could we get some water?"

I point towards Indio up at the front. "You can order at the register, and I'll come to bring it over."

"Yeah, but you're already right here. Why would I go do that?" He scrunches his rugged face, drawing attention to his bushy eyebrows. My stomach flops sideways as Aaron darts his eyes to the ground.

I nod reverently and take a quick headcount. Back behind the counter, I gently elbow Indio and motion to the group crowded together at the booth. They're all shoving one another's phones into their neighbor's faces, laughing throatily with illegible grunts.

"Can you grab six glasses of water and take them over to those guys?" I wave a hand in front of my co-worker's thousand-yard stare. "And the guy wearing the hat wants to know if you can change it to something else."

That finally catches Indio's attention. He snaps his head around fast, his baby blue triangle earrings dangling aggressively against his neck. "What?"

I point to the two tables, tapping a finger to the counter with my commands. "They need water, and he wants to watch something else."

By the look on Indio's face, you'd think Hoodie Boy was asking him to donate a kidney. He clumsily grabs the remote and pauses the screen on a weepy, scantily clad Sophia. He leans his pencil-thin body across the counter to get a good look at Hoodie Boy's side profile.

He squints hard. "Tell the uptight prick to find somewhere else to loiter."

I roll my eyes and grab a stack of red plastic cups off the rusty drying rack. "Whatever. Can you get water for those guys then? They go to my school and I sort of hate them."

"You hate everyone," he remarks, resuming the episode. "And yeah, in a minute."

"I don't hate everyone!" My brow furrows. Rather than stand there and attempt to argue with someone who barely knows me, I take a few deep breaths and fill all six glasses with ice. The faster they get what they want, the sooner they'll leave. If only I could pull Indio's head out of *Dawn Heights*.

A loud rattling noise suddenly erupts from Hoodie Boy's side of the booth. He slips the Lakers hat off his head for a brief moment and fluffs his sweaty mess of short brown hair. He slaps the cap back on his head before I can get a good look at his face. Were we in any of the same classes? I just couldn't place where I'd seen him before.

"HELLO? ARE WE EVER GETTING THAT WATER?"

Julian is practically standing on top of the booth, nearly toppling over onto Aaron and the others who hoot him on obnoxiously.

Indio scrunches his nose and grabs one cup at a time, running each under the tap without breaking his focus on the show. Losing my patience, I grab a tan serving tray off the bar and set all six glasses on top. I march them over to the team's table while muttering a cold "thanks for nothing" to an unphased Indio.

I set one glass in front of each of the boys, trying my hardest not to slam Julian's in front of him and see it rain over his head.

"Thanks, Aunt Flo." He smiles.

Indio could say all he wanted about Hoodie Boy's loitering. At least he'd actually ordered something. I was starting to wonder if Julian found out I worked here and only came to order water and make my life a living hell without getting detention for it.

As much as I'd love to stand there and stare at Aaron, who seems to be the only one in the gaggle showing a hint of humanity, I quickly move off to check on Hoodie Boy. As I come closer, the source of the rattling becomes apparent. He aggressively empties the contents of a pill case into the palm of his hand and downs a handful. Great. If he wasn't a bank robber, he was a drug addict.

"Are you still good here?" I sneak up behind him, causing him to jump back a second time and mutter a curse under his breath.

"Yeah!" He squawks. The pills explained his jumpiness.

"No luck on getting him to change it to *Killer Klowns*." I place a hand on my hip and wag my head in disappointment. "But to be fair, this is a different form of scary."

He muffles a laugh that sounds vaguely like a barking seal, causing me to grin like an idiot. "If you really want to piss him off, spoil the ending. Someone plants a bomb in the school, and the fate of Noah and Hunter rests in limbo till next season."

"You watch this show too?" I inwardly judge him. Was I really the only human on the planet who didn't watch *Dawn Heights*?

Something like that," he yawns with a stretch. His long arms wrap around the booth.

"Thanks for the spoilers," I offer, trying not to frown. Julian and his band of basketball jerks shoot straw wrapper spit wads at the ceiling that will keep me here scraping way past closing.

"Why do you let those guys treat you like that?" Hoodie Boy's comment takes me back.

"Like what?" I play dumb.

He pokes at the water glass in front of him, rhythmically sliding it from hand to hand in the trail of condensation. "I heard one of them bossing you around."

I point to the glorified teal shirt/apron combo. "I work here. They're allowed to boss me around."

"There's a difference between being a customer and being an asshole."

I bite the inside of my cheek and itch the top of my head with a lost shrug. "Guess there's no difference in the real world."

He shakes his head, visibly disappointed. His thick eyebrows peak an inch above his overdramatic sunglasses. "Still better than *Dawn Heights*, though."

"That I won't argue with." I tap one of my sneakered feet against the grimy tiles and nervously smooth the apron flat against my legs. "We close soon, just a heads up. Unless you want to stay and help clean up the new ceiling mural they're making."

"Tempting."

I spin my heels towards the counter where the latest episode Indio has been enthralled by finally comes to an end. He puffs out his cheeks, silky black hair falling into his eyes.

"Why is this show so addictive?"

"Campiness? Brain-dead dopamine? Hot, shirtless men?"

"Definitely the last one." Indio's face melts into a pleasured puddle of satisfaction. "Dear god, the things I would do to

Rowan Adler. At least, the shiny blonde version of him. Did you know he shaved his head?"

I grimace. "Isn't he a little young for you?"

"Barely. I'd wait for him."

I playfully gag. "What happened to the thing with Izzy Ezra?"

"What thing?" Indio huffs. "Izzy gives me coffee, I say 'thanks, see you next time', and then I drive home like a lonely creep and listen to an emo playlist for the next six hours."

About a month ago, a new coffee shop called Stillwater opened a block from our neighborhood. It replaced the supposedly haunted Little Caesars that doubled as a secret underground drug ring. It had become Indio's go-to caffeine destination before coming here, and not just because the coffee is good.

He came in last Friday night at the start of his shift, holding his cup of coffee up to the fluorescent lights like the newborn son of Mufasa.

"Hot Barista is named Izzy Ezra!"

"You finally got their name, but you didn't ask for their number?" I'd ask.

"There's a natural flow to these things in real life." He'd turn his thin nose up at me and toss his to-go cup in one of the overflowing garbage cans. "You don't run up on the love of your life and start making out like in one of your decrepit movies. You ease into things."

'Natural flow' was clearly the opposite of 'perpetually too shy to make a move,' even if I was more experienced than Indio gave me credit for. My first and only kiss happened freshman year during a study session with a boy I'd had a crush on for months. We locked eyes in the library over calculus and I went in too aggressively with my forehead. The misfortunate mid-kiss collision caused his nose to bleed all over his chess team blazer. That was the beginning and the end of that relationship.

Right on cue, Julian and his friends all begin to make a ruckus as they loudly exit the booth. There are multiple back slapping thuds and cheers of 'good practice, see you at the game Wednesday night' before they file out the door one by one.

Julian pauses before the door can groan in celebration of his exit, making sure to catch my attention with an informal salute and his infamous evil smirk.

"Till next time, Shark Week!" Because this night couldn't get much worse.

I sigh. I'm about to hang my body over the counter in dramatic self-condolence when Aaron the Actual Giant steps forward and slips a crisp five-dollar bill to Indio.

"Water is free," he laughs.

"I know." Aaron shrugs. "But you earned it."

I resist the urge to hang my mouth open like a Venus flytrap, taking the money and plunking it into the half-full tip jar. "Thank you. It's appreciated."

"I'm sorry about him." Aaron cocks his head out the door to Julian. "He can be kind of a jerk sometimes." Only sometimes?

"What can I say?" I hold my hands out towards my sides, "I'm an easy target."

He grins. "Do you have plans tomorrow night?"

I'm not sure whose eyes get bigger, mine or Indio's. He turns his back towards the kitchen to listen in on whatever gossip the fry cooks are spreading. His nosiness couldn't be more obvious.

I scour my brain, instantly wanting to mutter an audible *damn it* when I remember I'm scheduled to work tomorrow night.

"Here. Unfortunately."

"Oh." Aaron's oily skin glimmers under the unflattering

light. His bright expression instantly goes dim. "There's this block party thing for Halloween tomorrow night. It's lame, but I thought maybe you'd want to come."

"My little sister was telling me about that!" I instantly regret the words as they leave my mouth. Way to make it sound like I hang out with an eleven-year-old for fun, even if I do.

Aaron reluctantly nods. "Well, thanks anyway." He smirks a final time with a friendly wave to Indio, who is still pretending to not pay attention. The dead doorbell comes to a shrilling halt before an explosive smile spreads onto my face like a soft pad of butter.

I glance towards Indio, who already knows what I'm about to say and has his middle finger pointed at the ready.

"What was that about a natural progression?"

"Whatever." He shakes his head and aggressively tosses his apron onto the counter. "I'll count the register if you wanna clean the floor. The sooner we can get out of here, the sooner I can get home and be insanely jealous of you."

"Fine, but there's nothing to be jealous of. I literally just learned his name an hour ago."

"And I'm going home to spend the night with my stepmom and her three cats. Life's a real fucking picnic."

Indio would be a catch if he wasn't so... Indio. He'd recently said he was single enough that Spirit Halloween could take up residency up his ass.

I offer a look of gentle encouragement before squatting down beneath the sink and reaching for the arsenal of cleaning supplies. It's still thirty minutes to closing, but even the cooks know we hardly see any customers this late and have begun turning off the stoves and washing dishes.

I reach for a mop when I notice Hoodie Boy still hunched over his table, as he had been since I'd last left him. His shoulder blades move up and down in smooth rolling motions, his head perfectly still as he focuses intently on his empty cup of water.

"Told you he was a problem," Indio mocks. His small black lip piercing jets out whenever he puckers his lips. "Go tell him we're closing early or something."

A rock drops into my stomach. If this guy really is a problem, I don't want to be the one to set him off. Not when I saw him downing pills not too long ago. I drag the dry mop behind me like a lifeless mannequin, hoping he'll see it and get the point before I have to say anything at all.

Then it gets weird.

He doesn't look up from the table as I approach. He doesn't even jump back in startled terror as he had before. My expression goes from timid to concerned as I hunch down slightly and see his head hanging lifeless above the table.

"Excuse me." I raise a finger to poke his arm carefully. "Sir?"

Not even a flinch. Hesitantly, I crawl my finger up from his arm towards his face and peel the glasses down to the bottom of his nose, where I feel warm breath slowly escaping. His eyes are pinched back tightly, a loud snort rattling from behind his lips and causing me to toss the mop onto the floor with a high-pitched shriek.

He's asleep. Hoodie Boy is asleep.

CHAPTER 4
ROWAN

MY ORIGINAL PLAN was centered on food, as all good plans are. I'd find one of those rodent-infested halal carts, eat a gyro, then peer up at the skyline and wish Grandma were here to enjoy it before hauling ass back to the hotel. By chance, if Lexi walked in or Alex woke up, I'd lie through my teeth about needing to go downstairs and ask someone at the front desk about the Wi-Fi. It's a solid alibi.

Except I don't follow my original plan. Like, at all.

I make it out onto the sidewalk and immediately see the soft, green glow illuminating from the entrance of the Chambers Street subway station. That's when I do what any runaway in my position would do—load a MetroCard, board a subway without a destination, and hope I wind up somewhere decent.

I ride the C train for a solid half-hour, trying my best to watch everyone around me while keeping any attention drawn to myself to a minimum. Sporting a disguise that vaguely resembles the *I swear I'm a civilian and not a superhuman* starter-pack isn't helping. I go back and forth between wearing my sunglasses and shoving them back into my pockets, my self-consciousness rising with every stop.

Just months before, while sitting in a makeup trailer, my co-star Ashanti Nath got an exclusive first look at the buzzcut heard 'round the world.

"I always thought you were a natural blond!" She gasped. "You'll be so much harder to spot in public now!"

I ran a hand over my hairless head. "The hair makes the man?" I'd ask.

Her round, olive nose would bunch in her usual bubbly way. "A lot of other things make the man too, you know. *Hair* is so much more to Rowan Adler."

Dad jokes aside (and she came locked and loaded with them), Ashanti always had a knack for saying the things I needed to hear. I quietly wondered what she would think if she were here now, unsure if she'd be cheering me on or calling me a complete dumbass.

Our first day on-set together involved a hot and heavy make-out session I was both underprepared and under-experienced for. After meeting in her trailer for the first time and openly discussing how weird it was, she decided to develop a safe word we could use if either one of us started feeling uncomfortable.

"Grapefruit?" I'd repeat.

Her wide eyes blinked in the glare of the trailer's flimsy blinds. "Yeah! If we feel like it's going in a place that makes either of us want to reevaluate, say grapefruit!"

It would've been great in theory if both of us hadn't spoiled nearly every take by bursting out in laugher mid-kiss and shouting 'grapefruit' just to screw with one another. It was never weird with us after that. In fact, nothing was off-limits. We may have been Hunter and Sophia to the rest of the world —teenage toxicity at its finest—but off-screen, besides Alex, she'd become the only real friend I had.

Ashanti had been raised in the spotlight by famous Bolly-wood parents. She knew how to navigate the shitstorm of publicity that came with fame. After the hours worth of advice she had offered to help me through the first horrible year of *Dawn Heights* mania, I gladly would've taken a bullet for her.

You did take a bullet for her, my conscience reminds me. *How else did you fall into that stupid fight?*

A tight pinching sensation shoots down my left arm as the train screeches to a stop at Kingston Station. I rise to my feet and jump out the door as a mad scramble of people rush to claim my vacant seat. If I kept moving, maybe it would eventually force every ounce of anxiety out of my brain. That's what I was going with anyway.

I march up the long stairwell out of the subway tunnel and freeze. The earlier sunset is a distant memory as the sky transforms into a thick cover of murky black. In my pea-sized brain, it was still only three o'clock. Time change jet lag strikes again!

The streets around me are loud and bustling with the sound of car horns whizzing past and trains taking off underneath the station. A handful of people walking their dogs or sullenly marching home from work shuffle past. I know I'm somewhere in Brooklyn, but if you asked me exactly where I was, all I'd be able to refer to is the small convenience store loudly blasting a K-Pop song and a nearby laundromat with a broken sign that says LANDMAT instead.

Digging into the back pocket of my jeans, I reach for my cell phone to check the time and arrogantly swallow any panic that swells up when I think of what messages await me from either Lexi or Alex. I hadn't been gone *that* long. Surely, they couldn't have noticed by now.

My feet instantly become one with the sidewalk. My phone isn't there.

I reach into my hoodie pockets, only to feel Alex's roll of money, the gum, and the pill bottle. I dig into the next pocket and every other nonfunctional pocket my jeans possess, praying to every god who can possibly hear me to somehow cause my phone to magically reappear. The gods meet my plea with a resounding *piss off.*

I'd left my cell phone in the hotel room. I'd LEFT it there. Not only had I run away, but I'd also left the one thing behind that could help get me back.

Don't panic, Rowan, I tell myself. *You practically spent every summer in New York as a kid. You can fake your way around for an hour.*

Retracing my steps wouldn't exactly work when I could barely piece together what those steps were. How many stops had there been before I wound up here? Had I taken a local train? Express? Exactly how long would it take an Uber to get here if I miraculously found the last remaining payphone on the planet and called Lexi? Most importantly, would she kill me inside the car, or would she wait till we were back in the hotel to cover up the crime scene?

An older woman carrying a gallon of milk brushes past and clocks my shoulder hard, screaming at me to move out of the way. I bounce my frozen calves up and down the pavement and force myself to start walking again, where to remains TBD. As if being lost in an unfamiliar place with a wad of stolen money and no cell phone isn't bad enough, my stomach continues to whale in protest of intermittent fasting. I'm so hungry, I feel like I want to throw up. However that works.

I pause along the wall of a shuttered church building and take a deep breath, snapping my eyes shut and taking a moment to center myself and steady my shaken nerves. A sputtering engine zooms past and shatters the Zen, drawing my attention towards the end of the street.

A row of old brownstones with overflowing garbage cans out front line the block, a dark alley dividing two of the more battered buildings. You could have put a plaque at the entrance that read *Batman's parents were murdered here*, and I'd believe it.

Sitting on the corner across the street from the apartments sits a shack with a turquoise awning hanging over a long, exposed window. Puke yellow lights bleed out and illuminate the sidewalk, casting just enough light on the sign at the top of the awning to make it out from a distance. King Kone.

I take a few moments to walk up and down the graffiti-stained sidewalk, determined to find anything else that might serve as a better food option. Other than the corner convenience store and the 'landmat,' the neighborhood is mostly residential. Not to mention, there is definitely a bald homeless dude with missing teeth approaching me from behind one of the dumpsters in the alley.

Desperate times call for desperate measures. In my case, desperation is crappy fast food.

A doorbell chime that sounds vaguely like a masturbating robot pierces the air around me as I speed walk inside and pounce to the front counter. A guy with silver eyeliner hunches his thin body over the register, looking up at the digital clock behind him.

"Welcome," his nasally voice whines, "what can I get for you?"

My hands jitter like mad as I tug at the two strings on my hoodie, yanking at both ends and praying he doesn't take a good look at my face. I look down at one of the ketchup splattered menus stuck to the front and run through my options. Nothing sounds appetizing, but I'm hungry enough that the mere thought of food causes me to salivate.

"Ehh, cheeseburger and fries. That's it." I deepen my voice as much as possible, trying to make it sound natural but nervously coming out more as *Hi, I have strep throat.*

"Anything to drink?" the cashier asks. He makes eye

contact with me for a brief second before looking back at the clock once again. He really doesn't recognize me?

"Just water, thanks." I square my shoulders upright, shoving a twenty-dollar bill in front of his face before he has the opportunity to look up and read my total. The register opens with a loud ching as he counts what I'm owed. I hurriedly throw it into a tip jar that reads *Afraid of change? Leave it here!*

The guy slides the receipt over the counter, saying dully, "thanks. Have a royal day."

I plunk myself into the torn plastic seat in the farthest booth from the window. Exposed foam peeks out from the broken seem and makes me wish I'd grabbed hand sanitizer instead of just about anything else. Oh, and you know, my fucking cell phone.

Just eat something and then ask someone for directions. I steadily drum my fingertips on the table. *Everything is going to be fine.*

The robot moans again as a clamor of footsteps hurries inside, a female voice unsettling the eerie quiet. "I am so sorry I'm late! My sister needed help with dinner!"

"You're lucky Armani isn't here," the male cashier huffs, "you'd never hear the end of it. I call remote privileges!"

A burly-looking fry cook with a grease-stained apron marches over and carelessly throws a basket of food in front of me that looks like it's been microwaved and then sat on. I could care less. I dive into the burger and allow the taste of fake cafeteria meat to melt over my tastebuds. My eyes about roll back in pure delight. I pluck the tomatoes out of the bun and have the entire thing demolished in under a minute, coming up for oxygen only once.

The ice-cold air conditioning smacks my face with a strange sort of relief as I lean forward and pound my straw out of its wrapper, twisting the paper around my thumb till it's perfectly thin and flat. It's incredible how much a cheap meal eaten in a carnivorous rage can make you feel slightly more like yourself. The relief is short-lived as the reality of my recklessness comes whooshing back in one fell swoop.

All I could do was picture Alex back in the hotel room, frantically pacing from corner to corner, shouting my name like some twisted game of hide and go seek. Meanwhile, Lexi was probably on the phone with the cops, going on about cheerleaders, potential kidnapping, and the clusterfuck known as Archive of our Own.

"Care for me to get your table?"

The familiar female voice from earlier comes up beside me. Without thinking, I dig into my jacket pocket and pull out the sunglasses. *Sure, Rowan. This doesn't look suspicious at all.*

Her voice trails off as I look up and feel my heart jump into my esophagus. The flat screen hanging on the wall behind her head is playing... me. Rather, a close-up of Hunter Cade inside Heights High, preparing to confront his English teacher about impregnating his mother.

I mindlessly reply to her comments, trying to keep my head low and make it seem less obvious that I'm casually on TV for everyone to see.

"Do you go to Bedford Academy?" The girl asks gleefully.

"Uhh, yeah. I'm a senior." I say it almost too quickly, figuring lying is better than getting caught. I'm coming up with a quick embellishment about transferring to really sell it when I worriedly glance up and get a good look at her.

She's laughably short with a pale complexion. Her dark hair hangs wild in ringlets over her puffy cheeks. The lighting isn't doing anyone any favors, but I'm finding it challenging to save face and look back down. She's... nice.

My eyes dart back to the screen, feeling humiliated by my

performance as she asks if there's anything else she can get for me.

"Unless you can convince that guy to turn the TV to just about anything else."

"I hear Webstream added *Killer Klowns from Outer Space* just in time for Halloween." Her smile is bright and causes my cheeks to turn red. I'm not sure what's more embarrassing—this version of me or the one on TV yelling about unprotected sex.

A group of loud guys busts through the door of the restaurant, causing an obnoxious scene. One of them hollers over to the server as he smacks the top of the doorframe, drawing her attention away from my table. Here I am trying not to be noticed and simultaneously feeling my self-esteem shrink as I lose a complete stranger's attention. I can almost see Ashanti in the background, slowly shaking her head in disapproval. If anyone knew how bad I was at flirting, it was her.

One of the first personal questions Alex felt comfortable asking after being hired was if Ashanti and I were a thing.

"Not that it's any of my business," he'd carefully follow up with.

Everyone seemed to think so by how close we were. There were at least seven hundred Instagram accounts dedicated to Adshanti alone—only the best ship name ever, according to Ashanti. I guess I missed the rule where you can't work in Hollywood and have any sort of non-sexual relationship with your co-star. It didn't matter how many times I pivoted the question in interviews. I could downright deny it, and people would still find a way to pull up photos of us grabbing coffee and call me a liar.

"No," I'd answer Alex. "She's actually seeing someone else."

Alex would low whistle through his teeth with a smirk. "He's a lucky guy."

I cautiously glance over my shoulder and listen as the self-important doorframe smacker goes off on the girl about a glass of water, forcing my blood to boil.

Grandma always had a saying: 'I'll love whoever you grow up to be, unless you grow up to be an asshole.' It stuck with me long after she died and carried me once I was in the thick of Hollywood. I'd experienced my fair share of assholes in the last two years, and quickly understood exactly what she'd meant. There was never an excuse for somebody's arrogance.

The fight at the club flashes before my eyes as Grandma's saying repeats on a loop. I'm about to turn around and comment on what's happening when I abruptly see her smile at one of the guys at the table who looks like he has more game than I ever will. Especially when I'm sitting in a virus-infested booth, disguised as the She Doesn't Even Go Here guy from *Mean Girls*.

Just to recap all the mistakes I've made in the last seventy-two hours: I started a fight by sticking up for a friend, got single-handedly renounced by my own fan base for exhibiting 'toxic masculinity', and put my contract renewal in jeopardy. I risked my safety by leaving the hotel room where I'd been asked to quarantine until the publicity died down, left with someone else's money, and forgot my cell phone. To top it off, I'm tempted to start yet another fight with someone who looks like he could step on me because his friend was a dick to a waitress I find slightly attractive.

Passionate, but stupid about sums it up.

I massage my temples with my fingertips, the dull lighting making my vertigo worse than it normally is. My breaths start coming in shallow spurts. I repeatedly lick my lips to save off the sloshing nausea brought on by meat I'm almost positive wasn't cow.

A lightbulb goes off in my head as I dig into my pocket and

pull out the orange tube of medication. I pop off the lid and pour two pills into my palm, swallowing them dry and sucking down the last bit of my melted ice. If I was going to eventually go back to The Four Seasons to be murdered by my aunt and bodyguard, at least Zoloft might help calm me down first.

"You still good here?"

"Shit!" I mutter, dribbling water onto my jacket. It's the girl again, wearing a forced smile if I've ever seen one.

"No luck on getting him to change it to *Killer Klowns*." She sighs. "But to be fair, this is a different form of scary."

I unleash a laugh that sounds vaguely like the robotic sex door, embarrassed all over again. "If you really want to piss him off, spoil the ending. Someone plants a bomb in the school, and the fate of Noah and Hunter rests in limbo till next season."

"You watch this show too?"

"Something like that." I yawn with a bone-popping stretch. These meds never usually made me drowsy. *Weird*. She's about to turn away and rejoin Silver Eyeliner at the front register when I mindlessly state what I'm thinking. "Why do you let those guys treat you like that?"

"Like what?"

"I heard him bossing you around."

She points to her uniform, me being a total creep by trying to find any sign of a nametag.

"I work here. They're allowed to boss me around."

"There's a difference between being a customer and an asshole." My tone comes off harsh and defensive.

"Guess there's no difference in the real world," she says.

I weigh the accuracy of her statement, all the muscles in my face hanging loose. "Still better than *Dawn Heights*."

The girl's voice slowly starts to run on in my head, her words mushing together into one, long, high-pitched warble noise. I yawn for a second time, my eyelids feeling heavier with each passing second. Was I finally cracking under the pressure of life, or was I having a stroke?

Once she's marched off toward the front, I pull the pill bottle out of my pocket to read the potential side effects.

"Oh no," I whisper.

It's not Zoloft. *That* pill bottle was probably sitting happily next to my cell phone somewhere back in my hotel room. I'd just taken two of the sleeping pills Lexi had given me earlier. The pills she only told me to take half of.

The anxious vertigo I was feeling minutes ago suddenly turns into something else entirely. My chest pulses rapidly. The room is still spinning, but instead of making me feel sick, it feels like I'm levitating. I dream of flying off and crashing into the ceiling, making sure to hit the flat screen on my way out so nobody in the restaurant ever has to see my stupid face ever again.

Seconds later, drool slowly leaking out the corners of my mouth, everything goes dark.

"GO TOSS him in the alley across the street with the other weirdos. Problem solved." Clearly, Indio doesn't see the sleeping customer in King Kone as a problem whatsoever.

"I can't do that!" I panic. "What if he dies?!"

"Then he shouldn't have been doing drugs!" Indio reacts aggressively. He signs the bottom of the tally sheet for the night and shoves the money inside a small blue banker's bag to leave in the safe. "Wanna count out the tips?"

"Indio!" My volume increases. Hoodie Boy doesn't move a muscle. If I hadn't felt for a pulse and found one, I would be sure he was already dead.

Indio's shiny eyeliner flickers under the moody, half-switched lights. "What the hell do you want me to do about it? Call 911? Call the homeless shelter?"

"He goes to my school! He told me so!"

"Do you know his parents?"

I hesitate. "This was actually the first time I'd ever met him."

Indio's face falls flat. His patience has been worn from thin to nonexistent. "I don't make thirteen dollars an hour to care about what happens to high school drug addicts, Josie."

"So, you're just going to leave him here?"

"Yes." He zips the blue bag with a smug grin. "Consider it the Indio Byun version of *Scared Straight* or something."

I raise my arms and cock my head. My body temperature rises rapidly, along with my concerns. "You want to leave a high school drug addict—your words, not mine—locked in King Kone all night with several hundred dollars lying in the office? Free to steal and use as he wishes, all because you didn't want to deal with it?"

Indio, in a rare moment of silence, pauses to absorb my theory. "Well shit, when you put it like that..."

"Exactly!" I sass. It's rare that I get to be the smartass in any given conversation. I allow myself a moment to enjoy it before going right back to freaking out.

Indio groans into the depths of the spit-wad dotted ceiling, doing nothing to rattle the drooling customer in the middle of us.

"Do you have any friends who might know who he is?" Indio asks.

"What friends?" I laugh.

"First of all, thanks for proving my point." I roll my eyes at his rude remark. "And second? Josie, I have to get home."

"To do what? Watch more *Dawn Heights*?"

"To live my life! Maybe you should get one!" Indio turns towards the office before I can muster another insult.

I instantly feel awful, Indio's 'proving my point' comment burying itself underneath my skin. By no means was I a social pariah. I had a handful of people I spoke to at school regularly if a particular assignment required it. Plus, I had Hannah back in Ohio. So what if we'd spoken once in the last three months since she started working on the yearbook committee and dating that guy on the track team? That didn't make me a friendless outcast.

Did it?

"Josie," Indio's faint voice sighs from the kitchen, peering his eyes through the hot plate slit in the window. "Leave him in the alley. He'll wake up there, freak out, and never do anything like this again. Trust me. Public intoxication isn't a look."

I untie the apron around my waist and aggressively toss it into the dirty towel bucket next to the sink. Indio strides past me without a second glance, marching out the door and shooting me a peace sign from outside the window. Before he disappears down the road towards his car, he fogs up the glass, mouthing 'good luck!'

Easy for him to say. He wasn't the one being roped into dragging an unconscious six-foot teenage boy into a makeshift homeless camp across the street.

I look up at the digital clock on the wall overhead. It's inching closer to nine thirty. If Pru didn't hear me walk through the door in the next ten minutes, she'd likely break curfew by hopping out of bed and walking across the street in her rainbow pajamas to make sure I was alright. Or worse, she'd call our mother. Mom was already concerned enough about leaving us. I couldn't rock that boat on the first night.

I quietly switch off the remaining lights inside King Kone to make what I'm about to attempt look less incriminating than it actually is. The last thing I need is for someone to catch me dragging a lifeless body into an alleyway.

Gently, I poke at Hoodie Boy's shoulder, trying to stir him one final time.

"Hey!" I poke again. Leave it to me to notice how firm his arm feels underneath the hoodie. I shake my head. *Remove the body now. Thirst over it later.*

It's hopeless. This guy isn't just asleep, he's likely somewhere projecting into an ancestral plane. In one final attempt to try and contact his relatives, I carefully dig through his jacket pockets to see if I can find a phone or ID. I come up fruitless, unless you count the crumpled stick of gum.

Trying not to overthink it, I gingerly start to prod my way through his pants pockets, remembering to confess this the next time Mom dragged me to one of those awkward Mass services on Christmas. Rather than anything useful, I locate a gigantic wad of cash and a pill bottle. I can't pronounce the name, it's something that starts with the letter H, but it has one glaring piece of evidence in the description: *sleep aid*. Was it even possible to be addicted to sleeping pills? Questions only school-marms like me are poised to ask.

Carefully tilting his head, I lower his sunglasses, and shove them into his jacket. I take a good look at him to see if I can place his face from the hallways of Bedford. His cheekbones are hollow and defined, puffing out only slightly as he rattles out heavy snores that reek of raw onions. It's driving me crazy that I can't figure` out what his name is. How would I walk by a face like this and not look twice?

"Okay." I exhale to myself. "You can do this, Josie."

I pull Hoodie Boy's body off the bench with a grunt and prop him upright, leaning him over one of my arms. What he lacks in size he more than makes up for in height; if there was ever a time to hate being five foot two, this was it. He flops over me lifelessly as I drag him across the filthy floor I could care less to mop tonight.

Once I finally pull the two of us out the door, I swing my foot out to hold it open, pulling him alongside me. He rests against my arm for half a second before dropping hard against the ground as I fish for the store key Armani leaves tucked behind the mailbox out front.

"Oh god!" I cry loudly. It garners the attention of the home-less gang across the way. I cup a hand over my mouth and crouch down to inspect his head. His Lakers hat had fallen off and rolled into the slimy gutter, but there wasn't any sign of a concussion. I pull the hood off his head to be sure, revealing a soft, sweaty mop of dark brown hair.

"Everything okay?" One of the homeless guys, balding and toothless, shouts at me. He lights up a cigarette and takes a long drag.

"Yeah, thanks!" I sing way too enthusiastically. I pull him up onto his feet once again and lean him up against my opposite arm.

"A little too much ice cream, ehh?" The homeless man winks devilishly. "We'll take care of him if you want."

I try not to throw up at the man's implications. The longer I stare at the group of people across the street, passing around bags of god-knows-what while sitting on a box-spring exposed mattress and attempting to ignite a fire using the dumpster, the greater my apprehension becomes.

I can't leave him with them, I tell myself. *Nothing good can come of this.*

I look across the street to our apartment, the wheels in my head spinning on overdrive as his body grows more challenging to hold. Mom's rules required Pru be in bed by nine, which meant she was probably already safe and snug in her bedroom, waiting for me to knock on her door to let her know I was home safe. Tomorrow was Saturday, so she wouldn't be setting an alarm to be out the door by seven for school, and would likely be sleeping in like all of us did on weekends.

If I managed to sneak Hoodie Boy into my room and try to have him awake and out of the apartment before Pru woke up, I could sleep on the couch, and she would never suspect he were there. I'd be able to get his name, make sure he was alright, and send him home safely. It was almost too perfect. At least, some weird and twisted equivalent of perfect.

Hoisting him further up my arm in preparation for the

short journey, I quickly begin dragging him along the street, trying not to cry as I lift him over each and every stair leading toward the main door of our building (fourteen, to be exact— this was the first time I'd counted). His high-tops scrape against the stoop as I pull him up and launch the two of us inside, never having been so grateful to live on a bottom floor in my life.

I take a moment to pause and dry heave, my sides aching from the workout. "Enjoying your ride?" I look at his incapacitated face and chuckle to myself, secretly groaning.

Refusing to drop him a second time, I press him up against the wallpaper with my left palm, pressing in the four-digit code to our keypad and pushing it open with a low squeak. Success!

The living room is dark and motionless. Usually, Mom would still be awake when I'd come home from work, toiling away on a canvas in the corner as I told her about my night. She'd end our conversations by offering to make me a late-night grilled cheese that was borderline inedible. Not having her here made the house feel twice as empty.

You're carrying the lifeless body of a classmate who overdosed on sleeping pills. I roll my eyes. *I'm sure your mom would love to hear that story.* I didn't want to know what might happen if Mom knew what I was up to. If my plan worked, he'd be out of here before anyone could ever find out.

Pru's bedroom is at the end of the hallway across from our mom's. Hopefully, she wouldn't hear me as I quietly grunt my way through the apartment en route to the first door on the left. I can't get to my bedroom fast enough. I open the door and click on my desk lamp with a loud twist.

Once I'm able to see beyond the soft moonlight streaming in through the windows, I carefully set Hoodie Boy onto the edge of my twin bed and give him a good, hard shove onto his side. He wheezes with a soft, dreamlike chuckle as I step back and admire, mostly in horror, what I've just accomplished.

There is a boy sleeping in my bed. And I have no clue who he is.

I rub my eyes with a low whine, exhausted and energized all at once. Reaching beneath my bed, I pull out a lavender plush blanket my dad had bought on a business trip to Scranton years ago. There was no significance to it other than I was seven and going through my purple-everything phase. He picked it up at a local farmer's market and said it reminded him of me. It was far too small for me to use now, let alone anyone else. Considering every other extra blanket we owned was still sitting somewhere in a box, it was the only hospitality I could come up with at a moment's notice.

I reach into the top drawer of my dresser and grab a pair of grey sweatpants and a black tank top to serve as pajamas, taking one last look at him before slowly backing away towards the door. Despite how weird the situation is, and by god, it's weird, there's something curiously peaceful about him. It's almost like watching someone sleep for the very first time. *Way to creepily romanticize the moment, Josie.*

After brushing my teeth and throwing on my pajamas, I give Pru's door a single knock and hear her shout "Goodnight!"

I tiptoe back to my bedroom, clicking off the lamp and shutting my door with a slow, quiet turn of the knob, trying to keep things sounding as normal as possible. With Hoodie Boy safely tucked away, my footfalls return to normal. A swell of confidence bursts up inside me as I fall back onto our old tan sofa and grab one of the flattened throw pillows, stuffing it under my mess of hair with a fluff.

I helped that boy, I think to myself, stifling a giddy squeal face down into the pillow. Part of me wondered if this is how my dad felt after rescuing my mom from the subway platform of doom. My eyes grow heavy as I blissfully daydream about my part as his personal King Kone savior.

Out of nowhere, a faint buzzing noise begins rattling from the burgundy desk near the front door, the one that sat there collecting dust and junk mail. I sit up with a yawn and notice my cell phone lying on a stack of envelopes. I shake my head and ignore it as I flop back down onto the couch. It was probably just Mom telling Pru and me that she was getting ready for bed and wishing us sweet dreams.

A few more moments go by, and the buzzing starts again, shaking a pile of coupons off the table. By then, I'm already in a blissful sleep of my own.

THE ROOM WAS ILLUMINATED by a sea of tinted lights. Dark red velvet curtains lined the walls and swayed back and forth as loud bass thumped on the dance floor. The air was thick with fazer smoke and smelled of expensive perfume and alcohol. Unfamiliar faces whizzed past in a daze, most of them briefly stopping to wave and say hi despite me not knowing who any of them were.

"Calm down, Michael!" I point a finger to his face and feel his hot breath run up the sleeve of my blazer. "You're drunk!"

"You calm down, shithead!" He fires back. "Stop defending that bitch!"

It happened so quickly. I lunged forward, and without even thinking twice about it, my fist was crunching loudly against the bones in Michael Brewer's face.

Instantly, everything in the room turns to white light. I sit upright in a cold sweat, gasping for air as I press my head towards my chest and fold my shaking hands around my knees. I'd been having nightmares about the fight ever since it happened. It was part of the reason I hadn't been sleeping.

A bead of sweat rolls from my eyebrow directly into my eyeball, stinging like lemon juice in an open wound. I feverishly rub my eyes and toss my head back to look up at the ceiling. Bare white with detailed crown molding that hadn't been dusted since the day it was finished.

My knees make a satisfying clicking noise as I lower them beneath a soft purple blanket the size of a baby quilt. The sheets are a pale shade of blue with small gray heart patterns. I may not have spent enough time in my hotel room to notice every little detail, but this was definitely not my bed at The Four Seasons. A fresh batch of sweat begins to pool up underneath my arms and soak through my shirt.

Where the hell am I?

The walls are an unforgivable shade of pink. One might call it salmon if they were sophisticated, but Pepto Bismol is more like it. Paper-thin lace curtains explain the blinding sunlight shining in through the window. There's nothing personal about the space to provide any evidence of where I could possibly be. No posters, no artwork, not even a single picture, just some worn furniture and a loaded bookshelf. If it weren't for the neatly organized erasable wall calendar hanging above the desk, you'd think the room was abandoned.

I toss the hilariously small blanket off my legs and swing them off the side of the bed. The floorboard underneath me sounds like it's about to cave in underneath my weight. I approach the bookshelf and run my fingers across a horizontal row of colorful spiral notebooks. The edges of the paper inside are stained and torn from wear. Next to it are a series of old English textbooks that scream *I was stolen from a library!*

Stacks of DVDs fill the rest of the shelf, their plastic spines tightly packed. I recognize several of the titles from my grandmother's old movie library. *An American in Paris, Breakfast at Tiffany's, It Happened One Night,* and *A Streetcar Named Desire.* Whoever lived here had the overall taste of a ninety-year-old.

Who is it? I think to myself. Whose house was this, and why was I here? The details fuzzily ran together. I was in the hotel, I left, and then... *shit.*

I'd been gone all night. I'd been out of the hotel room, cell phone-less, for an entire night. The air in the room abruptly feels twenty degrees colder, my feet turn into frigid ice pops encased in disgusting sneakers.

In my head, I replay everything that happened right up until I blacked out. I'd taken two of Lexi's sleeping pills, thinking they were my anxiety medication. I planned to get up and ask someone at the food place for directions on how to get back to lower Manhattan. After that, it all goes blank. It's as if my brain is an old VCR, and someone is hitting rewind and record over the tape at the same time.

The door slowly cracks open with a low creak, a small voice following in a whispered tone.

"Hey Jo, sorry if you're still asleep, do you have any sciss—"

I'm not sure which one of us freezes harder. Me, as I casually snoop through the bookcase or the gangly little girl standing in front of the open door looking for scissors. At least, I think that's what she's about to say before she drops the handful of colorful strings she is holding. They all go floating onto the floor like strands of freshly cut unicorn hair.

Neither one of us says anything for at least half a minute. Both of our faces turn green and gape in disbelief. Long, auburn curls run past the length of the young girl's arms, a pair of square glasses sits on her nose and magnifies her amber eyes. There's an unfamiliar familiarity about her I can't quite place, mostly because I'm internally bracing for her to start screaming for the police at any second.

She clicks her tongue to the roof of her mouth, ending the silence. "Do you know who you are?"

Unfortunately, I muse. "Do you know who I am?"

The girl nods, her fuzzy white slippers making a tapping noise as she takes two giant steps forward. "Rowan Adler?"

I offer a lopsided grin. "Guilty."

The room goes quiet again after that. She bends down to pick up the string while keeping her focus locked on me. The least I can do is reach down and help her collect them. She gasps as I lower to my knees and we accidentally reach for the same one.

"Did you sleep with my sister?" She abruptly accuses.

"What?!" It comes out more convicted than I'd meant for it to.

The girl points a finger to the sky. "This is my sister's room. You were in her bed."

"Who is your sister?"

"Bold question for someone who potentially slept with her."

I toss the handful of orange and yellow strings into her palms, staring coldly. "I didn't sleep with your sister."

"Okay, so then how did you get in here?"

The dizzying pink walls are starting to make me feel like I need actual Pepto Bismol. "That's a good question."

She nods her head thoughtfully, ruminating in my confusion. Maybe it's the glasses, but she is one of the most intellectual-looking children I've ever seen in my life, minus the fuzzy slippers and rainbow-striped pajama pants.

"I'm about to make some friendship bracelets." she dangles the strings in the air. "Care to help? Maybe explain why you're in my house?"

Being an only child could be partially to blame for the way I behaved around kids. Their energy and enthusiasm always freaked me out. I didn't get those same uncomfortable feelings with this kid. Even if she seems way too okay with having a perfect stranger in her house, famous or not.

"Uhh, sure?"

She smiles, revealing two very large front teeth. She hands me the strings to hold while she repositions her knees and goes crisscross onto the floor, pointing up to the dresser covered in faded scratch-and-sniff stickers from at least a decade ago.

"Josie usually keeps her scissors in the bottom drawer with all her extra school stuff," she chimes. "Can you grab them for me? They're silver with a red stripe."

I nod and casually reach over to the dresser. *What the hell are you doing, Rowan?* I internally panic. *You should be getting back to The Four Seasons! Not playing arts and crafts with a living American Girl doll!*

A vein in my forehead throbs out of discomposure. Alex and my aunt were most likely out on a frantic search trying to find me. Why was I about to sit on a stranger's bedroom floor and sift through different shades of yarn? What the fuck was in those sleeping pills?

"These?" I open the drawer and hold up the first pair of clippers I see.

"Uh-huh!" she sings, leaning forward and ripping them out of my grip blade side down. "I'm Prudence Bradford, by the way. Pru for short."

"Rowan." I awkwardly wave, bending to the ground and attempting to copy her crisscross position. "We've established that you already knew that, though."

"Kind of." She bobs her head from side to side, her long hair sweeping the floor. "Only by association. I'll sneak into the living room late sometimes and find my mom watching your show."

"Sneak?"

"She says it's too 'mature' for me. Ironic considering I'm currently binging *Gossip Girl*." She darts her eyes to the sky. "No offense, but this experience is wasted on me."

"None taken." I reach to grab a single green string. "So, how exactly do you do this?"

She excitedly lies three long strings out flat on the ground and hovers her hands over the top like a magician performing a sleight of hand. "Marsha Delacross says the key to the perfect braid is getting the right length the first time."

"Who?" I itch my head.

Pru holds up the hardcover book she's kept safely tucked underneath her armpit. A middle-aged woman who looks like she belongs on the box of a 1950s ready-made dinner folds one hand underneath her chin with a resting bitch face that peers directly into my soul. *Arm Candy: by Marsha Delacross.*

"She's the queen of the cross!" Pru announces.

"That's not semi-heretical at all," I murmur.

"You take three long stands and then cross them over," she explains while taking three strings in different shades of blue and using them as an example. "Then, you tie a knot at the top with a loop and divide the six strings into two sections..."

"You've already lost me."

"...then you take the two sections with the three strands and braid each of them separately. Once you've finished both strands, tie the two braids together at the bottom into a chunky knot that fits into the loop. Voila!"

In the time it takes for her to run over the process, she's already grabbing another three strings and beginning work on a second bracelet. I give up entirely before I've even started. I opt for trimming strings for her to work with instead.

"You're not going to ambush me with a million questions?" I wonder aloud. If I were her age and a celebrity randomly walked into my house and offered to help me make friendship bracelets, I'd have at least a few. This really was a wasted experience on her.

"I didn't want to be direct," her sassy tone snips. "Do you not remember or something?"

I reach for my back, itching at the center. "I was at some little burger shack last night eating dinner, and then I took sleeping pills on accident. I must have blacked out. I woke up in here." The condensed Disney Channel version made it sound much more innocent than it actually was.

Pru peers up from her work and flairs her large nostrils. "Did the shack have a wide window out front? Kinda smells like chocolate and rotting flesh, lots of Vin Diesel pictures on the walls?"

"I didn't notice the Vin Diesel pictures, but yeah. Definitely the rotting flesh thing."

Pru grins. "That's not a burger shack. That's King Kone! It's across the street. My sister works there!"

More pieces began falling into place. No wonder Pru looked so familiar. Her sister was the server at the restaurant! Of course, that still didn't explain how I'd wound up in her bed.

Carefully, I set the scissors onto the floor and begin giving the room a once-over for pom-poms.

"Your sister isn't a cheerleader, is she?" I ask, my voice trembling.

"Josie doesn't have an athletic bone in her body," Pru giggles. "She wants to be a writer who writes movies."

"A screenwriter," I correct her, secretly impressed by the aspiration. Filmmaking isn't exactly a career you see many people vying for at high school job fairs. I guess screenwriting tracked with all the full notebooks and old movies on her dresser.

Pru finishes her fifth bracelet and tosses it into her small pile. She yanks one of the freshly cut yellow strings out of my hands. "I guess you'd know, huh? You probably know a lot of them."

It was bold for anyone to call the people behind *Dawn Heights* 'writers.' When the show was pitched by Webstream, it was labeled a realistic depiction of teen issues, told with relevance for today's teens. The first season started off innocently enough with a touch of melodrama occasionally sprinkled in to give the show some flavor.

Unfortunately, melodrama was all Webstream viewers wanted. They fired all the original writers and hired a bunch of morons for the next two seasons who had driven the show into the ground with hollow, fake woke plotlines and predictable, shocking cliffhangers. I couldn't remember the last time I'd read a script I'd liked.

"My guess is that she helped you," Pru continues. "My sister, that is. She's good at helping people, but she won't admit it."

"Makes sense." I shrug. "Do you know where she is?"

"This is her room, obviously." Pru holds up her current braid to her glasses, inspecting for any split strings. "Either she's on the couch in the living room, or you killed her, and her body is under the bed."

"You're not at all concerned it might be number two?"

"You didn't kill her. You can't even tie a knot."

I burst into laughter. "Harsh, Pru."

"I mean, I haven't ruled it out entirely," she declares. "I saw on Instagram that you got into a fight with Michael Brewer. I guess you've got a dark side somewhere."

My laugher turns to a simmering whimper. Life wasn't going to let me forget about that damn fight, was it? Changing the subject is all I can think to do without spiraling into a full-blown panic attack.

"You have Instagram, but you're not allowed to watch my show?"

She tilts her head. "It's for my business."

"Business?"

"Duh!" She grabs the stack of finished bracelets and holds them up over her head.

"This is a business?"

Pru clearly doesn't appreciate my cynicism, pulling her cell phone out of the pocket of her striped pants and loading the app for me to see her account. *It must be nice to have a phone*, I secretly envy.

"See?" She hands me the device and points to the screen. The account is @pruslooms. Each of her posts showcases a different colored bracelet accompanied by a dull, white background. A bed sheet, I'd suspect. There were at least fifty posts so far. Her inventory was admittedly impressive.

"I only have thirty-seven followers," she notes the ticker at the top of the page. "They're mostly from my school. I'm selling them for five bucks each."

I hand the phone back with a reverent nod. "A little cheap considering the effort, don't you think?"

"All supply, no demand," she argues. "Don't tell her, but I'm collecting the money for my sister's college fund. I've only sold two so far, but that's still ten bucks she didn't have before."

Without even really trying, Pru has become the only kid I've ever liked. I fish for one of the bracelets in her pile. It's black, white, and yellow. The vivid colors remind me of a honeybee.

"Sounds like she's lucky to have you."

Pru's eyes sparkle behind her glasses, straightening her shoulders and leaning back with a proud toss of her hair. "I know," she sings. "You can keep that one if you want."

I grasp the bracelet and run it between my fingers. "For free?"

"You're decent labor." She points to the scissors. "Consider it payment. Do you know how they're supposed to work?"

"It's a friendship bracelet. What's there to know?"

"Marsha Delacross says that you should wear it, then when you find a person you care about, give it to them so they'll always remember you."

"So... a friendship bracelet then?" I smirk. She sticks out her tongue and rocks her head back and forth, earning another laugh.

Pru dives back to work on her next bracelet as I tie the thin cord around my wrist. I loop the large knot into the clasp and pull the sleeve of my sweatshirt down to keep it safely tucked in place. I'd been given a lot of pointless gifts in the years since *Dawn Heights* started. This was one of the few I actually liked.

"So, it's just you and your sister then?" I ask.

"And Mom." Pru instantly picks up on my concerns. "But don't worry, she's not here! She's out of town for a few days." Thank god. The last thing I needed was another parental figure breathing down my neck.

As if she planned it, Pru's lock screen illuminates with a new message from *Mom* as she finishes another bracelet. I nosily turn my head to read the notification bubble.

Morning, love! Stay safe tonight if you decide to go trick-or-treating without your sister! Be home by eight and text me!

I glance to note the date and time. 10:04 AM. Saturday, October 31st.

"It's Halloween, isn't it?" I play stupid as if I haven't just learned that from her text.

She frowns. "Yeah, but my sister is working. Unless I get a last-minute invite from a friend, I'm probably going to be stuck inside watching *The VelociPastor* and solo eating a pint of rocky road."

"*The VelociPastor?*"

"It's a horror movie about a priest who becomes a dinosaur antihero and kills evil ninjas."

"No way that's a thing. I would know. I'm the king of bad movies." That was what Ashanti dubbed me as after I'd introduced her to the masterpiece train wreck known as *Plan 9 From Outer Space*. I'd never been particularly proud of the title till I heard Queen of the Cross and realized it wasn't that bad.

"IT'S ON WEBSTREAM!" Pru loudly cheers. "Wanna stay and watch?"

I'm not sure what the most bizarre facet of this situation is. That she's asking me to stay, or that I sort of want to. This had been the most unusual fifteen minutes of my life, but sitting here making bracelets with a random kid on a stranger's floor still managed to feel more normal than my life on any other given day.

Before I get the chance to say another word on Pru's proposition, the bedroom door swings open with a loud squeal. The baseboard spring whirrs like a car engine as it slams back. Pru's sister stands in the entrance, pajama-clad with her pupils shrinking to the size of pencil dots. Her mouth hangs open.

"Holy shit," she quietly moans.

Pru turns to her sister, slamming her strings onto the floor with a deep scowl.

"SWEAR JAR, JOSIE!"

CHAPTER 7

JOSIE

MOM SAYS I inherited Greg Bradford's ability to sleep through a tornado, which I actually did once back in Ohio. The compelling combination of sunlight streaming in through the living room mixed with an all-new chorus of text buzzing finally pulls me out of a deep slumber.

Still only half awake, I pull the pillow from underneath my head. I clutch it up towards my chin, my face falling onto the cardboard cushion with an uncomfortable smush. I take a few seconds to collect my thoughts before omitting a loud gasp and jumping to my feet. I pace back and forth on the freezing floor next to the couch in sheer panic.

There is a boy in my room.

There is a boy *sleeping* in my room.

Failing at keeping the floorboard croaking to a minimum, I tiptoe towards the hallway and peek my head around the dark corner. The door to Pru's bedroom is still shut. She must still be sleeping. I breathe a sigh of relief.

My cell phone continues to buzz away on the front table with an irritating hum. I would continue to ignore it if it weren't for the loud crash that immediately follows after yet another *burrrr* sound. It had vibrated itself off the table and onto the floor, taking a stack of envelopes down with it.

I run and frantically lunge down to reach for the device, shushing it as if it could possibly hear me and shut itself up. My head tilts sideways in vexed misery as I notice the small, new crack on the bottom corner of the screen. Mom was going to be furious with me. However, I'd happily accept her anger over this than what she'd do if she found out I'd snuck a guy into the house without her permission.

"What the—" my voice trails as I scroll through pages worth of missed notifications. Fifty text messages and fourteen missed calls, all from Indio. Each of the fifty texts were sent at various points in the night, and they all say the exact same thing.

CALL ME!

I duck into the corner of our small kitchen, near the air fryer Mom pointlessly bought in an attempt to start cooking more. I tap my fingers against the ugly vinyl countertop and hurriedly locate Indio's name on my list of contacts, gripping my phone tightly as he picks up after half a ring.

"MOTHER OF GOD, JOSEPHINE. REMIND ME NEVER TO CALL YOU IN AN EMERGENCY."

"I'm so, so sorry!" I softly whine into the receiver. "Is everything okay?!"

"You're not going to believe this," Indio's congested voice cracks with a giddy sort of sadism. "Remember that guy from last night?"

How could I forget? He was sleeping in the next room.

"The guy who fell asleep?" I reply, putting on my best performance of Cher from *Clueless*.

"Yes! Don't you think he looked familiar?"

The crack at the bottom of the phone scrapes against my fingertips, reminding me how dead I am. "Sort of? He goes to my school, remember? I've probably seen him around."

Indio responds by snorting into the phone. His vague taunting is officially starting to irritate me.

I rest a hand on my hip and lean my head against the sticky, blue wall. "Can you please just tell me what warranted an all-night freak-out?"

"Josie," he breathes with a low whisper, "I think that was Rowan Adler."

An image of Hoodie Boy's sleeping face flashes into my head like one of those fast-paced murder reenactments from an episode of *CSI*. Bright green eyes, well-defined facial bones, long eyelashes, and bushy eyebrows. I wasn't exactly looking up pictures of Rowan Adler in my free time, but there was without a doubt an uncanny resemblance between the two.

"What makes you think that?" I nervously chuckle.

Indio takes a drawn-out breath. This could only mean one thing: A long story with a plethora of pointless details is imminent.

"You know how I'm like, obsessed with The Fizz, right?"

"Of course," I say.

He's referring to TheFizz.com, a website devoted to digital media, emphasizing gossip and entertainment. They were primarily known for their pointless, time-wasting quizzes such as *I Guarantee We Can Guess Your Favorite Pizza Topping Based on Your Enneagram!*

"I was watching the next episode of *Dawn Heights* when I got home last night while scrolling through the news," he elaborates. I try not to neg him about what he considers news. "I saw a headline about how Rowan Adler was seen arriving at JFK with his entourage earlier in the day."

I shrug as if he can actually see how unimpressed I am by his detective work. "So?"

"So, I obviously freaked out because he's in New York. Duh."

"Along with a zillion other celebrities, Indio."

"Just wait, let me send you the article." He pauses for a beat. "There. Did you get it?"

My phone buzzes. I see the latest notification from Indio, a welcomed sight in the flood of 'call me' messages. I tap on the link. It leads me to an article with a quintessentially Fizz-esqe headline: *Rowan Adler is in New York, and I'm Emotionally Unstable.*

"Okay?"

"Read it!" Indio urges.

I thumb down and read on. The author of the article starts off by gushing over how big of a *Dawn Heights* fangirl she is and reminds readers that The Fizz is based out of Manhattan, meaning that she and Rowan Adler are currently 'breathing the same air.'

"Oh please." I purse my lips inward.

The following paragraph goes into detail about the supposed fistfight that took place between Rowan Adler and one of his co-stars at the season three premiere party over in Hollywood a few nights ago.

"*Neither Rowan Adler nor Michael Brewer have come right out and addressed the rumors yet,*" the author states, "*but sources say that both underage babes were drunkenly throwing blows at one another, while goddess and patron saint of all things pure and wholesome, Ashanti Nath, watched on in horror. Both of them had already left the scene by the time the cops arrived.*"

Indio's voice crackles loudly through the receiver. "Have you read it?!"

"I'm currently cringing over 'underage babes.'"

"Josie, scroll down!" The desperation in his voice is palpable.

I skip past the rest of the lengthy article and pause as a

series of sleazy paparazzi pictures loads at a snail's pace. The first few are far away and pointlessly grainy. It's the last one in the photoset that causes me to sink down the wall, my knees going out from under me.

"No. Freaking. Way."

Indio squeals in delight as I slouch on the floor in awestruck terror. "AM I RIGHT OR AM I RIGHT?!"

There's no denying it. The guy in the last photo is the same one I'd dragged into our apartment and thrown into my bed last night. Same dark hoodie, same douchey aviators covering his perfectly chiseled face, and if that wasn't incriminating enough, he was even wearing the same Lakers hat that had fallen into the gutter. If the boy in my bedroom wasn't Rowan Adler, I was currently housing one of the most creative cosplayers on the planet.

"Real question," Indio says between maniacal giggles, "did you end up leaving him in the alley?! And is he still there?!"

There is no good way to explain it. *Actually, I felt sorry for him, thinking he was a cute classmate, and I brought him home to detox. He's currently asleep a few hundred feet away. I was going to offer him a granola bar or something on the way out.*

"Indio," my voice trembles, "he's here."

"What?"

"As in, he's in my house."

His laughter comes to an abrupt end. "You're shitting me."

"Negative."

The silence on his end becomes unbearable to listen to. I crack and begin hyperventilating loudly, covering my mouth to mute my sobs and rocking myself back and forth on the floor like a baby.

"Josieeee!" Indio sings the end of my name like a high note. "HOW THE HELL?"

"I dragged him to my house!" I whisper yell. "I felt bad and was worried that the homeless people might do something weird to him!"

"Where is he now?!"

"In my bed!" I don't realize how risqué that sounds till it's come out of my mouth.

"In your what?!"

"I slept on the couch!" I explain. "I put him up in my room! I was going to wake him up and sneak him out before my little sister woke up!"

All I could envision in my head was the image of a dumbfounded Indio sprawled out on his bed, probably sporting one of his signature shades of colorful eyeliner, silently judging me. I couldn't exactly blame him, could I?

"This isn't a prank?" He questions. "This isn't some bad joke you're pulling because you didn't get remote privileges last night? He's deadass in your house right now?"

I'm becoming unjustly defensive over something I claim to feel so ashamed of. "What? Do you want a picture or something?"

"OH MY GOD!" Indio shrieks. I hold the phone away from my ear to salvage what's left of my hearing. "JOSEPHINE BRADFORD!"

Fearful tears begin to puddle up under my eyeballs and slowly roll onto my cheeks. Why was I crying about this? I hadn't done anything wrong. I thought I was helping a guy from school who'd made a bad decision. It's not like I intentionally set out to steal a celebrity and hide him in my bedroom.

"Josie," Indio's tone softens, "are you crying?"

"No," my watery voice sniffs.

"It's really not that big of a deal!" He snickers. "I mean, it totally is, and I kind of hate myself for not giving two shits last night, but seriously. Just tell him you were trying to help!"

I wipe the remainder of my tears and exhale with a puff of

my cheeks. *Everything can still be okay,* I attempt to convince myself as I beat my head against one of the cabinet doors. I can still wake him up, explain the misunderstanding, beg him not to call the cops, and send him on his merry way. With a granola bar!

"You know what I would do though," Indio mischievously adds, "take a picture and give it to The Fizz. Tell them your story and watch it go viral."

I gasp, knitting my forehead together into a single tight line. Great, now my inner mom was jumping out.

"That's awful!" I exclaim. "Why would I sell someone out like that? Especially when they have every right to call the cops on me!"

"For what?" He questions. "Being hospitable?"

"Put yourself in his shoes." I run a hand through my hair. "Would you want someone reporting on all your mistakes?"

"If I fucked up enough to deserve it."

There's no way I'm winning this argument, never against Indio. The man lives his life on a different planet. He once spent an entire four-hour closing shift explaining his thoughts on why cornflower blue is the most underrated crayon color. Four *hours.*

"I'm just saying," he grunts, "websites like The Fizz would devour this. Think about how much gossip sites paid to publish those crappy pictures from JFK. It's easy money."

Easy money. The phrase rings in my ears like a firehouse alarm. If there was one thing I presently needed in my life, other than a way out of this situation and for my mother to never find out, it was easy money.

Out of nowhere, I hear Pru's pipsqueak voice bounce off the walls towards the back of the apartment. My throat goes drum-tight, my phone nearly dropping onto the floor and shattering for the second time.

No. Please, no...

I pull the phone away from my ear, mouthing an indistinct "imgonnahavetocallyouback" to Indio before ending the call and hurrying to my feet.

I dash towards my bedroom in an unnerved frenzy, slamming the door wide open and looking upon my younger sister as she happily toils away bracelet making. Sitting across from her, with his legs gently folded into his lap, is a disheveled and visibly well-rested Rowan Adler, looking up at me with his piercing green eyes.

I almost fall to my knees. "Holy shit."

CHAPTER 8
JOSIE

"YOU KNOW ROWAN ADLER?!"

Pru's comment makes me want to spontaneously throw up. Their body language is easygoing and relaxed. The two of them sit on my floor wearing smiles like two old college friends who are reconnecting after years apart. Rowan sports an impressive display of bed head, while Pru taps at a vacant spot on the floor next to her and waves me over to join them.

I point to Rowan as if he were a dress I wanted to borrow out of my mom's closet. "Umm, can we go into another room for a minute?"

Rowan's face still had indentations from where my sheets had bunched up on his cheeks. I would call it semi-endearing if I wasn't about to go plead my innocence.

The outside corners of his eyes twitch upward. "Yeah, it's kind of necessary."

Pru looks up at Rowan as he rises from the ground and gives the back of his jeans a brush, removing the dust bunnies that multiply in my room faster than members of the Duggar family.

"Thanks for your help!" She waves.

He playfully bows and offers to shake her hand. "T'was an honor, Prudence."

Does Rowan know her name? Rowan Adler knows my sister's name?! How long had they been hanging out in my room while I slept my life away, completely oblivious?

As Rowan slides past me and moves out toward the living room, I catch the sly twinkle in Pru's eyes, shimmering like confetti behind her lenses.

"I like him," she mouths with a thumbs up.

I crease my head and respond with a silent "no" closing my door behind me. It's not like that. Absolutely not like that. Not in this reality or in any other.

It goes without saying this is easily the most awkward position I've ever found myself in. Seventeen-years-old and walking around in my see-thru pajamas as one of the most famous actors in the world wanders around my living room and admires my mom's paintings. These are the types of scenarios you only find in fanfiction, certainly not in the middle of a run-down apartment in Brooklyn.

"I like that one." Rowan points to one of the larger canvases hanging above the couch. Mom practically stabbed the concrete wall with a jackhammer to display it.

It's an interpretation of a bench in the middle of an abandoned park, fresh rain on the sidewalk reflecting the barren trees overhead. The sky is illuminated with a flood of red and yellow lights. She called it *Fall in New York*. The crazy part is that she painted it while we still lived in Cincinnati, years before she lived here again.

"Thanks. My mom painted it." I itch my neck, self-consciously tugging at my shirt. "She's not here, by the way. She's in DC."

"That's what your sister said," he smirks. "Secret government mission?"

More like pleading for money so I can get the hell out of this dingy shoebox. Not that I'd ever admit that to Mr. Most-Likely-a-Multi-Millionaire.

"Classified," I tease. "So, about all this..."

He ruffles the top of his head to unflatten one side of his hair. "Yeah," he says. "All this."

I take a deep breath, preparing to do the only thing that comes naturally to me—tell the truth. "You fell asleep last night while I was closing up. My co-worker had left and I panicked. King Kone is right across the street. I decided to take you home instead of calling the police. I thought you went to my school. So..."

Rowan almost smiles. "Probably shouldn't have lied, huh?"

"I mean, coming right out with it might've been a bit much for a Friday night."

He reaches his hands into his pockets and rocks on the balls of his feet. "Thank you," he says. "This whole thing was, *is*, one huge mistake. I took sleeping pills thinking they were something way milder. You should never have been put into this position. I appreciate you bringing me here and not calling the cops. That could've been—"

"A scandal?" I question. Rowan nods.

His *one huge mistake* comment pricks more than I expect it to. He's not wrong. This whole ordeal sounds like one freak misunderstanding on both of our accounts, but to imply that it should never have happened feels like giving providence the middle finger. Perhaps I was naïvely expecting to relive whatever magic had happened with my parents on the subway platform all those years ago.

"Would I be able to shower?" Rowan abruptly asks. "Then I'll be on my way. My skin feels like it's crawling."

My ears burn. You would think I'd never heard of a guy showering before.

"Sure! Wait here!" I enthusiastically respond—way, way too enthusiastically.

I march down the hall into Mom's bedroom and start digging through her discombobulated nightmare of a closet. Her office clothes dangle off the sides of her smock hangers, a sexy red dress from two pregnancies ago lies on the floor, collecting pile of dirty old sneakers.

Finally, I stumble upon a small stack of Dad's old clothes tucked away in a dusty corner. I settle on a plain t-shirt and a dark Cincinnati Law hoodie—what all the hipster lawyers of Ohio were wearing. My father was a good fifty pounds heavier than Rowan, but that didn't stop me from offering them anyway with a solemn smile.

"Thought this might help you stay incognito." I point to his jacket. "Sorry I can't help you with the underwear." *Sweet Jesus, Josie. Stop talking.*

"Thanks," he chuckles. "Another weird question. Would you be able to lead me towards a subway that takes me to lower Manhattan? I need to get back to The Four Seasons."

Oh boy. How would I explain to him that since moving here, I'd only ridden the subway to and from the hospital to see my dad? I hadn't stepped foot in one since the funeral. That's too much to unpack this early, especially when I'm already making thoughtless comments on the boy's undergarments.

"Sure." I shrug. "I can use the maps app on my phone and walk you over." I'm explaining it more for my peace of mind than for his.

I guide Rowan to mine and Pru's abomination of a bathroom. It's roughly the size of a broom closet with a shower and toilet, a mystery brown substance growing between the grout in the tiles. If that weren't bad enough, my mother was currently using our shower curtain as a drying rack for her lacy, black bras. I could die. Actually die.

"Soap and everything else is in there." I swiftly grab her belongings, failing to mention all of our soaps are acutely flower-scented.

"Thank you again," he repeats with a kind smile, tightly clutching my father's clothing. Just seeing them outside the closet for the first time in over a year felt like the emotional equivalent of Mentos being dropped into a bottle of cola.

I slowly back out of the bathroom to offer him privacy, but not before my overzealous hospitality gets the better of me. I poke my head through the door a final time.

"Hey, do you want a granola bar?"

Rowan's expression goes blank, his eyes morphing into two thin slivers. "No thanks?"

I nod. "Right."

The door shuts right in my face, and with it, any chance of playing it cool.

I'LL ADMIT IT. I'm finding ways to stall. I'm terrified of what awaits me in that godforsaken hotel room. So much so, I'm avoiding the obvious choice to borrow Josie's cell phone and call Aunt Lexi to tell her I'm alive. Why go through the rigmarole if I'm planning to return with my tail between my legs?

Just my luck, the train I'd taken the night before wasn't running towards the area I needed to get to. The line had closed over the weekend for maintenance. We'd been walking up and down the block for ten minutes, trying to find a route that would require as few transfers as possible. To make things even more uncomfortable, I'm staring at Josie way too much, and there's a good chance I'm starting to freak her out.

Unlike uber-suave Hunter Cade, I've never been subtle when it comes to girls. In the seventh grade, I asked Piper Tully to the middle school winter ball. I chose to do so after spilling an entire container of chocolate pudding on my pants in the cafeteria during lunch. Needless to say, she said no.

"I think the station is this way." Josie looks down at her phone and points the way, her teeth chattering against the wind. We pass King Kone and images of the night before come rushing back, causing me to feel secondhand embarrassment all over again.

"You think?" I blow warm air into my hands. The hoodie she'd given me had been worn to death. The material droops off my body, thin and faded from countless cycles through a washing machine.

"I don't take the subway much." She stares down at her sneakers.

I force a laugh. "How is it possible to live in New York and not take the subway much?" Grandma used to steal me away for summer getaways at her studio in the East Village as a kid. We took the subway everywhere we went. The only time I'd seen her behind the wheel of a car was when she'd moved upstate and started driving me everywhere

"We haven't lived here for long," Josie explains.

"Really? How long have you been here?"

She extends her phone like a metal detector, directing us to the corner up ahead where she signals us to take a right. If I knew any better, I'd say she didn't have a clue where she was going.

"Since last August." Josie finally replies.

I wave my hands to the sky, too cold for my liking and full of depressing gray clouds. "That's like, an entire year."

Josie lifts a hand to her mouth and starts chewing on her thumbnail without making it obvious that's what she's doing. The oversized black sweatshirt she's wearing swallows her petite body whole and makes her look like she's dressed as a Magic 8-Ball for Halloween.

"Yeah," she laughs nervously, "I don't go places very often. Besides school and work."

"That sounds miserable." Like I was one to talk. I was the one currently being held under house arrest by my own aunt.

Things between us grow quiet as the entrance to the

subway looms ahead at the end of the sidewalk. The surrounding streets are full of more copy/paste-looking brownstone buildings. Some have small front porches decked out with iron gates, mini grills, and plastic yard chairs. Others remain empty or littered with discarded living room furniture. It's cozy in a melancholy sort of way.

Josie motions to a small storefront across the street. The exterior of the mint-colored building is surrounded by braided vines and white orchids. Thin white letters hang overhead, reading Stillwater Coffee.

"That's a new coffee shop that just opened up a month ago. I've been in there." She sounds defensive as she points it out. Almost like she's proud of having been to one unfamiliar place in the entire year she's lived here.

"Is it any good?" I ask. The thought of coffee causes a visceral reaction. I never drank it till I started working early mornings on a set. Now I was one of those annoying caffeine addicts that baby boomers made Minion memes about. I would turn into a monster by midday if I didn't consume at least two cups.

She rocks her head from side to side. "Definitely a step above Starbucks."

"Wanna go in?"

Josie pauses along the sidewalk. Her eyes shift from my head to my feet. "For real?"

"I could use some coffee. Plus, I owe you for saving my ass."

She fights a smirk but eventually breaks as she locks her phone and slips it into the pocket of her skinny jeans. "I wouldn't say no to a flat white."

"That was my nickname in elementary school!" I joke. Crickets.

Ugh. That was the kind of dad joke that would've made even Ashanti Nath say 'too far.'

Josie approaches the corner to methodically press the pedestrian signal. I wait for a car to pass and casually jog across the stretch of road to the coffee shop. Josie's eyes bug out of her head as she frantically looks both ways and follows my lead with a run that could only be compared to a penguin waddle.

The corners of my mouth perk up. "You're a bit of a rule follower, aren't you?"

"What about it?"

"Nothing. It's just, everyone in the city jaywalks. It's natural, like breathing and cursing."

"Thanks for the tip," her voice warbles.

Another reason I tend to strike out with girls is because I have this less-than-awesome ability to mistake being a know-it-all for flirting. Backpedaling to save face, I open the door to the coffee shop and insist she takes the lead. I might be an idiot, but at least I'm a gentleman.

The flowers outside of the shop are a prelude to what awaits inside. The walls and tables are covered with various autumnal blooms, each in different warm orange and mustard yellow shades. Mason jar bouquets sit on each round table, alongside miniature pumpkins and unlit tea candles. The condiment bar and registers still have that new store sheen to them. The shop almost feels too nice to be in such a blue-collar neighborhood.

Josie's serious expression immediately softens as a guy sitting on a velvet couch propped against the merchandise wall recognizes her and extends a crooked smile. I get a good look at him from behind my sunglasses. It's the same guy she talked to at the restaurant the night before, the tall one who made me feel inferior in every possible way.

"Hey!" He stands to his feet to greet her with a wave. He's wearing a sweaty white basketball uniform and sucking down a green smoothie from a half-disintegrated paper straw.

"Hi, Aaron!" She tucks an unruly curl behind her ear, only to have it pop forward half a second later. "I'm guessing there was practice this morning?"

Aaron tugs at his wet jersey. "Yeah, every Saturday morning. Grabbing coffee?"

"Yeah, just running an errand and stopping in."

It's me. I'm the errand. *Hotel room prisoner* suddenly sounded like a term of endearment.

"Who's this?" Aaron points to me, the awkward boy standing next to her wearing a hoodie and sunglasses indoors. This whole *don't draw attention to yourself* thing was drawing an awful lot of attention to myself.

Josie fumbles for words. Rather than watch her fold under the pressure, I chime in first. "I'm her cousin."

"On my mom's side," she quickly adds. "This is... Hunter."

There's a beat between us. I half expect him to recognize me as he sizes me up from top to bottom.

"Hey, man!" Aaron extends one of his hands. I grab it firmly and give it a weak shake before wiping his sweat onto the thigh of my jeans. *Too close.*

"We can't stay long." Josie motions to the subway station right outside the door. "Hunter has somewhere to be."

"No worries, I'm actually about to head out myself." Aaron stretches his muscular arms over his head with a flex so pronounced, he might as well ask if she wants to go to second base right there on the couch. "Are you still working tonight, or is there any chance I'll get to see you at the party?"

Josie's cheeks glow as maroon as the flowers on the tables. "I wish I could, really."

"Here." He whips his cell phone out of his back pocket. "Since Julian isn't here to give me shit about it, let me get your number."

Her rich brown eyes melt into swooning pools of warm goo.

Not only was I an errand, but I was also making for a terrible third wheel.

The two quickly exchange numbers as I watch the scene unfold with a puzzling sort of jealousy. How was it possible to have perfect strangers willing to throw themselves at you daily and still be unable to catch the interest of the one stranger you want to notice you?

Aaron taps her lightly on the sleeve as he marches past us. "See you later, Josie. Nice to meet you, Hubbard!"

Hubbard. Never in my life had I felt less like a Hubbard.

A long line of customers had grown in the several minutes I waste watching the two of them stare longingly at one another. I move to the back with an impatient scowl. If there is one thing that can't be taken away from me, at least it's coffee.

"Sorry about that," Josie chuckles with an exasperated sigh. "He goes to my school."

"Looks like you're about to see all sorts of new places." The words spill out of my mouth before I can ask myself if they're necessary.

"It's not like that." she shakes her head. "I barely know him."

In my experience, at least in Hollywood, you could do a lot of things with people you barely knew. I remove my glasses and fold them closed into my palm, rubbing the bridge between my nose and eyes, praying this line moves faster.

"Sorry," I state. "I don't mean to be a jerk."

"It's fine." By her tone of voice, I can tell it's absolutely not fine.

After eight of the longest minutes of my life, we finally reach the register and order our drinks—a flat white and a black coffee, respectively. Alex's wad of cash burns with betrayal in my pocket as I unwind yet another twenty-dollar bill and hand it to the cashier. I slip five bucks into the tip jar as if karma will bypass me for giving a shit.

"Thank you for the drink." Josie sips loudly. "Mom started me on bougie coffee young."

"No problem. Pretty sure I owe you more than coffee at this point."

She relaxes her hardened demeanor. "What can I say? I'm nice."

"Until it's time not to be nice?"

Josie nearly does a spit take with her coffee. "Did you just quote *Road House?*"

"Thank you for appreciating it," I smirk. Long live the king of bad movies.

She chews on her upper lip to lick off a glob of foam. "I was out of first grade with the stomach flu one day and my dad stayed home to take care of me. He let me sit and watch it with him. My mom nearly murdered him when she walked in."

I blow a puff of curling steam from the top of my open-faced paper cup. "Is he with your mom in DC right now?"

She gulps hard and moves toward the door, swinging it open forcefully. "He, umm, passed away shortly after we moved here."

The awkward tension between us abruptly stretches beyond the length of the Grand Canyon. Why wouldn't *bring up her dead father* turn up on my awkward conversation bingo card?

"I'm sorry," I offer with a shaky voice. "That sucks."

Josie reaches up and pretends to flick a stray lash away from the corner of her eye. I might be painfully oblivious to things, but even I'm perceptive enough to know she's dabbing a tear away. Way to make things even worse.

As much as I'd hoped it would somehow disappear in the time it took for us to continue stalling and get our drinks, the train station out front sits there unmoved. Josie pulls out her phone again and begins scrolling through her screenshotted directions. "This says if you take the L train for eight stops, you can transfer to the six and get off at 56th Street."

"I should be able to find my way from there." I nod.

It could be the muddy black coffee hitting my empty stomach like a lead balloon, but the longer I stand there, continuing to not move towards the stairs, the more I can't bring myself to do it at all.

It's not just facing Lexi again that scares me. It's all of it. The thought of going back to that hotel feels like me giving permission to hundreds of people who don't care about me to keep making decisions about how I should live my life. Flashbulb snapshots of the future fill my head with an unbearable image of myself. My hands tremble as they attempt to maintain a grip on the coffee cup keeping them warm.

"I can't go back." The words come out of my mouth sounding like the final plea of a victim in a horror movie.

Josie frowns. "I'm sorry?"

"I can't go back," I repeat, bouncing on my heels.

I suck in one deep breath, and in an instant, I'm Reckless Rowan from Rochester all over again. Grabbing Josie's hand, I pull her along with me as I lead us down the subway tunnel to the corroding silver turnstiles. I ditch the dregs of my coffee in a nearby trash can as her cup sloshes all over the ground.

"Where are we going?!" She cries.

I whip my MetroCard out from the pile of money. I methodically slide it till I hear the satisfying beep of the machine. Once I shove my hips through, I reach over and hand the card to Josie.

"Come on!"

"Come where?!" She rattles.

"Come and do something!"

"Do what?!"

I hand her the card, signaling for her to swipe it. Her face floods with panic as she attempts to move the card through the machine, a less cheery beep greeting me from the opposite end.

"It's not letting me through!" She cries. "It says the card was just used."

"Shit," I mutter under my breath. "Just jump it then!"

"WHAT?!"

"JUMP IT!" I repeat. The heat of the moment courses through my body like static electricity. It's like we're being chased by a pack of rabid dogs, and the longer she takes to convince herself, the closer we are to being devoured.

"I can't..." Josie trails off.

I aggressively shake my head. "Break a rule for once in your life!"

The comment hits her with a dumbstruck sort of agony. Her forehead bends into a single fold, her round cheeks so rosy, you can practically feel the heat radiating off them. She hesitates for a second more before swinging one leg over the cold metal bars and then the other.

"Oh my god," Josie gasps. She does a double-take and looks behind her, frantically waiting for someone to pop out and scold her for the crime she's committed. "I just did that!"

A wicked sense of pride swells up in my chest as I grab her by the hand again and lead us through the tunnels at full speed. I glance at the signs overhead, not having a clue where any of them would take us. Grandma would be ashamed. I finally settle on an A train that has pulled up to one of the long corridors. A small group trickles out of the car in a hurried scramble.

"Hurry!" I cry to Josie, tugging the two of us into the first open car as the automated voice warns us to stand clear of the closing doors.

Josie hurls herself into an available seat, doubling over in breathless gasps. I clutch tightly to one of the metal bars and watch as a series of bystanders lower their eyes to the floor in typical unphased fashion. I'm realizing if I wanted to go unnoticed, a New York subway is probably the best place to be.

As the wailing metal tracks begin screeching forward, I plop myself into the empty seat next to Josie, knocking arms with a burly male nurse on the opposite side.

"That was... the craziest thing... I've ever done!" Josie rips at her sweatshirt as she huffs, then pats her heart to ensure it's still beating. "This... is... the first time in almost... a year... I've... been on a subway!"

Her adrenaline-fueled confession infuses the moment with even more absurdity. I completely unfold into tyrannical laughter, covering my face with my hands to muffle the embarrassing wheezing noises. The nurse offers an annoyed grunt before moving three inches to his left.

Josie glances over at me in petrified silence before she starts laughing too.

"This is so stupid!" She exclaims, wiping a stray tear off her cheek. "Why did we do this?!"

The train makes four stops before the two of us come to our senses and start to catch our breath, honing in our hysteria by looking at one another in a unified pact of confused desperation. Everyone coming in and out of the station must think we're on something, not that it's uncommon to see freaks in a subway car.

"Rowan," she sniffs in a hushed tone, "seriously. Where are we going?"

I respond the best way I know how to. "Wanna eat?"

CHAPTER 10

JOSIE

I DIDN'T PLAN on going along with the whole Fizz idea until we were at the turnstile. I was simply going to drop Rowan at the subway station, maybe get an autograph for my sister, and then turn around and go home, giving Pru the whole story and beseeching her to never speak of it again.

Then Rowan grabbed my hand and that plan went to hell.

Between frantic confusion and trying my hardest not to run directly into any subway station pillars, Indio's words came rushing back to me. *Tell your story and watch it go viral.*

I'm not proud of what I'm planning to do. In fact, condemnation rises up in the pit of my stomach with such intense fervor, I don't know how I still haven't seen the half coffee I consumed work its way back up.

Once we're off the train and roaming around an unfamiliar neighborhood, I cautiously whip my phone out to text Indio. Rowan evaluates the shops ahead in passing, searching for a decent place to grab a late breakfast. I feverishly pound at the screen, trying not to make my treachery seem too obvious. I proofread it quickly and hit send.

Can you give me a call? I think you may be onto something. I could use your help.

"Check it out!" Rowan stops in front of a tiny storefront with Mystic Dough written atop a dark red awning. A spattering of hot pink tables and chairs sit outside the front window. The two of us press our foreheads against the glass like kids staring into an aquarium, our breath leaving two foggy ovals.

"Are those... rainbow bagels?" I ask.

Rowan scrunches his nose and repositions the bridge of his sunglasses. "Only one way to find out."

They're rainbow bagels, alright. Vibrant shades of red, purple, green, and blue are twisted together into imperfect circles of dough. Next to the tray of colorful pastries lie silver baskets filled with standard bagel shop fodder. Everything, jalapeno cheddar, cinnamon raisin. Every option looks incredible, my stomach grumbling at the first whiff of freshly toasted bread.

"Is that cream cheese with mini marshmallows?" Rowan laughs like a kid in a candy store. I suppose marshmallow cream cheese isn't all that far off from candy.

My phone vibrates in my pocket, Indio's name flashing across the caller ID. Thank god he was better at answering his phone than I had been the night before.

"Hey." I lean over to Rowan, "I need to go take a call outside. Meet me at one of the tables?"

"Want me to get you anything?" His thoughtful offer only makes me feel worse about what I'm conspiring to do.

"Surprise me."

Outside, I tuck my unruly hair behind my ears and hit accept. Indio wastes no time talking.

"WHAT HAPPENED?"

"Correction: What's happening."

"No way," he interrogates, "he's still in your house?!"

"Not really. In fact, I have no clue where we are. That's kind of why I need you."

A clamoring of footsteps booms into the earpiece. It sounds like Indio is climbing a flight of metal stairs. "Don't tell me he kidnapped you."

I grind my teeth together. "Very funny. It's a long story. We're talking Stephen King long, but I was wondering if you still had your camera."

"I'm a photographer, Josie. Why would I not have it?" Sardonic venom drips off his words. To his defense, dumb questions deserve dumb answers.

"Look," I sigh, "do you remember what you said earlier? About selling the story to The Fizz?"

"Yeah."

"What if I did it? Or, maybe not The Fizz, but—"

"Josie," he cuts me off, "back up. Where are you guys right now?"

I peer through the window and observe Rowan as he attempts to order from the cashier while keeping a distance and twisting his head to hide his face. I'd almost feel bad for him if he hadn't dragged me here without any warning. Literally dragged me here.

"He doesn't have his cell phone," I explain, "he asked me to help get him to a subway so he could go back to his hotel. I was about to send him off when he freaked out and pulled me onto the train with him, and now, we're at this place that sells rainbow bagels getting food."

My CliffsNotes version excludes the part where I run into Aaron Lopez at Stillwater and he asks me to give him my phone number. That joyous happenstance would somehow become the least exciting part of my morning.

"Gaygels?!" Indio cheers. "You really are living my dream."

"He's having some sort of midlife crisis level breakdown." I take a seat behind one of the pink tables, hunching over in a fatigued slump. "I don't think he plans on going back to the hotel. I'm fairly sure he wants to wander around the city or something."

"Let me guess." The metal clanging behind Indio finally goes silent. "You want to follow along for as long as possible to get the dish on him being a rogue actor?"

"Precisely. It was your idea, really. I thought maybe if I kept you informed on where we were going, you could do a loose follow. Like, an amateur paparazzi?"

"Why would I do that?" He asks.

"Besides the clout?" I tease. "Because anyone could make up a story like this, but the proof is in the pudding. Or, in this case, the pictures."

I lick my lips and glance back through the window again. Rowan has his back leaned up against the wall. His hands are shoved into his pockets as he patiently waits for our food. He peeks up from the ground and waves to catch my attention, offering a kind smile. It's unfair of him to act so polite when I feel so abhorrent.

The background noise rattles again. How many metal stairs was Indio climbing? "What's the endgame here?" He inquires. "I mean, I'm about it, but why the sudden change of heart? This is so un-Josie."

Which version sounds less pathetic? Because my family is poor? Because my mom shouldn't have to beg for money from her classist parents? Because I won't be able to move to Cincinnati and go to college if I don't raise several thousand dollars in the next few months? Because I'm secretly afraid I'll be stuck here working at King Kone and existing in a three-block bubble till the day I die? They all sound pretty damn valid to me.

I snap my eyes shut and rest my elbows on the table, settling on a quick response. "The college money would be nice. Plus, we could split whatever we're offered 50/50."

"Uhh, yeah," he agrees. "It's my day off. I'm throwing it away to sink to scumbag paparazzi levels without any guarantees."

"Where are you?" I finally ask, the banging noise becoming too much to handle.

"I was leaving my apartment to go to Rough Trade, but now I'm going back upstairs to get my camera and find wherever the hell you are."

"Gaygels, remember? It's called Mystic Dough."

He pants into his receiver. "Just keep me posted on where you guys wind up, okay? If he ditches you at any point, try to follow him and don't get caught."

I nod. "Got it. Thank you, Indio. I really think this could pay off for both of us."

"Try to find out what his motive is," Indio suggests. "This story won't be reputable if it looks like we're a bunch of obsessed fans following him around. Dig up some dirt nobody knows about him."

"And you claim you're not a scumbag paparazzi." I smirk.

"Fuck you. Text me!"

I end the call not knowing if I feel accomplished or internally vile. I lean towards the latter as Rowan walks out of the bagel shop carrying a tall brown bag full of multi-colored deliciousness.

"Hope you're ready for a sugar coma!" He shoves his sunglasses into his pocket, lifting his eyebrows with glee.

Rowan opens the steaming bag and unveils two sandwiches. The first is a rainbow bagel covered in edible glitter and marshmallow cream cheese. The edges are dunked into glossy neon sprinkles. The second looks like candy corn in bagel form, smeared with a bright orange spread I can only assume is pumpkin spice flavored by the pungent scent of cinnamon and cloves. It smells like cremated unicorns and icing and happiness, and it makes my mouth water.

"I figured we could go half and half." Rowan takes the seat across from me, his back strategically turned towards the street. It made me wonder if all celebrities had to learn tricks on how to exist in public spaces without being seen all the time.

I peel back the parchment paper on one of the halves of the pumpkin spice bagel and sink into a corner. It's warm and crunchy. A blob of the spiced orange cream cheese splatters onto the brown bag underneath.

"This tastes like fall in my mouth," I rudely state mid-chew.

He grabs the other half of the sandwich and demolishes it in five bites. "Gotta go hard on Halloween, right? By the way, was everything okay?"

It takes a moment for me to realize he's referring to the phone call I'd been out here taking for the last several minutes.

"Yeah. It was just my mom making sure Pru is still alive."

He starts to unwrap the unicorn sandwich, diving in with a soft groan. "This is everything five-year-old me ever wanted."

I giggle, still munching on my first half. It was cruel to have my moral conflict clashing with my hunger so intensely.

"Your sister is kind of awesome," Rowan mutters, swallowing a bite.

I pick at a fleck of cream cheese and lick it off my finger. "I hope she didn't bother you too much this morning. Pru's been all about making bracelets lately. She can be annoying about it."

"I didn't mind. Plus, I scored this for free." He lifts the sleeve of his jacket to reveal a braided band with a bright pop of yellow string. Leave it to my little sister to give a friendship bracelet to Rowan Adler.

"You're lucky. She won't even give me a handout."

Rowan grabs one of the napkins inside the bag and wipes a stray purple sprinkle off his chin, accidentally making eye contact with a nearby bystander and immediately putting his sunglasses back on. He rushes to make small talk.

"How long is your mom gone for?"

"Only a few days. She's visiting my grandparents." Hearing myself say it gave me goosebumps in the worst sense.

"Without you and your sister?" Rowan wonders.

I reach for the unicorn sandwich and allow the sweet, marshmallow fluffiness to melt over my tongue. "They're not exactly our biggest fans."

He lowers his glasses and narrows his eyes. "Did you kill their cat or something?"

"It was their dog," I joke. His face turns pale. My eyes crinkle as I swallow another bite. "I'm totally kidding!"

"Not funny." He sneers.

I give my hair a fluff and sink a hand into my cheek. "Let's just say their daughter marrying our free-thinking father didn't exactly match their yacht club aesthetic."

"Ahhh," he exclaims. "So, they're the... conservative type?"

"That's the nice way of putting it," I scowl.

"Why is she seeing them then?"

I bite down on my lip, hesitating. "It's complicated."

Rowan doesn't press the matter, pouting with an understanding nod.

People watching comes naturally to me. I can tell what somebody is thinking more by how they react than what they say. Subtle brow movements, quick shifting of the eyes, uneasy twitches. People don't realize how obvious they can be when they don't mean what they say. With Rowan, it's near impossible to gauge anything. You can't exactly study how he reacts when his face is perpetually covered up. I'm left to unravel his thoughts based on body language. So far, he hasn't seemed uncomfortable with anything I've had to say. Whether or not it's an act, it's a nice feeling.

"Complicated," he repeats my word with a scoff. "I get that."

I slowly slide the rest of the unicorn sandwich towards Rowan like a burnt offering. "Does it have anything to do with not wanting to go back to your hotel?"

He grimaces. "Everything, actually. I didn't exactly have permission to go out last night."

I squint my eyes. "You need permission? How old are you?"

"I turn eighteen in thirty-eight days. Not that I'm counting or anything."

"Imagine having to wait until May to claim your independence." I attempt to lighten the mood. "I've always thought it was kind of weird how parents stress that you're under their rules till the minute you turn eighteen, then you're supposed to have the whole adult thing figured out on your own."

Weird, yes, but I barely had any experience with this specific concept. If anything, Mom was constantly calling me too dependable and sorted out. The only act of rebellion I'd performed was staying out too late with Hannah once. It was only because we didn't realize the PG movie we were going to see ran past my curfew.

"I'm not sure about that." Rowan shrugs, my dad's baggy jacket bunching around his stomach. "I mean, I guess it's true, but I can't remember the last time I got to make a decision for myself. I don't see that changing anytime soon. Just once, I'd like to do what I want."

Indio's voice comes back and haunts me. I didn't need to try and dig up any dirt on Rowan Adler. He was handing me the shovel himself. It was surreal. I was sitting in front of one of the biggest stars on the planet, someone who could ask for anything and get it at a moment's notice, and all he wanted was a break.

A city bus whooshes by with a hot burst of exhaust, a thought bubbling out of my head. "You have today. You should make the most of it."

Rowan quickly eats the last bite of rainbow bagel and licks his lips clean. "Impromptu vacation?"

"Consider it doing what you want for once." I rest my hands on the table. "If you could have twenty-four hours to do whatever you wanted, without anyone interfering—managers, parents, whoever—what would you do?"

Rowan leans back in his chair, thoughtfully contemplating my question. He snaps his head over his shoulder to look back in the direction we'd walked from. His hood nudges towards one of the more significant-looking buildings at the end of the street. It has dark tinted windows with an embossed gold pig pressed onto the outside.

"Would you believe me if I said that was one of them?"

I look in the direction he's staring. My lower jaw nearly unhinges from my face. "You're serious?"

Rowan stands to his feet and collects the trash into the discarded brown bag, my face unmoved from the golden swine. "I'm going to toss this and see if they have a bathroom," he explains. "Are you up for it?"

I didn't exactly have a choice anymore, did I? I'd already made a commitment to Indio—we were doing this.

"Sure. Why not?" I fake a smile.

Once Rowan is back inside the store, I reach for my phone and spot a new text from Indio.

Driving over now w/ my camera. Are you still at Mystic?

I nervously look around to make sure nobody is hovering

around me, wiping a beaded sprinkle off my hand as I reply quickly.

In the neighborhood. Park near Pig Skin.

I think Rowan is getting a tattoo.

AUNT LEXI recently asked how I wanted to spend my eighteenth birthday. She tossed around several ideas, one of them including a private blowout at our house with all of my closest friends. Considering I only had two, it wasn't presumptuous of me to assume the rest of the guest list would be her associates and celebrities who didn't have anything better to do. Lexi proposed we hire a DJ and possibly invite a photographer from Vogue to do a spread so press wouldn't hound the event for photos.

I turned her down. "I don't want a party. I want to get a tattoo."

"No tattoos," she'd react sharply. "Tattoos limit the types of jobs you're offered. Hunter Cade doesn't have tattoos."

I hated it when she referred to me as 'Hunter' as if her nephew had somehow died and been possessed by the spirit of his television alter ego.

Even with her disapproval, that was before the fight at the premiere. Hell would freeze over before I got the okay to attend any Hollywood parties in the near future, let alone my own. That only left the one option on the table.

"You're still seventeen, Rowan. Are you sure they'll even

let you do this?" Josie's levelheadedness teeters between aggravating and endearing.

Pig Skin, the tattoo shop down the street, didn't open for another fifteen minutes. Josie and I have camped out at the bus stop a few feet away, gawking as a variety of strange humans steadily trickled passed us.

"Do you think that guy was really a priest or was it just a costume?" I point to the Father with a bleached Mohawk hailing a cab. Living in New York must feel like a perpetual episode of *What Would You Do?*

Josie ignores the question, deciding to tip more towards aggravating. "You don't even have your ID, do you?"

"I haven't thought that far ahead," I answer through gritted teeth. It's not like I could call Alex and ask him to come run it down here for me. If this was going to work at all, I'd need to turn up the charm to eleven.

Josie frantically studies her surroundings, looking more paranoid about being caught than I am.

"Relax," I urge. "What's the worst that could happen? They give me a colossal no, and we leave. Big deal."

"I suppose that's true," Josie huffs. Her eyes are locked onto a car parking down the road.

"*Suppose,*" I mock with a playful nudge. "Pru told me you wanted to be a screenwriter. Must be why you're so well-spoken."

"She did?" Josie acts surprised.

I quickly point out the Walter White walking down the street, complete with the yellow hazmat suit. "Do you write much?"

She shakes her head, clasping her thumbs together and flicking at a broken cuticle. "Not as much as I should for someone who wants to do it professionally. It used to be a fun thing for me."

"Used to?"

"I mean, it still is," she contradicts, "but these days, it's more about trying to get into college so I can actually take it seriously."

"You know fun and serious aren't mutually exclusive," I protest. "It shouldn't stop being fun, especially if you want to spend your life doing it."

Kinda like acting, my brain reverberates loudly—stupid brain.

Josie looks over with a soft smile. "I guess part of me just doesn't want to suck at it."

"Anything you like to write about in particular?"

She glances away and pinches her shoulders back. "Don't laugh, but I'm a sucker for a good love story. I know it's trite and cheesy."

"Have you seen my line of work?" I laugh. "Who am I to judge?"

Josie tosses her head back. "What was it you said in that episode last night? When you confronted your English teacher—"

"Slash, future stepfather," I interrupt with an eye roll.

"—about your mom?" Josie mimics Hunter's hysteric angst. *"You don't know what it's like to live off love! Love, and Minute Rice!"*

I facepalm. "Can you believe one of the producers improvised that line on-set?"

"Darn, I thought you came up with it on your own."

I wince. "Gonna need some Neosporin for that burn."

"Really though." She grips the edge of the bus bench. "Your show is sort of awful. No offense."

How I felt about the show hinged less on offense and more on embarrassment. Deep down, I secretly feared *Dawn Heights* would be my legacy. I'd be stuck on the show till Webstream finally decided to ax it in favor of something newer and hotter. Then I'd forever be known as the talentless teen actor from that one show someone's mom watched when they were in high school. Goodbye, reputation. Hello, Hallmark Channel Christmas movies.

I shrug my shoulders, yanking on the sleeves of the weathered jacket. "Don't get me wrong. I'm grateful for the show. I wouldn't be here without it, you know?"

She leans into my dithering. "But?"

I sigh. "I'm afraid of winding up like all those C-list celebrities you see on *Dancing with the Stars*. I don't think I'm above the show, but I think I could be a better actor if I was given a chance to do other stuff. Does that make sense?"

She nods. "It does, and for the record, I think most people are naturally above it."

Looking beyond Josie, I spot a tall woman in a pair of Doc Martins marching towards Pig Skin. She pulls open her messenger bag and unlocks the door with her giant carabiner full of clanging silver keys.

"Now or never?" I smirk.

The hesitation on Josie's face slowly returns. "I'm getting the impression that 'never' is never on the table with you."

We wait another few minutes to allow the woman to open up the shop before running in and ganging up on her. Josie anxiously looks down to respond to a text, bouncing her feet up and down on the concrete. Once the shop's glowing red OPEN sign is flashing, we prepare to make our move.

"Here's what I'm thinking." I wave my hands. "If she asks to see my identification, you go along with the whole 'he's my cousin' thing again."

"Okay, then what?"

"I don't know," I recoil, "it'll come to me."

Josie's face falls. "Fantastic." She shoves past me and opens the door to the studio quickly to hear the rejection she expects.

I'm not sure what I was expecting the inside to look like, but it certainly wasn't whatever we walked into. The walls are painted a similar shade of gold as the pig embossed on the window, shimmering under the dull light. Various sketches and pieces of artwork hang in neat rows along the walls. The weird part: every single one of them is a different style of pig. Caricature pigs, Warhol pigs, pin-up pigs, if you can picture any type of cartoon pig in your head, it was probably on Pig Skin's wall.

The woman looks up from behind the counter, her bright blue eyes caked in thick, winged eyeliner. I can imagine she's what Amy Winehouse would've looked like if she'd lived to be in her fifties.

"Hi!" I wave innocently like I'm not about to mercilessly lie about my age. "I'm wondering if I could maybe—"

"Shut. Up." The woman's bright red lips part slowly, revealing pearly white teeth. She rises to her feet, her boots adding another half foot to her already monstrous height. She cups her mouth with her hands and starts squealing. "YOU'RE ROWAN ADLER!"

JOSIE STANDS behind me with her left leg in a diving position, ready to run back out the door and drag me with her if necessary.

"I'm sorry." I reach for my hood, tucking my hand underneath and itching the top of my damp hair with a nervous chuckle. "I think you—"

"I would recognize you anywhere!" The woman cuts me off before I can finish.

She shuffles from behind the counter and bounds her way in front of us, lifting one side of her high-rise shorts and revealing more of her nether regions than I ever cared to see. The graphic display reveals an inner thigh tattoo that wraps all the way around to her butt. The scary part? The tattoo is of my face.

"One of the guys did this for me a couple of months back! My fifteen-year-old daughter and I LOVE *Dawn Heights*! We've already binged season three twice!"

The new season debuted on Webstream less than two days ago. There were twenty episodes, and each was almost an hour-long. How the hell had they managed to watch it twice already?

I shake my head, dumbfounded. I'd been wandering

through the streets of New York for the last twelve hours without being recognized once, only to be outed while wearing my disguise in a random Brooklyn tattoo parlor. Of course that would happen to me.

The woman starts fanning her eyes, holding back tears. "When your character had the car accident at the end of season one," she sniffles, "I was a complete mess! Hunter means so much to me!"

The compliment, while bizarre, still gives me that comforting, itchy wool blanket feeling. The whole reason I decided to chase acting was because I wanted to tell stories and hope they made people feel something. Hunter might have been the farthest thing from who I was in real life, but he managed to mean something to a middle-aged mother covered from head to toe in tattoos, and that was still pretty cool.

"Look." I lower my hood and remove my glasses. No use hiding anymore. "I'm technically not here," I explain. "We passed by the shop, and we were wondering if there was anyone available for a quick session?"

The woman tugs at a tattered string on her denim corset. "I'm the only one here for the next hour. This is a slow time of day for us, though. What are you looking to get?"

I look back at Josie, who appears to be wondering the same thing. I inch backward a few steps and hold out my hand. "Can I borrow your phone? For like, ten seconds?"

Josie clutches it tightly to her collarbone, swiping away at a text. "It's actually cracked and super fragile. I can search for you!"

Weird, but okay. I raise an eyebrow. "Search for 'rose tattoo by Ink Pros.'"

Josie types and swipes away at yet another text, trying to make them vanish off the screen before I'm able to quickly see anything at a glance. A lump in my throat rises. They're probably from the hot basketball player. It would explain the secrecy. I wouldn't want anyone to witness my flirting either.

As the website loads, I instruct Josie to scroll down till she gets to the photo at the very bottom of the page. She holds it up to the woman, who pulls a pair of readers from her back pocket and observes the design. I'd had the webpage saved to my laptop for ages. It's a small black tattoo of a rose in bloom with thin, delicate petals. Simple and not overly tacky.

"Oh yes," the woman sings with her midwestern accent. "That shouldn't take me more than twenty minutes. Do you have your ID on you?"

I shake my head. "I can't easily get to it right away. Is that going to be a problem?"

She presses her lips into a thin red line, a streak of lipstick smearing onto her teeth. "Have you had a tetanus shot before?"

"I think so?"

"Look, hon." She taps her fingernails together with a sigh, "If you can get my daughter an autograph, you can have whatever you want." She bends over, revealing an overwhelming amount of cleavage in what is either an ill-timed stretch, or she really is genuinely offering me *anything*.

I suck back a gag. "Thank you."

The excited woman lowers her glasses and grabs a stack of papers off the front desk, marching towards the *Employees Only* area masked by a jangling curtain of bacon beads. "Give me a few minutes to draw it up! It shouldn't take me very long!"

Josie and I find seats in the waiting area. It looks more like a doctor's office than a tattoo parlor. It's clean and organized with boring plastic chairs lining the back wall. An impressive stereo system sits in the corner thumping alternative rock. It rattles the long glass coffee table filled with outdated gossip magazines.

"So." I clear my throat. "That worked out."

"Or something like it," Josie remarks. "Is it weird to constantly have women hitting on you like that? Older ones included?"

I scrunch my nose, digging through the magazines for something to read. Surely there would be a Men's Health somewhere in the stack of US Weeklys.

"I mean, I thought it was cool the first few times, but I was also fifteen and stupid. Now, it's just gross."

Josie sheepishly raises a copy of Word on the Street. It's a tabloid notoriously known for fake stories and causing havoc on red carpets. Unprofessional reporters would stop and ask questions like, 'if you were a banana, how big would you be?' The *Dawn Heights* cast had been their main source of creative fuel since the moment the show premiered.

I frown when I see the front cover. It's a distant, blurry photo of me the night of the fight. The headline: **Hollywood's Newest Bad Boy? Drunken Rowan Adler Attacks Co-Star!**

"Does this have anything to do with all that complicated stuff you mentioned?" Josie asks.

I tear the magazine out of her hands and study the picture. My face is red and contorted into an unflattering scowl. My tight-fitting casual suit is sweat-stained, and my fists are curled up into two tight balls. I note the incense burning over by the front door and wonder where I could find the lighter so I could ignite this thing.

"Yes, would be an understatement." I slam it back onto the table. "Another mistake. I make those a lot."

Josie rests her elbows onto her knees and cups her chin in her hands. "I don't know. An impromptu tattoo doesn't seem like a mistake to me."

Her humor falls flat. I rub the sides of my head, giving my

unruly mess of newly grown hair a scratch. "The fight wasn't intentional."

"Is any fight intentional?"

"You clearly don't watch pro-wrestling." I slowly flutter my eyes. "We were all at a club after the premiere. One of the directors of the show cornered me and made me do a tequila shot with him"

"Made you?" She sounds unconvinced.

I glance away from her. "Peer pressure or something. Anyway, right after, I saw Michael Brewer harassing someone, and I stepped in. Things got..."

"Out of hand?"

I jokingly point to my fists in the photo. "Hands were definitely involved."

"Who was it he was harassing?"

Every fast-paced moment of that night comes rushing back like some horrible found footage movie. I bounce my knee up and down, hanging my head low.

"Ashanti Nath."

Josie's eyebrows shoot up. She looks like she has at least one hundred questions to follow up with, only to be silenced by the return of Knockoff Amy Winehouse, waving a slip of tattoo paper in the air like a white flag.

"Are you ready to see?!"

The woman might be eccentric, but her work is flawless. It's an exact replica of the picture on Josie's phone. The longer I look at it, the more I convince myself to go through with it. I give the woman an approving grin and thumbs up.

"Guess I'm going for it."

"Hop on over, babe!" She directs us over to one of the long, shimmery chairs in the back. "You too, babe's friend!"

It takes Knockoff Amy several minutes to get everything in place. Testing her gun, sterilizing her needle, pouring a fresh bottle of dark black ink onto her small canvas. It gives me just enough time to wonder if I'm making yet another decision I'm going to regret. Josie grabs one of the black plastic chairs from the waiting room. She pulls it up next to mine, continuing to mindlessly text with determined focus.

"Where do you want this thing?" The woman asks.

I pull the borrowed hoodie off my back and raise the sleeve of my shirt, pointing to the space just above my forearm. Lexi may have had a point in saying that tattoos make it harder to get jobs, but she clearly underestimated the value of well-hidden placement. Plus, had she never heard of makeup? Plenty of A-list actors are covered in tattoos and you'd never know it while watching them.

The woman tells me to lie back in the chair, making me instantly more nervous than I already was. Once my arm is cleaned and positioned, the woman pulls a case of AirPods from her pockets and shoves them in her ears.

"Hope you don't mind if I listen to music while I work. I can't stand the sound of these damn guns. Helps me focus." I could care less what she does as long as she knows how to draw straight lines.

Loud metal music begins pouring out of her ears, the hypnotic buzz of the gun chatters as she dips it into the ink. Seconds later, there's pressure on my arm, followed by a slight burning sensation that becomes more intense. It feels like being scratched by a feral cat with a personal vendetta.

Josie leans over and offers a supportive smile. "Remember, you wanted this."

"Still do," I play it cool.

"If I'm allowed to ask, why a rose?"

"What? Not manly enough?" I jest.

"Just curious." She leans back.

Riding an adrenaline rush, I give up the answer. "My grandma's name was Rose."

She lowers her phone and sets it onto her lap. "Oh. You two must have been close."

I fight the urge to whine as the burning sensation becomes genuinely scorching. Instead, I keep talking to mask my pain.

"She kind of raised me. I never met my dad, and my mom —" I pause mid-sentence. Why am I telling her this? Nobody knows this about me, not even people like Alex or Ashanti who knew things even my aunt didn't. I concede and finish my sentence anyway. "My mom loved a lot of other things more than me."

Josie hangs on my words, soaking them in with interest. "That's rough."

Childhood memories flip through my head. "I'm actually from upstate New York. We lived in this old house in Rochester. My mom would take off for weeks at a time doing whatever the hell she did, so Grandma Rose would always come to stay with me and make sure things got done. She'd lived in the city for decades and was almost famous on Broadway."

Josie's face glows. "Really?"

I nod, the woman grabbing my torso to hold it steady. "She'd take me with her into the city over the summer. I loved it here. I'd always ask if I could come and live with her. Instead, when my mom took off for the last time, she moved into the house for good. She died a few years later, and I went to live with my aunt."

The conversation is cut short by the sound of the tattoo gun, spitting ink as she twirls her wrist in a circular pattern. It was oddly liberating to talk to someone about all that. It felt like I'd been trying to manage a suitcase full of rocks on my own for the last eighteen years, and someone had finally come up beside me and offered to give me a hand carrying it.

"I guess the acting thing must have skipped a generation," Josie says, meeting the heaviness of my story with welcomed levity. "That's really cool, Rowan."

"DONE!" Knockoff Amy Winehouse cries. She sets her gun onto the metal tray and wipes my arm with an alcohol-soaked paper towel.

Josie stands and hovers above me with a smile so wide, her round cheeks cause her eyes to disappear. The woman holds up a mirror for me to see it. It's better than anything I expected. Clean lines, tight shading, and just visible enough that I'd still get to see it without having to work too hard to cover it up. I'm tempted to run my fingers across to feel the risen skin, but smart enough not to.

The image of Grandma's face in my head sears more than the afterburn does. She hated tattoos, but deep down, I hoped she would've liked this one. If I could survive losing her, I could handle anything, even all the bullshit that came with being famous. This was the best reminder of that I could have.

"It's perfect." I grin from ear to ear.

Once the tattoo is bandaged, the woman gives me instructions on properly caring for it, telling me the name of a good aftercare lotion to pick up from a local drug store.

"How much will it be?" I ask.

She waves a hand and winks. "Consider it a gift."

I protest. It's unfair not to charge me for her work, even if she continues to claim that touching me has been 'one of the greatest pleasures of her life.' I unwind a thin stack of money from my pocket, willing to fight with her reluctance if necessary.

"Do you guys do piercings?"

Josie's comment comes out of the blue as I insist, yet again, that Knockoff Amy take the money.

"We sure do!" The woman beams with a hand on her hip. She's in full salesperson mode.

I slip the hoodie back on and tug it tightly over my head. "You want a piercing?" My surprise comes off sounding almost condescending.

Josie tugs at her earlobes and admires the wide variety of rings and studs in the glass case near the register. Some of them look less like earrings and more like objects of torture.

"Just my ears." Josie lowers her head. "Do you guys do ears?"

"We do everything." The woman winks.

Josie's straight face delicately mops up the information like a sponge. She offers a tight-lipped smirk as she reaches for the doorknob. "Thanks. I'll remember that."

I stretch my non-bandaged right arm out to clothesline her, refusing to let her go any further. "No."

"No?" She questions sarcastically.

"You want your ears pierced. Clearly."

"Yeah." She relaxes her shoulders. "Eventually."

I slip another twenty-dollar bill to Knockoff Amy. "Could you help her out? She's had her shots too."

The woman enthusiastically nods her head. "I'll go grab another gun!"

Josie's mouth hangs open wide enough to trap a few stray city pigeons.

"Rowan!" She scolds, stomping her foot like a child.

"Josie." I point to my upper left arm, "I just got a tattoo on a whim after wanting one for years! And it's amazing! How long have you wanted your ears pierced for?"

She rocks on her feet, going quiet as she chews her lip and

thinks. "Since I was ten, maybe? I hate needles. I avoid them unless they're to actively ward off plagues."

"You're not getting needles. You're getting earrings," I joke. She still looks skeptical. "Come on! You're the same girl who didn't think she could hop on a subway or jump a turnstile, and you've done both today! You are Josie Bradford! You're a badass!"

A crack breaks through Josie's sour expression. She stares at me and reflects back on her choices like this is the first time in her life she's ever considered herself to be cool enough to do something so mundane. Truthfully, she's not, but neither am I, and I think that's why I'm starting to like her.

"I'm a badass," she repeats to herself, quietly repeating it twice more for good measure. "I'm a badass who's about to get her ears pierced!"

CHAPTER 13

JOSIE

I THINK **I see you guys**

Holy shit, I can't believe you ate bagels with Rowan Adler

No, that's not you guys

Where ARE you guys?

Are you inside the tattoo place? The windows are dark!

Okay yeah, I see you

He's really getting a tattoo?!

Has he told you anything good?

Got a few pics from the window through the door

ARE YOU GETTING SOMETHING PIERCED?!

I somehow manage not to audibly groan with every new notification. Had I known asking Indio for help would result in fielding five text messages a minute, I would've gone about this whole thing by myself and considered the logistical details later. No amount of money was worth the man's high maintenance.

My ears burn swollen and hot, now the proud owner of two small, holographic silver studs. I can't stop looking at them in the reflection of the glass countertop as Rowan signs a personalized piece of paper for the tattoo artist's daughter.

"Please." He waves a finger at her. "Don't mention meeting me here, at least not to anyone besides your daughter. I'm just in town hanging out with a friend. I'd like to avoid making a spectacle of it."

With a friend. Was that supposed to be me? I guess we *had* bonded over enough blood and needles to form some sort of lifelong bond. Well, that and the deeply personal story he'd chosen to share while getting stabbed. I feverishly burned the information into my brain to compile later, all the while, not feeling any more unworthy of the 'friend' title.

The tattoo artist begins crying again as she agrees to his terms and wraps Rowan in a bone-snapping hug, swearing that meeting him was all she needed to survive her divorce. It sounds disturbingly more like a pick-up line than it should.

Walking out of the parlor feels like taking one long drag of fresh air. I fear the scent of vape smoke and ink are permanently embedded into my hair follicles. Down the road, I see Indio sitting outside Mystic Dough, inconspicuously munching on a bright purple ube bagel and pulling his bucket hat down over his stringy, dark hair. He's wearing a green leather jacket and rocking a pair of cat-shaped sunglasses. Between him and Rowan, I'm not sure which one is trying harder.

"Where to next?" Rowan greedily rubs his hands together.

"I'm picking?"

He nods. "Have you ever been to the Brooklyn Bridge?"

My face falls. "You're really asking me that?"

"That settles it then." He claps. "I refuse to let you live in Brooklyn and not cross the bridge. It's a rite of passage." It must be like how he refused to let me live in Brooklyn and not walk around with piercings and break transportation laws. Were those also rites of passage?

I attempt to lock eyes with Indio from afar as he glares down at his phone. "As long as it's what you want to do."

"It is," Rowan proudly boasts. "I think we passed a subway station that could get us there. It had Brooklyn Bridge on the sign. Can you search for directions?"

"That's the only reason you're keeping me hostage, isn't it?" I coyly shake my head. "Limitless phone data."

Rowan timidly sets a hand into his pocket and pulls out his sunglasses. "And the company. You're a good listener."

I know he's just being nice, but there's a certain thin honesty to the way he says it that causes my heart to practically skip a beat.

The entrance to our designated train station is less than two blocks away. When I finally have a vague idea of the general direction we're headed, I screenshot the map and send a quick text to Indio.

Headed to Brooklyn Bridge by way of High Street!

Inside the station tunnel, Rowan loads his MetroCard with more funds and surprises me by handing me a small yellow card of my own.

"Consider it a ticket to limitless possibilities!" He extends his arms to the sky as he swipes and passes through the turnstile. "At least, until it expires."

"Sort of dramatic, don't you think?"

"That's my job," he laughs.

The two of us wait on the platform for several minutes, odd

bodies skirting around us left and right, including a man selling bags of beta fish from inside his trench coat. I half expect Indio's head to pop out from any random corner, only to remember he's a complete germaphobe, and would rather drive in New York traffic than take public transit anywhere. He's probably already halfway to the bridge in his decrepit silver Prius.

"You really don't go anywhere in the city? At all?" Rowan asks yet again. My remote existence is apparently so unbelievable, it bears repeating.

I twiddle with my thumbs. "I just don't see the point, really."

"Why is that?"

"Because I don't plan on staying here." My statement comes out sounding sharp and a touch too loud.

The train pulls up a few moments later. Rowan and I shuffle down the length of cars to find one with two empty seats. We run towards one near the back that's mostly empty, minus the person wearing one of those inflatable tyrannosaurus rex costumes and reading the Wall Street Journal. I'd say 'it's because it's Halloween,' but more accurately, it's because it's New York.

"What's your plan then?" Rowan picks our conversation back up. I would've been just fine leaving it on the platform.

"My plan?"

"You said you wanted to go to college, right?"

Crap. I *had* said that. On the one hand, telling him doesn't seem like the worst thing. God knows he's been vulnerable enough with me, and it's not like my disdain for our move here comes as a surprise to anyone who's met me. My apprehension stems more from how backhanded it is to tell him about my goals when I plan to exploit him in order to achieve them.

After a few loud moments of howling track noise, I cave.

"I'd like to move back to Ohio and attend University of Cincinnati next fall. They have an excellent filmmaking program."

"Is that where you're from?" Rowan asks.

"Yes and no." I teeter a hand. "I was actually born here, it's where my parents met, but they moved to Ohio a few months after I was born."

He snaps his fingers. "You are a city kid then!"

"Hardly," I argue. "My whole life is practically in Cincinnati. My friends, my school, my—"

"Was." Rowan cuts me off. "It *was* there."

My face knits into the shape of a pinched oval, his flippant comment stinging more than the piercing gun had. "What is that supposed to mean?"

Rowan hesitates for a moment. He folds one leg over the other in an attempt to weigh down the foot he's just shoved into his mouth. By the way he nervously shifts, he knows he's crossed a line. Rather than apologize, he doubles down.

"You act like you're stuck here."

"I am stuck here," I hastily respond with a sarcastic laugh.

"Josie," his tone sinks low, "you're not stuck. You're frozen."

This sounds like an offshoot of one of Mom's 'you'd love it here if you actually gave it a chance' lectures she'd given me once a week since we arrived. Except he actually has a valid argument. Coming here hadn't stalled my life the way I claimed it had. I just wasn't doing anything with it.

"People would kill to be in your position," Rowan continues. "I'm only saying, for a romantic, you sure don't romanticize your life very much. Don't be in a hurry to leave because you want the comfortable stuff back."

The comfortable stuff, also known as the flat gray area I'd idolized since the day Dad died. It was the reason I stayed in and studied more than I hung out in the city with my mom and sister, the reason I desperately wanted to get back to a city that was far too small for my ambitions and hang out with a friend who had clearly moved on with her life. It was the endless nights spent in my room watching old movies on my laptop because the thought of knowing I could lose something real again was too much to bear.

"Hey." Rowan gently places a hand on my wrist. "I don't mean to make you cry."

It's not until he's pointed it out that I realize salty tears are quietly rolling down my squirrel cheeks. My freshly pierced ears radiate with pain and embarrassment. Inflatable dinosaur guy has officially come into competition for *Worst Thing You'll See on a Subway Today*. Instead of telling him how I feel, anger rises up and overtakes my ability to act rational.

"What about you then?" I wipe a tear with a scornful laugh.

"What about me?"

"You're the one complaining about how stunted you feel in your career. Why don't you do something about it then? Stop playing the victim for once and think about how lucky you are compared to some of the rest of us!"

The decree flies out of my mouth and clangs against the metal walls. Rowan slips his hand away and pulls it tightly to his lap. His nostrils flare as he makes every effort to pinch his mouth shut and keep from retaliating in some way. So much for the friends thing.

The two of us sit in painful silence throughout the rest of the trip. When we finally get to the High Street exit, we jump to our feet and nearly shove one another down as we race onto the platform, pushing past each other to see who can make it out of the subway tunnel first.

Bright sunshine unexpectedly greets us on the outside. The overcast clouds have parted and given the chilly morning air a much-needed infusion of sweet autumnal warmth. Many of the tall trees around the bustling neighborhood are already barren, having shed their red and orange leaves all over the sidewalk in a dried up and bruised heap. Had I been brave enough to come a few weeks earlier, the sight probably would've been breathtaking.

"I'm not frozen, Josie!" Rowan's statement comes off like a kid who sat in his bedroom after being punished and came up with a good comeback an hour later.

The two of us continue to march together with a petty, angered swag, following signs for the bridge up ahead. The weather is completely gorgeous, meaning we're suddenly surrounded by a sea of strange faces making their way in the same direction. I'm not sure if it helps or hurts Rowan's cause. His continued outburst doesn't do us any favors either way.

"Why do you think I'm doing this?!" His temper boils, clenching his teeth down hard. "My aunt is my manager. We're in town to talk with the producers of the show today. Each of whom would gladly sell my soul to Satan if it meant keeping me on a contract for another ten years!"

His voice jumps higher and higher the more he confesses. I pat the air in an attempt to hush him up. "Rowan, I'm—"

"I don't get to make decisions, Josie! Decisions get made for me, and I'm told to shut up and act like it's fine because I'm good at it and it makes me money. It's bullshit! So please, don't preach about me getting to be the lucky one when you're free to run back home and live your own life!"

The words sink into my skin. I'm forcing myself to hold back tears all over again. Had he really thought I was running, and from what?

Rowan hurries ahead of me with furious speed. Had my ulterior motives not lingered in the back of my mind, I gladly would've let him continue walking without me. Like cruel, universal clockwork, my phone buzzes with a new message from Indio.

At the entrance to the bridge. It's packed. Keeping my eyes peeled for you!

I'm impressed you've stuck it out this long!

If only he knew the toll I was paying to make that happen.

CHAPTER 14

JOSIE

THE SAD THING about this whole scenario is, as much as I'm banking on Rowan, he's also banking on me. Who else knows who he is, is willing to protect his identity to keep him from getting mobbed, and offer him free use of their phone to route him wherever he wants to go?

His desperation shows in the way he tries to ditch me as we work our way onto the start of the Brooklyn Bridge. He takes two steps back in discreet pause whenever he sees my short legs starting to lag behind. Rowan may be pissed off, but he's also helpless, and that's the advantage I'm finding it harder and harder to leverage.

Indio's green jacket shimmers like a beacon of hope straight from Buffalo Exchange. He lingers near the side railing and holds up his expensive-looking Nikon. He's making it appear like he's taking pictures of a bird that's several yards in front of Rowan. He sends me a text a few moments after we pass him.

Following, but it might be tricky.

That was an understatement. The sheer volume of people on the bridge reduces me to claustrophobia I never knew I had. There are at least two gazillion tourists on both sides of the walking path and bike lane, knocking one another down to get a decent picture. Cyclists zoom by with barely enough time for you to hear their bells chiming before they've plowed you down.

My mind is pulled in a torrent of directions. Staying close to Rowan, keeping an eye on Indio, actually trying to enjoy the walk along the bridge, and the crippling awareness that Rowan may be right and that New York isn't the problem, I am.

I allow myself to get lost in the gothic architecture for a moment, looking up at the towers and cables that stretch far and long, some in wheel-like circular patterns. The buff railings are littered with gum, half-removed band stickers, and various acts of vandalism, some as inspiring as *It gets better*, all the way down to *DM me, I'm lonely*.

Had you asked me earlier in the day what made this place special, I wouldn't be able to give you a good answer. I would've responded with a desponded and smart aleck 'it's just a bridge' and moved on. Now, after having walked halfway across and seen the entire city skyline come alive in front of me like a pop-up book, I was starting to understand why everyone needed photos so desperately, not that any could adequately capture the scope of it.

The Flatiron building jumps out first, then the Empire State Building and the One World Trade Center. For some strange reason, I find myself smiling like an idiot every time I recognize another familiar landmark I'd seen in a movie hundreds of times before. Every reference is put to shame in comparison to experiencing the wind-whipping, car whoosh-ing, *how does this all fit onto one small island?* sensation of the real thing.

"WATCH IT!" A voice hollers. My arm slams hard into a nearby older gentleman walking his dusty black schnauzer. After apologizing, I tell myself to ogle less, pay attention more.

It turns out to be a fortunate collision because it helps me locate Rowan, who had wandered away from the crowd and wound up hiding out near a lamp pole. I wipe the sweat off my forehead in sweet relief. I was starting to wonder if I was following the wrong guy with a dark hood and sunglasses.

Rowan is intently focused on something ahead of him. I could swear he's gazing out at the East River stretching endlessly in the distance, but as I get closer, the source of his interest becomes clearer. It's a bride and groom decked out in their formal attire. He's gorgeous, tall with a warm skin and tightly curled hair. His new wife is just as stunning, her off-white mermaid gown covered in tasteful sequins. The bottom of her train flaps in the wind as the man tries to kiss her without getting smacked by her long, copper hair. I'm not sure why this is interesting to Rowan, but internally, I'm dying.

I come up behind him and watch in awe as the photographer tries to position the couple in different, sexy poses. The combination of the wind and crowds refuse to play along with any of her ideas, forcing the two to burst out laughing in the middle of every intimate shot as someone walks by and whoops at them.

"They look happy," I gush.

Rowan turns to me with a forced smile. "Must be nice."

"Do you... have a girlfriend?"

It's a classic Josie Bradford moment. Ask the handsome actor you're currently trailing about his relationship status and hope he forgets about the explosive argument you had ten-minutes prior.

To my surprise, Rowan isn't fazed by the question. "No."

"Oh." My heart leaps. "You mentioned Ashanti earlier. Sticking up for her and whatnot. I just assumed it was for a reason."

He scoffs. "Because I would only make international headlines if I were fucking the person I was causing the headlines for?"

When he puts it that way, yes.

The groom's tuxedo crumples as he grabs his bride and swings her into a low dip, kissing her neck as the photographer goes wild and excitedly tells him to keep going.

Rowan heaves a sigh, lowering his head and folding his arms as he leans in close to me. "She has a girlfriend."

"What? Who has a girlfriend? Ashanti Nath?"

He loudly shushes me and quickly nods his head. "She's not out," he explains, "and the girl she's seeing apparently isn't ready to go public with it either because of all the attention it'll draw to them, so they have to be really careful. I only know because she trusts me to keep it a secret."

The confession floors me. I'm not up enough on pop culture to tell you anything significant about current superstars or their love lives, but I know enough that Ashanti Nath coming out and having a girlfriend would be huge. Break the internet huge.

I try to hold my hair down as it flies in all directions. "That's the reason for the fight then? That guy who plays Noah Lawrence found out or something?"

"Michael Brewer is an asshole," Rowan states proudly, unconcerned with who hears him. "He's always been this huge diva on-set, and he acts like being on the show is an automatic pass for all the dumb shit he does. He found out about Ashanti through someone on set and got drunk enough at the party that he came up and started pushing her around, threatening to expose her just to be a dick about it."

I work out the rest. "Aaaand, then you punched him."

Knowing the whole story in context, I would've done the same thing when put into Rowan's position. That is, had I possessed half the amount of courage.

Rowan stretches his freshly tattooed arm with a flinch. "It's not like I enjoyed it. It just sort of happened instinctively. Ashanti is one of the only friends I've had since the show became a thing. I feel protective of her. I know, that's barbaric."

It was hard to imagine someone as extroverted and personable as Rowan being friendless. Then again, I don't dare admit what it must be like to have any authentic relationships in his line of work, especially when you're only seventeen. His admirable loyalty unearths a cage of butterflies in my stomach that have no business being there. Not when what I've schemed up makes me as much a lowlife as Michael Brewer.

"It's not barbaric. She's lucky." I tighten my lips. "You're a good friend."

"Doing my part to keep love alive, or something like it," Rowan jokes. He nods his head towards the newlyweds. The beanie-clad photographer is leading them further down the center of the bridge, mouthing an aggressive 'let's go!' The two wrap their arms around one another's waists and whisper with coy smiles.

Abruptly, Rowan turns to me and leans in close with one shoulder.

"Hey, I'm sorry," he mutters. "I shouldn't have called you out and expected you to be cool with it."

"You're good at making mistakes, remember?" I gulp down my pride and prepare to eat my own serving of humble pie. "I'm sorry too. It's not fair for me to claim to know what your life is like. I can only speak for myself, and honestly? My life kind of sucks lately."

"I get that." He bows his head reverently. I catch an emerald flecked glimmer behind his sunglasses that makes me wish those stupid butterflies would make their way elsewhere. After a beat, he quickly adds, "it doesn't have to suck today, though."

I stare out to the wide-open city in front of me and pinch my eyes closed, allowing the sights and sounds to overwhelm my senses in the best possible way. In the distance looms the smell of warm, freshly baked bread that makes me want to attack the first pretzel cart vendor I find.

Rowan must be able to read my mind. "Hungry again?"

"You too?"

"If memory serves me correctly." He insistently raises a finger. "The end of the bridge leads right to the financial district of lower Manhattan..."

"Precisely where you don't want to be?" I confusedly wonder.

"*Precisely*," he teases. "We won't be too far from Little Italy, though. There was this one bakery Grandma would go to all the time. Up for another walk?"

"I live in New York," I state, "I'm always up for a walk."

Rowan and I finally time our steps in sync with one another, making our way to the end of the bridge and soaking in the very last bits of the skyline across from us before they loom over our heads like an industrial, corporate sized umbrella.

Somewhere between Rowan pouring his heart out and me standing there feeling like actual human garbage, I lost track of Indio. Rowan asks if I can pull up a map, but not before reading a few missed texts. The first, of course, being from my partner-in-crime himself.

Drop a pin or something. I can't see you.

I roll my eyes and immediately reply with something short and vague.

About to head off the bridge.

I tap on his name and have the foresight to set his messages to Do Not Disturb for the foreseeable future, lest I risk Rowan seeing anything incriminating. I'd had too many close calls at the tattoo parlor as it was.

The second unread text causes me to audibly gasp. It's from my mom, whom I, for a brief moment, completely forgot existed.

Everything okay there?

She knows, I internally panic. *She totally knows.* There was no realistic way she could unless Pru had told her, but she was a mother. Mothers have the unspoken universal superpower of being able to know when you're up to no good, even from several hundred miles away.

My treasonous hands trembling, I reply and hope my delayed response doesn't add to her suspicions.

We're fine, Mom. Pru is making bracelets. I'm reading. You sure are missing a lot.

"You must be starving," Rowan says, "your hands are totally shaking right now."

I load the map on my phone, clutching it tightly and gritting my teeth down hard. "You don't even know."

I'M GETTING the impression Josie is still pissed off with me after our fight. It's not like I could blame her. She was honest with me and I was a total prick. The worst part is, I wasn't even mad at her for what she said. I was angry at myself because she was right. I'm frozen too.

She coolly distances herself on our walk to the bakery, gluing her nose to her phone and making every effort to make her directions short as possible. As we skirt the outer reaches of SoHo on our way to Caffé Palermo, I try to pull her out of her despondent nature the only way I know how—talking about old movies.

"You're dead to me. I'm leaving."

I toss my head back with a laugh. "Seriously?!"

Josie points a threatening finger at my nose. "*West Side Story* is the greatest movie ever made, full stop."

And I had just told her I thought it was overrated. Nice, Rowan.

"Okay then," I change the subject quickly. "*The Sound of Music?*"

"Ooooh no," she sings playfully, "you're not allowed to pull yourself out of this one, and with *The Sound of Music*? That's cheap."

I shove a finger down my throat and flippantly wag my hands in the air. "Ooh! Look at me! I'm *Romeo & Juliet* with street gangs!" Josie punches my tattooed arm. "OWW!"

"Sorry!" She covers her mouth with an evil chuckle. "Fine then. What's your favorite old movie? And I swear to god, if your answer is cliché or something with James Dean, I will shove you in front of an oncoming car."

We make it to Walker Street and quickly cross the road in a break of traffic before Josie has the chance to chicken out and wait for the pedestrian crossing sign to light up. I rub the back of my neck as I ponder my answer.

"As much as I love *East of Eden*—please don't hit me again—it's this old movie called *Ziegfeld Girl*." Just saying the name fills me with instant hipster cred I otherwise don't possess in any other way.

"First of all, that movie is amazing." She grins. "Secondly, nobody on earth has seen that movie."

"Minus us. We're not nobodies."

"Speak for yourself." She points to my piss-poor disguise. "Seriously, you've seen it?"

I feel like I'm harping on the dead grandmother thing way too much, but I can't help it. The reason I turned out half as normal as I claim to be is because of her.

"It was Grandma's favorite." I explain. "We watched it every time I came to stay with her. I think she could relate to the whole Hedy Lamarr 'I'm gonna star on Broadway and then abandon my career to support my husband' thing."

"Did she?" Josie's face falls.

"In a way." I push up my sunglasses. "Grandpa Jim got sick when they were really young. She left the theater to take care of him. He ended up recovering, but she realized she didn't miss it as much as she thought she would. They settled down and had kids instead."

"Wow. Was she happy?"

"Grandpa got sick again when my mom and aunt were still young and eventually died. It was hard for her, but yeah, I don't think she regretted her choice."

Josie's stride noticeably slows. She folds her arms and bobs her head back and forth to some invisible beat. "How did he die?"

I sigh. "Cancer."

The word strikes her like a sucker punch, her cheeks caving in and her pink skin turning pale. "Same as my dad," she explains.

I remembered how visibly shaken she'd been earlier after I brought up her father. "How long was he sick for?"

She blows through her lips and counts on her fingers. "Maybe three months? The doctors said he was probably sick for much longer, but they only caught it after it had spread. Pancreatic cancer is no joke."

"That's terrible," I practically whisper.

At least when Grandma learned her heart was failing, we had time to burn. We spent the last year of her life ditching school and taking road trips to the Catskills to camp and talk about all the places she hoped I'd see one day. Josie blinked, and her dad was gone. People always talk about nature taking its course when it comes to death. When it actually happens to you, it feels a lot more like nature dropping its signal in the middle of the woods and leaving you stranded.

"It was hard on my mom," Josie goes on. "She and Dad were crazy about each other. Out of nowhere, she was expected to go on without him."

"Kind of like Grandma." I nod. "I can imagine having two

kids to raise alone probably doesn't help with the whole grieving thing."

Josie relaxes her arms and allows them to swing at her sides. "Pru seems to have rebounded. Mom is doing alright. She mostly just misses him."

Caffè Palermo pops onto the scene after a marathon of walking. The thought of food suddenly seems so insignificant compared to the weight of our conversation.

"It's kind of funny," Josie says. "People assume that love is dead or that people our age don't know what it's like to have a relationship. I don't think that's true."

"How so?" I ask.

"Because you have people like your grandparents or my mom and dad who would've been willing to sacrifice so much for one another." The color slowly bleeds back into her face. "I don't think the notion of happily ever after is ever about everything being perfect after you fall in love with the right person. It's choosing to admit that life can suck, but doing it with someone who is willing to stick by you makes the hard stuff survivable, maybe even good."

"Damn," I admire, "you really are a writer, huh?"

She blushes. "Or, forever alone."

As we approach the café, I allow the smell of warm sugar and rich espresso to flood into my nose and squash any ability to feel sad. Impressions of the bakery are vague at best. I mostly remember begging Grandma to bring me a box of their life-changing cannoli every time she came to visit. I'd swear it was the manna the Israelites lived off of if the Israelites were Italian immigrants.

Despite the open layout, the inside is dimly lit with crowded seating. A massive glass case sits against a narrow doorway. The refrigerated display houses various baked goods like amaretti cookies covered in a heavy dusting of powdered sugar. Right next to them sit puffed round disks filled with brightly colored jams and fillings. There is an army of chocolate-dipped cannoli and decadent cheesecakes seated on the top shelves, practically begging to have their way with you. I'm like a catfish sucked up against the glass, breathing harder with every tray of food I pass.

"You're uncomfortably excited about this," Josie prods. "You don't get out much, do you?"

"Ha-ha," I respond flatly. "I never get to eat this stuff. They always have me on some stupid diet."

"Diets aren't part of my religion." Josie shakes her head. "What should I order?"

"As a first-timer? A cannolo. Standard, classic. Maybe one of those lobster tails too, they're filled with this amazing cheesecake type filling. Or they have gelato too if you want something cold."

Her cheeks turn up. "How much do you think I eat?"

I wave a flattened hand over her head to make a display of how short she is. "Not enough."

We settle on splitting a box of various Italian sandwich cookies covered in sprinkles, two cannoli rolled in chocolate chips, and a couple of cappuccinos. I beat Josie to the draw as we approach the register to pay, handing the cashier my money as she bumps me with her hip.

"You got breakfast!" she argues. "At least let me contribute the few dollars I have."

"Not a chance. This is me trying to move past the *West Side Story* thing."

"That's never happening," she sneers.

The older male cashier hands me my change back, wagging a pointed finger at my face as he extends a broad smile to Josie and me.

"You look like that boy on the Webstream TV!" His thick

Italian accent is the equivalent of marinara sauce incarnate. "The sad one from the Connecticut show!"

I grip the box of cookies close like an edible teddy bear and slowly back away before he has time to connect the dots.

"He gets that a lot." Josie worriedly scrunches her nose and grabs my arm. "Let's go, *Hunter*."

Tourists and loud families are all packed around the tables inside, smushing more chairs together in order to make their guests fit. Loud dishes back in the kitchen bang and clamor, a few random kids in line start having meltdowns to the dismay of their screaming mothers.

Josie grabs our drinks from the barista and looks at me with wide eyes. "So much for laying low in here."

"Let's just go out!" I yell above the noise, gesturing to the tables out front.

I note the clock above the door that says 3:00. How had so much of the day passed without feeling like we'd done anything? I suddenly understood what people meant when they referred to a New York minute. You could come to the city for a week and still not see a quarter of it. I envied Josie for being able to experience all of it freely. There was no expiration date on her time here, even if she was convinced otherwise.

The time suddenly clicks in my brain like a trigger. Lexi's lecture in the limousine the day before comes to mind. Our meeting with the producers over at the Webstream building was at 2:00. I was gloriously, spectacularly late. Not that it meant much when Lexi wouldn't be able to find me in the first place. I'd spent the whole morning saving off the urge to have Josie search for my name on social media to see if any new headlines came up. Splash pages with shocking breaking news articles ran through my head, each worse than the last.

Rowan Adler Kidnapped! Sources closest to him say, 'it was probably that cheerleader from Florida...'

"Is your coffee okay?" Josie asks, gabbing the first open table she sees and freeing us from the deafening chaos inside the bakery.

"Yeah." I force myself to take a piping hot sip and brush a barrage of graham cracker crumbs off my seat. "Just thinking."

"About our next stop?"

No, I ponder. *About how I've scared the bejesus out of my aunt and bodyguard by disappearing for nearly an entire day and how there are probably NYPD cops hunting in dumpsters for my dead body all over the city as I stand here innocently and stuff my face with cookies.* Too much?

"About you," I squeak. Not sure where it came from, but I'm rolling with it.

"Me?"

"You said you were single. What about that guy from the coffee shop this morning?"

Josie clears her throat with a nervous cough, opening the plastic container with a loud crinkle and pulling out one of the butter cookies. She holds it up for me to make a selection. "Aaron?"

Aaron. I curl my lips at the mention of his name. Tall, smooth, never has to try too hard or worry about bleach causing his hair to burn off his head. *Aaron.*

"Sure." I extend an uneven smile.

"We're in the same homeroom." She twirls her hair. "Last night was the first time we'd ever spoken. He typically hangs out with this jerk named Julian who likes to make my life a living hell."

If Julian was the same friend who'd been jerking Josie around the night before, she didn't need to say anything else. *Jerk* is being overly considerate when it comes to entitled assholes like him. I would know—Michael Brewer was one of them. I'd had my fair share of run-ins.

"Why is that?" I bite into the cookie with a soft whimper.

Her chin goes rigid. "It's an awkward story."

"Well, now I have to know."

Josie's face sinks. She lowers the cookie before she's even taken a bite. "You're gonna laugh at me."

"You say that, and then I never do."

Josie sighs. "Fine. Let's just say I pulled a code red on the first day of junior year, and Julian made it his sole purpose in life to point it out for the entire class to see."

I raise an eyebrow, devouring the last of my cookie. "I'm lost. Are you saying he picks on you for having a period?"

"Yes. To be fair, he makes fun of everyone," she explains. "I happened to be a prime target that day, and the joke marked me for life."

I reach for the container and grab my cannolo. "Sounds like Aaron needs new friends."

She flicks at a fly trying to contaminate the goods inside the box. "I won't argue with that. I wasn't expecting him to ask for my number this morning. That doesn't exactly happen to me frequently."

I had a hard time believing that. Josie was the kind of pretty you wouldn't notice in one quick glance. The longer you looked at her, the more you noticed. Like the small wrinkles the crept up underneath her eyes whenever she smiled, or the tiny, square-shaped freckle on her chin. Each small discovery only made me want to linger and find more.

"Do you think you'll go out with him?" I stress eat a second cookie, fearing how my finely tuned, frequently starved body will react to all the sugar I've consumed today.

She smacks her lips together. "He wants me to go to this Halloween block party thing in the neighborhood tonight, but I'm scheduled to work. By the way, after five, you're on your own. Unless you want to hang with me at King Kone. I'm sure you already miss it."

The last half of her statement goes over my head. "Why don't you go then?"

"Because I just said I had to work."

"Get out of it. Find someone to cover your shift and go."

She cocks her head. "You're adorable when your 'I've never had a real job before' shows."

All I take away from that statement is *you're adorable*, and my stomach does this sloshing thing that nearly causes everything I've eaten to take a bow all over the table.

I feel my face turn purple. "Do you want to go? Like, no hyperbole. If you had tonight off and Aaron wanted you to go, would you?"

Josie thinks about it for a moment. You can see the wheels in her head turning like cogs on a machine as she weighs the question. It's yet another quirk I find way more attractive than I should.

"Yeah," she finally touts. "I think I would."

"Great!" I smack the table. "So, who are we getting to cover for you?"

"I'm sorry, what?"

"You're gonna text the guy you like, tell him you want to go to that party thing tonight, and you're gonna go and prove to yourself once and for all that you're a badass."

"I have a job, Rowan!" She protests, lowering her voice when she gets to my name.

"That's why we're going to King Kone after this to ask someone to work your shift."

"I can't do that!"

"Why not?"

Josie groans. "Why are you doing this?" Her voice sounds

exhausted and vulnerable. It's the same tone Aunt Lexi puts on after having to deal with my sarcasm for more than an hour.

Yeah, Rowan, I think. *Why are you doing this? Especially when you like this girl and have spent most of the day trying way too hard to impress her?*

Guilt is the first thing that comes to mind. I still felt terrible about how I'd exploded at her after getting off the train. I'll be eating those words for the rest of my life, but that wasn't the only reason. Maybe I was trying to perform some sort of cosmic justice for my sins. Going back to the hotel and facing whatever wrath awaited me would be far more worthwhile if I walked away from Josie knowing I'd been able to help her the same way she'd helped me.

"Because," I stutter, "maybe you deserve a little happily ever after."

The corners of her mouth perk up. "That was a cheap answer."

"Did it work?"

She finally grabs the cookie she's been going back and forth with and munches deep into the center. The creamy silkiness spreads onto her face with a soft glow of ecstasy.

"Perhaps."

I COME to a devastating revelation while eating an Italian sandwich cookie: I like Rowan Adler. Not in an ironic *I'm totally going to plaster a poster of his face on my wall after all this is over* way either. We're talking the full-blown fuzzy, swooning, clutch your pearls, *can he please kiss me like I'm Audrey Hepburn* feeling I always got whenever I watched a movie that made me wish guys like that existed in real life.

Don't get me wrong. Aaron is fine. He's gorgeous and considerate and the complete opposite of guys like Julian Varma, who deserved to die by process of natural selection, but I hardly know anything about him yet. Is he funny? Is he good at anything besides basketball? Would he drag me all over the city and tell me to stop wasting my life while making fun of my favorite movies? You know, the real stuff girls look for in a suitable match.

None of it mattered in the end. The more I thought about it, the more asinine it sounded. Me and Rowan Adler? It was like one of those cringy Tom Holland + Y/N fanfics Hannah used to send me whenever I needed to feel better about my creative writing assignments.

Not to mention, the only reason I'm still with him is

because I'm planning on selling him out to tabloids, a plan that feels dirtier and dirtier by the second.

That grimy 'I'm the scum of the earth' feeling is the reason I've actively been avoiding Indio's texts ever since we lost him on the bridge. I don't have the heart to tell him I can't go through with this. Not when Rowan has confided so much that doesn't deserve to be shared, and not when I'm starting to care so much about all of it. He may not be whisking me off into the sunset, but he also doesn't deserve to walk away from today with a broken heart.

"There's this guy, Armani," I explain to Rowan. "He's the manager at King Kone. He's working this afternoon. Maybe he'd be willing to stay late to cover my shift for me. I've never asked before, but that is because—"

"Great! Text Aaron and tell him you'll see him tonight then." Rowan slaps his hands together eagerly before I can finish the sentence. *But that is because he's kind of a creep who stiffs his employees on their tips and sexually harasses every woman he perceives as having an apple bottom ass.*

"And we for sure have to go to King Kone?" Rowan adds. "You don't have this Armani guy's phone number to call?"

I shake my head. I'd blocked his number after the one time he'd 'accidentally' sent me a shirtless picture he swore was for his mom, because normal guys totally do that all the time. After that, I'd tried to keep all of our interactions short and within the boundaries of King Kone.

The two of us dodder away from the café with our stomachs bursting full of sugar and caffeine. I follow Rowan's advice and shoot Aaron a text as we walk to the subway station.

Hey Aaron! It's Josie Bradford! It looks like I might be going to the block party tonight after all! Hope to see you?

I'm tempted to add a bit about my 'cousin' joining me but opt to leave it out.

My phone starts buzzing a few moments later. I half hope for it to be Aaron calling and asking where we could meet. Instead, my legs lock up, and I suddenly feel like dog poop. No, worse, what dog poop must feel like after it's stepped on.

It's Pru, whom I hadn't considered once since I left her at the apartment and said, 'I'm going to take Rowan to the subway, I shouldn't be too long' ...almost five hours ago.

"It's my sister." I turn to Rowan. "Can I take this really quick?"

"Sure." He points to a Starbucks around the corner. "I need to use the restroom anyway. Meet me outside when you're finished?"

I nod approvingly and answer my sister's call as Rowan jogs off down the street directly in front of a honking oncoming city bus. I was never going to get used to this jaywalking thing.

"Pru!" I cry into the speaker. There are at least half a dozen ways I could follow up that greeting. *I'm so sorry. It's a long story. You'll never guess what I got pierced*—it was hard to choose.

In evergreen Prudence fashion, she's cool as a cucumber.

"One," she lists, "can I have a sleepover at Emma's house tonight? And two, WHERE THE HECK ARE YOU?"

"Who is Emma?" I question. As if I have any right to ask about her friends. I might be the worst older sister ever, but at least my ability to mother her isn't lost.

Pru groans. "She lives down the street. You've met her once! She's in my class, her mom said she'd take us trick-or-treating at her dad's house in Williamsburg, and she promises we'll be back and in bed by ten. Also, WHERE THE HECK ARE YOU?"

I hold the phone away from my ear. "Stop yelling! I'm sorry I didn't call sooner, I was just—"

"Hooking up with Rowan Adler?" She adds a childish 'oooh' at the front end to set me off.

"Don't use 'hooking up.' You don't know what it means."

"Oh, I know what it means."

"Prudence!" I shout, earning the scornful attention of a few pedestrians. "Yes, I'm with Rowan, but it's an insane story, and I don't have time to tell it over the phone. I promise I'll tell you when I get back."

"When *are* you coming back?" Her voice gets whiney. I start to wonder if she's been more worried about me than she's letting on.

"Tonight," I promise. "I'll be back by tonight."

"Fine," she huffs. "Can I go to Emma's or not? And remember, before you say no, I have every right to tell our mother about how you let a strange boy sleep in your bed."

She'd be leaving out the minor detail that I was sleeping on the couch while said boy was in my bed, but it's still enough to rattle me.

"You wouldn't dare."

"Try me."

"Okay!" I scream again, earning more judgmental stares. "Text me once you're at her house and when you're done trick-or-treating tonight!"

She laughs. "That's hilarious."

I can't be angry at her insolence. I thoroughly deserve it, regardless of how annoying it is.

"I'm serious, Pru. Please let me know?"

"Maybe do the same?" She snaps back. "I really was starting to wonder where you went. There are only so many places on our block you can visit in four hours."

My shoulders slump. "Goodbye, Prudence."

"Use protection!" She shouts before hanging up. My face goes scarlet.

Rowan lingers in the bathroom a little too long for my liking. I'm standing outside the Starbucks for fifteen more minutes before he finally turns the corner with a sly grin.

"Was there a line?" I snip.

"You know, sugar makes most people happy. I think it just sucks your joy."

I ignore his jab and pat my pockets. "You ready? I have the directions loaded."

"No, you don't. We're making a pit stop."

I could strangle him for even suggesting it. "Rowan..."

"What? I asked the lady behind the counter for directions. I might be navigationally challenged, but my memory is a steel trap." He taps his head. "Thanks to script memorization!"

"Where are we going?!" I mean to sound firm, but it comes out more like a child having a temper tantrum while lying on the floor of the grocery store. I'm not sure I can handle any more of Rowan's improv today. It was fun at first, but I'm starting to lose my patience.

"You'll see." He leans in and lowers his sunglasses. I'm convinced the boy is part leprechaun. Nobody's eyes are that green without possessing some sort of supernatural magic.

Rowan leads us down the street towards a different subway station and silently points to the signs we need to follow. He eventually takes us to the uptown W platform, where a train is moments away from arriving.

"We're on this for eight stops," Rowan instructs as we hop on board.

"Where, though?" I ask. I peer up and notice a ticker overhead flashing the train's upcoming stops. Rowan catches me looking and pokes my arm.

"No spoiling it!" He scolds. "I promise, it'll be worth the hold up."

Every train we've boarded throughout the day has gotten progressively busier and busier. This one is no exception. There isn't a single seat available. The both of us grasp the same metal standing pole, hoping we don't lose our footing and go flying across the train to our deaths.

There are a few normal-looking people on board. A businessman who looks like he's fresh off of work at a bank, as well as a young mother with her sleeping toddler beside her in a stroller. The rest are all clearly on their way to various Halloween festivities. There's a sexy angel, an impressive lookalike Luke Skywalker, and a reasonably convincing Frank N. Furter from *The Rocky Horror Picture Show*. I don't think it's actually a costume, and I'm sort of obsessed with it.

Rowan looks over every few seconds to make sure I'm keeping my eyes off the list of upcoming stops. He eventually locks his gaze into my side profile and nervously puckers his lips into a duck face.

"Can I ask you something personal?" He says softly.

Great. We're about to have a repeat of the train fight from earlier.

I tap my fingers back and forth on the pole. "Is anything off-limits at this point?"

He wavers. "What do you miss most about your dad?"

My eyes instantly go wet. Anytime someone brought up my dad, I involuntarily lost control of my emotions and started sobbing all over them, making a complete idiot out of myself. Most of my teachers quickly learned to avoid the subject altogether.

"There are lots of things," I reply. I keep my focus glued to my shoes in an effort to save off any unfortunate waterworks.

I think back to all the adventures Pru and I had with him as children. Trips into the city to see the children's museum and the zoo, Cincinnati Reds games where Mom would always forget to pack sunscreen and turn into a lobster by the seventh inning ("you're wearing team colors!" Dad would say.) There were school events and dance recitals, and countless horrible dinners he made sure to be home on time for. He always made it a priority to be there for us, even when it inconvenienced him most.

All that aside, if one thing stood out about Greg Bradford, more than any of the sacrifices he made for others, it was the thing that set my dad apart from all the other dads on our block.

"He had this amazing 1970 Mustang. It was cherry red. He restored it himself."

"No way!" Rowan cheers.

Note to self: Rowan is a car person.

"It was gorgeous." I beam. "He bought it completely thrashed from some guy a few towns over after paying off some student loans. He spent years restoring it. It was the one nice thing he ever did for himself. I think I was fourteen by the time he was finished. It took a while."

"Clearly," Rowan remarks.

My eyes sting as I recall the memory. "The day he finished, he ran into the house freaking out and told all of us to get in. He said we were going for ice cream, but he ended up driving us through the city with the top down for the next few hours. We totally forgot about the ice cream, but we didn't even care. We just sat in the car and butchered old Marvin Gaye songs. I miss having adventures like that with him."

"Do you still have the car?" Rowan asks. "I think I would've noticed a car like that outside your house."

My throat tightens. "We brought it with us when we moved, but then Mom sold to some collector in Albany after he died to pay for his funeral and some hospital expenses."

His excitement diminishes. "Oh."

"We weren't mad at her," I explain, "we know she didn't have a choice, and she would rather Dad have a headstone than a stick shift none of us knew how to drive."

I keep waiting for the tears to come, for the pain to become too much and for Rowan to stand there and watch me fall apart. Only, it doesn't happen. This is one of the first times since losing my dad that I've been able to look back on his life and not think about how much we both missed out on because of him dying. For once, the memories were enough.

"A stick shift isn't that hard to learn," Rowan attempts to lighten the conversation.

"Says you," I chime. "He tried to teach me to drive the thing in an empty Kroger parking lot one time. I nearly had a nervous breakdown."

"Sounds like it would be a regular Tuesday night for you." I aggressively smack his tattoo again.

Eight short stops later, we finally arrive at Rowan's mystery destination: Broadway and 49th Street.

"We can't stay for long," Rowan explains, "the barista told me it could take a while to get back to Brooklyn from here, but I needed to see your face."

I'm about to ask what that means by that as we follow a long tunnel of stairs, but as the luminosity above ground gets brighter all around us, I'm suddenly left speechless.

I'm surrounded by the lights and towers of Times Square. The sun had started to set behind the skyline, backlighting everything in its path with bright sherbet shades of orange and pink. Twinkling billboards flash various ads for Broadway shows, makeup brands, musicians, and movies. Some of them wrap around entire buildings while others shoot straight up the sky.

The air smells like dirty fog machine smoke that's

somehow escaped into the streets, combined with a variety of foods from hot dog carts and nearby bodegas. Characters in costumes are speckled throughout the landscape, more than usual due to the holiday, I'd assume. It's utterly over-whelming to the senses, yet at the same time, oddly welcoming.

"Don't get pictures with the characters," Rowan warns me. "They'll want money and probably try to molest you."

The characters aren't what intrigue me. It's not even the buildings or the billboards or anything else wide, weird, and wonderful about the experience of being there. It's the people. So. Many. People. There are couples and children, solo trav-elers and tourist groups, each coming and going without any clue who they're passing or what their history is.

I'm surrounded by a sea of thousands of nameless faces who don't know me, and for the first time since moving here, it doesn't make me want to run away to where it's smaller and safe. The world feels vast and limitless and entirely mine for the taking, like all of this exists so I could be here in this moment to experience it. I'm not just another background char-acter in someone else's story. I'm the leading role.

"This face," Rowan finally says.

I catch a glimpse of myself in his glasses, looking like an absolute dweeb with sore cheeks from how wide I'm smiling. My skin is covered in goosebumps, feeling hot and cold all at once. If we weren't in a rush to get back for the block party, I could spend another hour here just soaking it all in.

"This isn't even the best place in the city," Rowan explains, "it's actually a massive tourist trap and kinda sucks, but as a starting point—"

Rowan goes silent as I abruptly cut him off and wrap my arms around his waist for a hug. Part of me expects him to shove me off and tell me to stop making a scene. Instead, he loosens his arms from my grip and hugs me back, tight and warm. Fire moves throughout my body as his grip intensifies.

"Thank you," I muffle, blinking away tears before I'm a complete disaster on the streets of Broadway.

"Anytime," he responds. If only he meant it.

I force myself to pull away and poke at the corners of my eyes. "Ready to head back to Brooklyn?"

Just as I ask, a new advertisement flashes across most of the screens on the strip. Rowan's face is front and center. Hunter Cade's bleached nineties boy-band hair hangs in greasy strings on his face. The screen zooms out to reveal Ashanti Nath with her arms around his chest, whispering a seductive secret. The rest of the cast pops up behind him like a poorly executed cat GIF. The wraparound banner reads *DAWN HEIGHTS: SEASON THREE NOW STREAMING ONLY ON WEBSTREAM!*

I'm mortified for him. I can hardly imagine how he feels.

"Yes," he lifelessly shouts above the street noise. "I am very ready to go back."

CHAPTER 17

ROWAN

THE IMAGE OF A BROODING, blond-haired Hunter Cade haunts me on the ride all the way to Brooklyn. It's not like I'd never seen myself on a billboard before. Trust me. I signed enough two-foot posters of my face at last year's first annual DawnCon in Hartford that I could hardly look in a mirror for a week afterward. As Josie stood there having an out-of-body experience in Times Square, I was spiraling into an existential crisis.

Weeks before the premiere, Aunt Lexi approached me about the contract meeting. We were at a members-only gym, and, like most of our sessions, my trainer was watching TikToks while I ran a fifteen percent incline on the treadmill for twenty minutes. I was about to keel over and pass away when Lexi walked up, a fluffy towel slung over her shoulder, her dirty blonde hair wrapped into a tight ponytail.

"I just got off the phone with some of the folks at Webstream!" She gushed. Her hair swung back and forth like a metronome.

"Cool," I huffed, "what about it?"

"We're meeting in New York at the end of October to talk about your contract."

My contract. I stopped the treadmill, much to the dismay of my trainer, who gives me five minutes to walk it out. I stood hunched over the screen, dripping beads of sweat all over the machine as I wipe my brow with my shirt.

"What is there to talk about?" I asked.

Her neon green athleisure blinded me with its obnoxious glow-in-the-dark shimmer. I had a conspiracy theory that Lexi never actually worked out when she went to the gym. She'd sit in on ten minutes of hot yoga before excusing herself from the class to answer emails, and up until a year ago, smoke half a pack of cigarettes outside. Alex said she only went with me to meet men with a Bally Total Fitness aesthetic, whatever the hell that means.

"I won't get into the specifics of it here." Lexi turned up her nose at the eighty-year-old guy going two miles an hour on a stationary bike nearby. "Let's just say they're willing to extend through another two seasons. With a substantial salary hike."

My eyebrows jump at the words 'salary hike' the same way hers do, for different reasons entirely.

"Are they afraid they're going to lose me?"

"They see your value," she corrects. "They know the competition is fierce."

We'd had at least two dozen lunch meetings with various studios in the last year who all wanted me for different projects, each of the opportunities falling through thanks to the show's hectic filming schedule. Either that or Lexi would advise me they weren't worth the commitment. That's also what she'd said about her last two live-in boyfriends.

"You say that like it's a bad thing." I blow my nose into my shirt.

Lexi steps back, batting her eyelashes. "Why would you think that?"

"I'm only saying, it's not the worst thing to branch out a bit."

"There isn't an if about it," she says snidely. "This could be huge, Rowan. Really think about it."

I had, or at least, I thought I had till I left that hotel room, and my entire mental state went up in smoke. Josie's lashing from earlier was still rattling through my ears, the words *you're not the victim* playing over and over on steady repeat. I may have felt like a slave to expectation, but at the end of the day, the decision was still mine to make. Not Lexi's or the producers, or anyone else's.

Now, I suppose it all depended on if there was still a decision to go back and make once all of this was over.

Josie jumps upright as her phone dings. Aaron's name pops up on the screen. As much as I want to be a better person and look away, I can't help but pry. I dart my eyes back and forth quickly to see their exchange. There are only two messages. One from her asking if he's still going to the party, and his response: **ysss!!!! see you l8er!**

He *would* be one of those douchebags who unironically used 'l8ter.' It didn't surprise me, but what did, were did were the two messages. I'd spent the whole afternoon thinking she was texting Aaron while we were at the tattoo parlor. Had she not been flirting with him then?

"Aaron says he'll be there!" Josie bounces in her seat. Why do girls bounce in their seats for l8ter boys?

"Awesome," I reply frigidly. *You're the one who told her to do this,* I remind myself. *Stop sulking over a girl who isn't interested in you.*

The streets of Josie's run-down neighborhood feel weirdly welcoming. A group of boys play a game of two-on-two at the park around the corner. Their grunts and yells echo in the air like white noise. A few young kids wander the streets in costumes with their slagging parents to pregame the primetime candy.

King Kone's illuminated window at the end of the road signals us. Across the street, next to Josie's apartment building, several homeless people are once again gathered in the alley, tossing heavy black bags of garbage into the dumpster and throwing matches inside to kindle a rancid fire.

"They do that every night." Josie pinches her nose. "They're mostly gone by the morning."

"How do they put out the fire?"

"I don't know, and I'm afraid to ask."

The fluorescent lights inside the restaurant burn my retinas through the sunglasses just as they'd done the night before. Two new employees stand behind the front counter. One is an older, burly man with biceps that could possibly give Alex a run for his money, and the other is a scrawny older woman with a purple streak in her lengthy, gray hair.

Hanging high on the wall behind the register, I notice the Vin Diesel photos Pru had told me about. One of his latest movies plays on the TV in the corner. It's about an ex-military guy who becomes the President of the United States —*Commando in Chief.*

"That's Armani," Josie leans into my ear and whispers, pointing to the muscly man.

"Thanks for clarifying." I jab her with my elbow. "I was really starting to wonder if it was her."

The older woman spots Josie and frowns. You can read the confusion on her face like a book.

"I thought you weren't working till five." She states.

"I'm not." Josie thumbs the door, "I actually wanted to talk to Armani about that."

The woman's eyes go wide. "Good luck with that." What was that supposed to mean?

Armani turns to face her from the reuben he's not-so-secretly eating on the far side of the counter. His feet thud with heavy clomps, a huge scar running down the side of his face towards his puffy lips. I take it back. This guy *did* give Alex a run for his money.

"Couldn't stay away?" His thick, syrupy voice booms. His words make me feel sticky.

Josie takes a deep breath and pleads her case. "I got invited out last minute tonight, and I was wondering if you could cover my shift? I'd be willing to come in and work for you any time this week after school!"

"No," Armani doesn't hesitate to decline.

Josie sucks in her cheeks and grabs handfuls of her hair, twisting them into a thick rope. "I know it's last minute and that by asking, I'm coming off as inconsiderate, and I'm sorry, but—"

"No."

"Jesus, dude," I crack, "what's your problem?"

"Ignore my cousin." Josie pats my chest with a thwack. Armani gives me a look that says he's three seconds away from Popeye punching me into the dumpster fire across the street.

I turn a deaf ear to their conversation for a moment and face the mostly empty restaurant. The booth in the back corner where I'd fallen asleep is now occupied by a single police officer, quietly eating a sandwich and casually watching the movie. I feel like my act of stupidity should be commemorated with a plaque the same way Vin Diesel's visit had been. *Rowan Adler sat here once and fell asleep after popping sleeping pills he thought were anxiety meds. Boy, he sure is a dumbass.*

Josie continues to infuse her negotiations with patience rather than sarcasm, something I sorely needed to learn.

"You can take my tips for the next week!" She offers.

The man shakes his head, his facial expressions as dull as a slice of toast. "I think you forget who you work for, honey."

The desperation in her voice begins to leak onto her face. "Come on! You've covered for other people before!"

"Like who?" Armani snaps back.

Josie's face calculates. I press a hand to my cheek to hide a smirk. This was not the time to have an embarrassing *god, she's cute* moment.

"Alice!" Josie snaps her fingers. "You covered for Alice over the summer! All the time!"

Rigid chords pop out of Armani's neck, his creepy stare bulging. "That was different. You're not Alice."

Defeat washes over Josie's face, the hollows of her eyes sagging into a frown only a creepy clown statue would be proud of. Several seconds of silent, uncomfortable staring later, she spins her feet toward the small opening in the counter and humbly walks towards her boss. For a moment, I fear she's about to grab an apron and throw it on over her sweatshirt. What she does instead shocks me.

"Is it because Alice let you touch her boobs?"

Armani's face turns white as a sheet. Every eye in the building suddenly turns to the two of them. In the corner, I hear the purple-haired woman laugh to herself and mutter a soft, "oh shit, this is gonna be good."

Armani makes a croaking noise before lifting his jaw off the floor. "I'm not sure—"

"Yeah!" Josie continues. "You remember Alice? Single Mom Alice? Worked here for two months? The one you 'forgot' to pay one time and you make her go back into your office and—"

"ENOUGH!" Armani cries. "That's a disgusting accusation!"

"You're a disgusting accusation!" Josie retaliates. She might've been a little too confident with that one. After taking a moment to cringe at herself, she fires again. "I quit, Armani."

Armani's dark eyes squint as he laughs in her face. "You quit?"

She repeats it again louder, sticking a finger in his face and adding a foot stomp as a flourish. "I QUIT!"

The purple-haired woman stands behind Armani, looking on at the scene. If it wouldn't put her job in jeopardy, I'd say she was tempted to cheer.

"I have never complained once!" Josie shouts. "I've shown up for every shift on time since I've started, I've covered shifts, I've helped on school nights, and I've put up with your creepy 'you had a dog hair on your back' butt grabbing!" She adds finger quotes. "I don't even have a dog!"

The cop in the booth looks over and raises his eyebrows. Armani's broad shoulders hunch, his face contorted into a smug/horrified combination that can only be interpreted as *at that moment, he knew he fucked up.*

Josie slams the counter with a flat palm as she makes her grand exit. The moment would be way more legendary if her sneakers wouldn't squeak every time her feet hit the tiles. I follow behind her like an awestruck puppy dog, watching as she turns around and throws her hands to the sky for one last statement.

"By the way, apparently Vin Diesel didn't even like his food!"

The doorbell screams in agony as we walk out of King Kone for the last time. I burst into hysteric whoops and cheers.

"Dude!" I hold out a hand for a high five. "You just quit!"

A smile explodes onto Josie's face as she thrusts her arm in the air and meets mine with a popping smack. In an instant, her expression changes. Her pupils grow large, and her lips part into a quivering V-shape.

"I just quit," she exasperates. "Rowan, I just QUIT."

I know, I want to say, *I'm sort of inspired.* "You never said your boss was such a perv! I'm so—"

She turns and begins panic-riddled walking down the sidewalk, running her hands through her hair and silently repeating to herself, "ohmygodohmygodohmygod!"

I run to keep up with her, internally thanking my trainer for sticking me on an uphill treadmill incline five times a week for the sole purpose of keeping up with people when they have a speed walking anxiety attack.

"Josie!" I call out again. "That was amazing!"

"No, it wasn't!" Her voice cracks. She sounds like she wants to cry. "Rowan, I needed that job!"

"You'll find another job!" I protest.

Josie pauses and waves her trembling hands in the air like a conductor. "It wasn't only for me! Most of my paychecks go to family expenses! And the small bits that don't go to my college fund! Why do you think my mom is in DC begging my grandparents for money?!" She pauses at that last portion like it was never intended to come out.

As her breaths come faster, shorter, and more intense, my pride diminishes to empathy. I'd never had to work a real job. I was thrust into my career at fifteen and cheated my way out of the struggle phase. I couldn't relate to how she was feeling about losing her job, and I didn't want to act as if I could. What I could relate to was her fear of what would come next after making a choice that scares the shit out of you.

Reaching out and loosely placing my hands on her shoulders, I lean in with a tight-lipped grin and say the only thing I think could possibly help.

"You'll figure it out. You are Josie Bradford. You're a badass."

ROWAN OFFERS to buy me a giant chocolate chip cookie at Stillwater before they close for the night. My stomach can't possibly take any more sugar today, but the thought of what just happened at King Kone requires some form of celebratory slash lamenting comfort food. I'd quit my job, the one steady thing I had in terms of college money.

Well, maybe not the only thing.

I scroll through my phone as Rowan goes to the counter and orders, finally reading the deluge of ignored messages from Indio. He'd finally given up around the time Rowan and I left the Italian bakery, sending me a middle-finger emoji and saying he was going home. I deserved every ounce of his anger. I'd left him high and dry all because I'd developed a conscience. Or worse, a crush. Surely between the information I had and the photos he'd managed to get, it would still be enough to sell a story.

This could still work, I think to myself, *just stay focused this time.*

Rowan walks over with a goofy smile and a planet-sized cookie on a plate. I secretly want to die. He didn't deserve to have his life thrown under a bus, but I didn't exactly want mine to wind up there either.

"I asked them to warm it up," he says. "Cold chocolate chip cookies are against *my* religion."

"Thank you." I break off a small piece and nibble the buttery edge. Inwardly, my response sounds more like 'CAN YOU STOP BEING SO GODDAMN THOUGHTFUL?'

"What exactly is this block party thing?" Rowan asks, helping himself to a massive bite.

I recalled what Pru had mentioned to us weeks ago when she and her school friend had planned on attending. "It's supposedly this big neighborhood event they have where businesses shut down early and open vendor booths with carnival games and stuff. The local Boys & Girls Club funds it to keep kids from causing trouble on Halloween night."

"Sounds like we're more than qualified to attend," he jokes. "How far is it?"

"Not far." I search the event on my phone and pull up the bland webpage for the event, reading the noteworthy bits aloud. "Boroughween. Festivities start at five. The live music starts at eight. Booths close at eleven. Oh, and there's an apple bobbing contest at nine."

Rowan shudders. "Followed by mono at nine-thirty."

"And yet, you make out with women on TV for a living."

He tosses a cookie crumb at my sweatshirt, darting his head down towards his dirt-stained shoes. "It's not fun when it's not real."

"You might be the first man alive to admit that."

"What can I say?" He pops the last bite of cookie into his mouth with a sly grin. "I'm old-fashioned."

I groan internally. Why did the boy straight out of all my fake scenarios have to be someone I'd never stand a chance with in real life? And why did knowing it would never work make it so much easier to stab him in the back?

"Hey." He points to the restroom sign in the back, "I'm gonna go unload."

Maybe he wasn't entirely dreamy. "Gross."

"Everyone poops, Josie."

"That doesn't mean I like to know when they do."

He rolls his eyes. "I'll be right back."

The mood in the café changes exponentially from morning to evening. It alternates from a fast-paced, big city coffee bar to a vibey, wannabe candlelit jazz lounge. It would be the perfect place to bring a date and bond over a warm, oversized cookie. Kind of like Rowan and me... minus the part where it was ever a date, and we're never going to see one another again.

"JOSEPHINE FUCKING BRADFORD!"

That voice. I know that voice. It's a voice that sounds like someone's nasal passages never grew properly. I hesitate to turn around in my chair, knowing I'm about to find a scathing Indio Byun on the other side, ready to strangle me with his camera strap.

I scoot my chair to face him and press my lips together, folding them in and making an awkward buck-toothed smile. "You're mad, huh?"

He folds his arms against his leather jacket, his bucket hat shoved into one of the front pockets. "What makes you think that? Is it the way I'm standing or the fact that you DITCHED ME, BITCH?"

"Shhh!" I press a finger against my mouth. "I'm sorry, okay? I had second thoughts!"

"About what?!" Indio sinks into Rowan's seat and leans over the table like he's convincing me to become one of Ocean's eleven. "He's famous and stupid, and you need money. It's perfect!"

"I know!" I lower my tone of voice. "We're back on, okay? I just went into King Kone to convince Armani to work for me and ended up quitting."

"YOU WHAT?!"

"SHHH!" My loud hiss sounds like a possessed rattlesnake. "It's a long story."

"Tell me about it! It's been a long day!"

I sigh, setting an elbow on the table and running a hand through my hair. I can feel how greasy I look after a day spent impromptu sightseeing.

"What are you even doing here?" I ask. "I thought you weren't working tonight."

"I'm not," Indio retorts, pointing to the register like a shy schoolboy. He finally lowers his voice, "I'm doing what I do every night, coming in and stalking Hot Barista."

He refers to the infamous Izzy Ezra behind the counter, taking a thin man's mocha order. Izzy could very well be the lovechild of David Bowie and Dua Lipa, who goes on to win *America's Next Top Model*. A bright yellow crop top sits above their high-waisted flair jeans. Ombre blue eyeshadow highlights their pale gray eyes, with matching sapphire streaks running throughout their full platinum hair. It was hard for me to picture Indio interested in anyone besides himself, but his crush on Izzy needed no explanation.

"That's not creepy at all," I tease.

"Says the girl who caved on our deal because she got a hard one for Rowan Adler."

I shove his arm lightly. "Eww!"

Indio arches one of his square eyebrows. "I followed you around for half the afternoon, Josie. You're officially one of us."

One of us, meaning one of the millions of teenage girls on the planet who thought they'd ever get a chance with Rowan. I was suddenly the Y/N in all those fanfics. I hated it.

I fight fire with fire. "Then why do I have a date tonight, hmm?"

Indio's quizzical surprise causes his hair to jolt. "You talked to a boy?"

"Another long story."

"Where is Rowan anyway?" He peers around the room to see if Izzy is still there. Who was Indio to make fun of me when he was the one spending his free time sitting at a coffee shop and hoping someone would eventually notice he existed?

"The bathroom," I explain, "and he'll be out any second, so if we're still doing this, you might want to—"

"Oh my god." Indio takes my hand and slides it underneath the table with a squeeze so tight, I nearly scream. "Is this really happening right now?"

Izzy waves to us from behind the bar, namely to Indio, whose smile is glistening brightly enough to beacon ships to shore. He releases my hand and daintily waves back. This was the most un-Indio I've ever seen him. I wasn't sure if I loved it or if I wanted it to stop.

"Did you need to break my hand?!" I grit my teeth, griping the air to check for broken bones.

"shutupJosieitstruelove," he mouths fast and quietly. "You should appreciate this."

"Appreciate what?" Rowan's voice nearly causes me to fall out of my seat and break my other hand.

Indio spins himself in wide-eyed terror. This wasn't the first time he'd seen Rowan up close, but it *was* the first time since learning who he was. Try as he may, the boy can't play it off to save his life.

"Hunter!" I cry with a chipper grin. "This is Indio! He works with me at King Kone!"

"Worked," Indio corrects, internally wounding me. "Who

are you? You seem familiar." *Oh god,* I panic. Was he really going to play dumb?

Rowan seems equally as alarmed, shoving his sunglasses so high on his face, they may as well be worn on his forehead. "I'm, uhh—"

"My cousin!" I nod, getting him to join along. "Remember? I was telling you about how he came in last night and pranked me with the whole sleeping thing? I didn't realize it was him? After you left...?"

One thing is for sure after that terrible performance: Rowan is the actor, I am not.

"Oh yeah!" Indio smiles, playing along. "Nice to meet you, Hunter!"

Rowan extends a skeptical hand for him to shake. "Likewise."

"You know." Indio wags a finger with a suspecting smile. "I told Josie you look a lot like Rowan Adler from *Dawn Heights.* You must get that often."

"Sadly." Rowan's face turns pale.

Indio's ad-libbing only seems to be making things worse. I quickly change the subject. "Indio was in the neighborhood and wanted to say hi."

Rowan lingers on Indio for what feels like slightly too long. That is, till he flatly states why. "Nice camera."

My stomach sinks, along with the half cookie inside it. My internal monologue sounds suspiciously like "Twinkle, Twinkle Little Star," only every word in the song is replaced with *shit.*

Indio looks at me like I'd make up anything better to lie about than he would. I quickly come up with something. "Indio is a freshman at the School of Visual Arts. He's studying photography!"

"Bird photography." He says robotically. "I've been

photographing birds. Today." The awkward pauses he takes between every other word only make this more unconvincing

"Really?" Rowan curiously pouts. "That's kinda cool." He pulls up a chair from one of the empty tables nearby and swings his legs across the back, immersing himself in our conversation. Did that fake ass alibi actually work?

"I was just stopping by to say hi," Indio reiterates. He must've missed the part where I already said that. One step forward, two steps back...

"And stalk the baristas," I prod. Might as well have some fun at his expense while he's here and ruining everything.

Rowan smirks. "Really? Which one?"

"Josie!" Indio clenches his teeth and shakes his head.

"That one." I point to the yellow crop top. "That's Izzy Ezra. Whom we refer to as Izzy Ezra because it's way more fun to say their first and last name together."

Rowan studies Izzy for a moment and approves with a devilish nod. "I can totally see you guys together."

The borderline compliment takes Indio by surprise, reaching to stroke the collar of his jacket.

"Really?" He scrunches his nose.

"We all could, but there's this small hitch where Indio here," I say, slapping his shoulder, "is too scared to tell them."

Indio dusts me off him like a piece of lint. "Says the girl who is going on her first date ever tonight."

Rowan's mouth goes agape. "You didn't tell me that it was your first date!"

"Because it's not!" I argue.

It is technically accurate. Aaron and I never established that it was a date. He'd casually asked if I was going to the party and then said in a text he'd see me there. I did what all ordinary people do by confronting their boss and quitting their job to get their time off approved. It was my own personal Cinderella story in the making, minus anything magical and non-musical subway rats. At least there were guaranteed pumpkins.

"What are you scared of?" Rowan folds his hands together like an inquiring therapist. Our efforts to distract him may have been weak at best, but one thing was for sure—the boy loved a problem.

"Other than rejection and the crippling fear of dying alone?" Indio scoffs. "I dunno. You tell me."

"Just go talk to them!" I urge. "If I can talk to my crush, you can talk to yours."

Rowan's jaw twitches at the word crush. Was it that obvious I was confused about the whole Aaron thing? And did Rowan even know he was the reason why?

"Natural flow, Josie," Indio snarls my name, his lips turning up into a Grinch-like curl. "You don't walk up to someone and say 'I like you' and have it all work out."

Oh no. I know what's about to happen before Indio has a chance to realize it himself.

Rowan tilts his glasses down, a familiar spark of rebellion exploding in his eyes like a firework. He pushes them back up and then swings his legs from around the chair and marches towards the register with his hands shoved into his pockets.

Izzy pauses whatever they're working on and squints their eyes as they move up to the front. "Can I help you?"

Rowan jilts his hip to one side and proudly waves one arm to our table, looking directly at Indio.

"He likes you!"

I cover my mouth with one hand and pinch my eyes shut, hoping this is the point where I wake up, realizing this whole day was one long nightmare. I'll awake comfortably in my bed and have a good laugh with Pru about the dream where I took Rowan Adler home from work and watched him run my life and sanity into the ground.

Indio's face burns so red, you can see his bright blue eyeliner melting at the creases. He's ten seconds from jumping to his feet, swearing off coffee for life, and running all the way back to his stepmom's apartment in total mortification.

After the day I've had, what happens next really shouldn't come as any surprise.

"You do?!" Izzy's voice is tight and childlike. You'd think Rowan had just told them he was sending them to Disney World.

Indio stands to his feet, itching his nape and doing this awkward half nod smile thing that counts as some form of yes.

At this point, everyone in the coffee shop is watching. A couple in the corner cuddled up in front of their computer whip their dual headphones out of their ears and watch the scene unfold, alongside the other baristas who treat the moment with the reverence of a marriage proposal.

After a long silence and more head shaking, Indio finally speaks up. "Why do you think I'm in here every day?"

I lower my hand from my mouth and place it directly over my heart. Apparently, art school assholes have feelings too.

Izzy bursts into a smile that can only be described as Christmas morning and seeing stars all at once. They sheepishly run their fingers through their silky hair (which forces me to wonder what the rules are here on server hygiene) and smacks their lips with a popping sound.

"My band is playing a show tonight. I'm off in twenty minutes if you want to stick around and come... with?" Izzy's hesitancy causes my heart to melt into a pile of gush on the floor. How was it possible Indio was the one living out my rom-com dreams?

The thought of tagging along with Rowan and me fades into a distant memory as Indio smiles wide and chuckles to himself.

"Sure?"

The couple in the corner starts clapping out of sync as the rest of the patrons watch on in silence, making the moment even more awkward than it already was. Izzy goes back to the drink they were making, looking back over at Indio every few moments to flash a weak-kneed smile.

Matchmaker Rowan marches back from the center of the room and boyishly slaps Indio on the back with a thump. "That's how it's done."

Indio still towers over the table as my butt stays firmly glued to my seat. He turns his head down and parts his mouth in tongue-tied astonishment.

"What the fuck just happened?" He mumbles.

"I think Hunter just got you a date," I say. My secret fake cousin for the win.

"If you want to thank me," Rowan states, pressing his hands onto the table and leaning his torso back, "point me to the nearest thrift store."

I furrow my brow. "Why?"

Rowan ruffles the mess of hair under his hood. "We're gonna need some costumes."

ASKING INDIO where a thrift store is located nearby is pretty much like having a personal bloodhound. He fired off at least fourteen of them within a ten-mile radius and knew the hours and sister locations of most of them off the top of his head. We settled on a small ten-bucks-or-less shop called Dress Less.

"Do you think they wanted to call it Dress FOR Less, but there was an issue with the trademark?" I wonder aloud.

"Maybe." Rowan shrugs. "Or they just really want to see you naked."

Dress Less is less than half a mile from the coffee shop. Indio swears that their clearance section is a gold mine. I'm mostly curious how a bargain store can have a clearance section.

I fire off a text to Indio on our walk, not knowing where our plan stood now that we were going our separate ways again. It's not like I was begging him to stick around and take pictures at the party. My desperation and my feelings were still at war with one another, and I had this sinking feeling one of them was going to win at the expense of the other. I just didn't know which yet.

Indio touches base right away.

Izzy's band is playing at the block party. Fate's Bitch.

I send a reply, my gut sinking.

I mean, I guess that is sort of ironic.

As we near the entrance, my phone buzzes with another response.

That's the name of the band, genius.

I laugh to myself, getting a suspicious stare from Rowan. I wave my cracked screen in the air. "Indio's date is playing the block party. He said he'd see us there."

He enigmatically quirks his lips. "That's ironic."

Tell me about it. Life wasn't going to let me slide out of my evil plan easily, was it?

Dress Less reminds me of this old thrift store I used to frequent back home called Save Rite. The lights flicker as if the store is haunted by the ghosts of fashion disasters past, very fitting considering the holiday. The floors are a dull white deco covered with mysterious black skid marks. This is definitely the type of place where I could see Indio finding a pair of cheap, designer combat boots and bragging about it till kingdom come.

Racks of clothes separated by size and garment are lined from wall to wall with different colored price stickers. Blue is five dollars, pink is eight, yellow is ten, and red is a dollar or less. Rowan immediately dives into the red rack, clearly having some idea of what he's looking for.

"No brainer." He shuffles through clanging plastic hangers. "A superhero. They wear a mask, and they're a dime a dozen at a costume party. Nothing to suspect."

"This wouldn't have anything to do with a secret desire to be in a Marvel movie, would it?"

"If you're about to tell me you hate superheroes, we can't be friends."

"No." I chuckle. "That's actually kind of great."

I admire a red cardigan vest covered in fluffy white Shih Tzus. Or, more accurately, stare at it in confused terror. Nothing on any of the clearance racks is sticking out to me, unlike Rowan, who has an armful of choices by the time I pick up one decent-looking pink sweater, and it's because I like it and not because I'm costume hunting.

"Exactly which superhero's aesthetic are you going for?" I ask.

"Did you ever see *Blankman*?"

"No."

"That's probably for the best." He pulls a pair of full cherry red long johns off the rack.

Once he's satisfied with what he's found, Rowan escapes into a bathroom that doubles as a dressing room to try everything on. I continue to scour the more expensive clothing, landing in front of the dresses and trying to come up with anything original. Everything is already so picked over. Apparently, everyone went thrifting for their costumes last minute.

Halloween was always a holiday Pru enjoyed more than me. I preferred to stay at home and pass out candy to the kids on our doorstep while Mom and Dad took her around the block to beg for chocolate. I could barely remember how we'd celebrated last year, probably at the hospital with Dad. I'd spent every waking moment trying to block the last year from my memory. Nothing in that window of time ever seemed like it was real. Today was the first day in ages I didn't want to instantly forget.

From the corner of my eye, I spot a tulle monstrosity hanging at the end of the dress rack. It's ivory with an off-shoulder neckline and bold lace embellishments on the bodice. The skirt looks like a bloated replica from that one *Cinderella* remake, swallowing half of the next aisle as it lies flat on the ground collecting dust. It's the nineties wedding dress to rule all nineties wedding dresses. And it's only ten dollars.

I hold up the hanger and examine it for any tears or unpleasant stains. It's definitely used (how used, I don't want to know) but otherwise, in fair condition. It's a size too big, and the length is going to be a hazardous nightmare on my short body, but it's not as if I have many other options.

The bathroom/changing room door opens. Rowan leaps out in a reasonably embarrassing superhero fashion. He'd really need to take some stealth lessons if he was expecting a phone call from Marvel.

"What do you think?" He spins.

The long johns fit well around his torso, but the legs stop just short of his shin and reveal his hairy calves. A long, gingham scarf is wrapped around his waist as a makeshift belt, and a thin faded *My Little Pony* comforter is tied around his neck like a cape. He's fully committed to the role as he blinks wildly through a plain black masquerade mask he's snagged off the accessory aisle. I'm not sure if he wants me to be encouraging or if it's intentionally supposed to be this bad.

"I feel like this is what would happen if Peter Parker was bitten by a radioactive furry instead." I force a smile.

Rowan holds up two thumbs up. "Then it's exactly what I want." He spots the dress I have not-so-inconspicuously shoved underneath my arm. "Did you find something?"

I raise the weighted hanger, fearing how many southern belles gave their debutant balls so this dress could exist.

"I think so? It's going to be huge on me."

"Better than highwaters." He points to his ankles. "Go try it on! Don't look inside the toilet, by the way. Unless you care to be scarred for life."

I know better than to argue with him. Dragging the dress with me inside the bathroom, I try not to overthink the putrid, brownish liquid leaking from the walls overhead. I pull off the sweatshirt and jeans and allow a day's worth of collected sweat to evaporate off my skin. I step into the gown and pull it over my chest, immediately feeling insecure knowing I'll have to ditch my bra in order for it to work.

Once I fight to get the thing zipped in the back and smooth the unruly skirt, I face the vandalized mirror to fluff my frizzy curls. For a second, I don't recognize myself, and it's not because I'm wearing a bitter divorcee's old wedding gown. A strange feeling swells up inside me and causes me to gulp for air.

This is *me*. Not the stereotypical, insecure Josie who locks herself in her bedroom watching old movies and studying to hide away from a world that hurt her, but the one who knows that even in grief, life can still surprise you with days like this one.

The world wasn't going anywhere, no matter how much I sat around and tried to wish it away. It's always been right there waiting for me to face it again. All the good, bad, and everything in-between. Wedding gown optional.

I collect myself before stepping outside the room and forcing the skirt through the door, offering Rowan a model-esqe twirl and nearly taking both of his eyes out in the process.

"Too much?" I ask, running a hand down my stomach.

The visible portion of Rowan's face falls. He doesn't say anything. Was that a good thing? I was starting to wonder between myself, arms nervously clamped over my braless chest, or him standing there speechless in his makeshift Fantastic Faux costume, which of us looked more ridiculous.

Rowan's mouth clamps shut, nodding his mess of sweat-styled hair in approval. "I think that's what you were going for."

"It's between this and a dog vest. I think the frontrunner is obvious."

"You clearly underestimate the sexiness of a dog vest."

We collect our clothes and hold them in piles, planning to plant them outside my apartment near one of the enormous flowerpots containing the rotting corpses of Mr. Chung's summer sunflowers.

"Do you really think they'll be cool with us walking out wearing this stuff?"

"Probably not the weirdest thing they've ever seen," Rowan says. "Plus, we're giving them our money."

His voice trails into indistinct chatter as I notice the small corner of the store labeled *home décor*. There's hardly enough there to call it a section, merely a broken desk and an old wooden dresser. What grabs my attention are the shelves full of picture frames, foggy glass desk lamps, and discarded scrapbooks. I could understand one's need to ditch a wedding dress if it brought back bad memories, but I never understood people who donated fully loaded photo albums.

A faint smile creeps onto my face as I bunch my dress into my hands and quibble over to the shelves. Rowan dutifully follows my lead.

"I live for this type of stuff!" I giddily explain.

"Old picture books?" Rowan puzzles.

I grab the first one off the shelf and wipe a trail of dust off the battered, mahogany leather. The spine opens with a crack, and out falls a stack of wrinkled papers that sink to the floor and dust the deco. Rowan bends down to collect them, revealing more of his exposed legs. It's impossible to take him seriously.

"W. McMillian, summer 1941 to 1942," I read the scribbled ink on the flyleaf. "This is so cool!"

Only the first few pages of the thick album are filled, mostly starring at a brunette woman with a tiny nose sporting the most expensive-looking Darlene dresses I've ever seen. At least, by 1941 standards. There are at least a dozen photographs of her with classmates outside a school building, some of her posing with an older couple I assume to be her parents, and several with a mystery man dressed in his military uniform.

"I think W had a mystery man." I suggestively raise my eyebrows.

"Not think," Rowan corrects, handing me the stack of papers. "*Did*."

I unfurl the letter on top and brush my fingertips delicately along the faded scribbles. There's no questioning these are from a man because the penmanship is terrible. The date is marked in the upper right-hand corner. May 14th, 1941. Reading the first line causes my heart to nearly burst out of my chest. *'Dearest Winifred...'*

"Military?" Rowan guesses. I point to the photos and nod, continuing to skim the letter and read all about mystery man's day at the army base.

"The pictures end after the few he's in," I sulk. "I wonder if he didn't make it."

Rowan reads over my shoulder and runs his finger across the bottom of the page. "Check this out!"

As the letter ends, the man concludes his long-winded tirade on barracks protocols by leaving a personal message to Winifred.

'I hope you don't mind that I told everyone about you. They've all been asking who the beautiful broad on my night-stand is. I tell them you're no broad. You're mine. Always yours, Robert.'

My bones morph into mashed potatoes, holding the letter like an artifact and closing it tenderly back inside the book. This was the type of thing everyone I knew would roll their eyes at, especially Pru, but to me, it was precious.

"I would love this," I sigh.

"The photo album or the dead boyfriend?"

"Not funny!" I yank his hipster utility belt. "I've always thought love letters were one of the best ways to get to know someone. There's something freeing about saying things on paper that you can't say in real life. You have permission to be cheesy."

"*Dearest Josephine,*" Rowan recites the greeting like a piece of Shakespearean theater. "I guess it beats Tinder."

Costumes in hand (or, more appropriately, on our backs), we approach the register to the aloof reaction of the redhead female cashier. She taps her long, clear acrylics on the counter and leans over to check the colors on our tags, typing each figure into her geriatric register.

"Told you this wasn't the weirdest thing," Rowan says under his breath.

The woman hits the tally button with a loud clicking noise. "Your total comes to $22.98."

Rowan unfolds the pants from his pile of discarded clothing and reaches to pull money out of his back pocket. A few moments of digging later, he looks over at me, minorly horrified.

"I'm out of cash."

My weight sinks into the floor. "You're kidding me."

"Between the tattoo and everything else today..." His voice fades off.

"That's really all the money you had?"

"I kind of borrowed it from someone in my camp." His eyes shift. "It's a long story."

"So, you were stealing from your entourage?"

Rowan hisses with a curse and points to my clothes. "Look, can you cover it?"

I bite my lip. "Pretty sure I only have ten dollars' worth of tips from last night."

Even with the mask, his expression is so quintessentially Rowan. You couldn't miss his shrewdness if you tried.

"You're telling me we can't afford clothes off the clearance rack?" This must be a hard pill to swallow for the guy who is used to wearing designer everything.

"We can still afford most of your clothes!" I point to the five-dollar long johns and mask. "That's mostly what counts right now."

"Hold up," Rowan smizes. "Let's try something."

This never ends well. I've only known him for a day, and I know this never, ever ends well.

The woman behind the register grows impatient with the two of us whispering back and forth. Her tapping ceases. "You got it or no?"

Rowan inflates his cheeks and leans over the counter, rubbing his thumb and pointer fingers over the nose of his mask like he's massaging a tension headache.

"No, ma'am," his voice goes raspy. "No, we don't... have it."

Dear god. He's becoming Hunter Cade.

"Then put it all back," the woman sluggishly demands.

"Please!" Rowan holds out both hands. "Just hear me out!"

The woman rests her head against the wall and tilts back in her stool. "I'm listening."

Rowan searches for his next line of dialogue, pouting and pointlessly brooding behind the mask. If I weren't actively playing a part in whatever this scheme was, I'd be rolling on the floor in blanched agony.

"This is my girlfriend." He motions to me, my chest thudding at the lie. "She's dying. She has a rare blood disorder, and her doctors don't think she's going to make it much longer."

I fake a mucusy cough as if that would ever have anything

to do with a rare blood disorder. Unfortunately, I know exactly where he's headed with this. My mother secretly watched enough soap operas during my childhood for me to accurately predict the outcome of every major plot twist.

Rowan licks his lips. "Her parents disapprove of us getting married so young, but I can't let her die without being able to spend at least a few days together as husband and wife. She says I'm her superhero."

I may actually laugh at that bit, briefly, and only because it's the most cringeworthy, *Dawn Heights* explanation for his costume he could possibly fabricate. If nothing else, the boy is damn convincing, even working up a few tears as he continues his dramatic monologue.

"Please," he pleads, "the man at the courthouse said he'd wait for us as long as we were back by eight. This sweet angel doesn't have much time left. Please, let her have this."

The woman listens intently, her face neither flinching nor showing signs of disbelief. She pauses for a moment to see if Rowan has anything further to add, but he's already buried his face deep into his hands to muffle fake, moist sobs.

She finally tilts forward and presses a button on her register. "Your total comes to $22.98."

Well, shit.

If your next guess were like mine, you'd assume we'd put our tails between our legs, humbly put all the clothes back, show up to the Halloween block party dressed in our street clothes, and make every effort to help Rowan blend in with the masses while managing my time with Aaron.

You'd be wrong. Because I, too, was very, very wrong.

"RUN!" Rowan screams.

As if it were some sort of immediate instinct, I grab my phone from my pants pocket, and the two of us drop our piles of clothes onto the floor. We bolt towards the front, me clumsily dragging the extra foot of skirt behind me and praying I don't trip on the way out. Rowan grabs the door and shoos me out, following closely behind. We book it all the way down the sidewalk till the only people watching us are the strangers on the street wondering what the hell they're looking at.

"I don't think she's even following us!" I gasp for air.

Rowan glances back and slows his pace to a steady walk, looking over his shoulder every few seconds and firmly positioning the mask on his face.

"That wasn't part of my plan," he breathes, "my plan was for her to buy that."

I clutch my aching side. "Stick with acting. Writing isn't your strong suit."

The reality of what we've just done sinks in. Alongside all of the other laws I have broken today for Rowan's sake, both providential and local, I can now proudly add 'stealing' to the list. When I said I saw a new and improved, confident Josie in that bathroom mirror, this is absolutely not what I meant.

"I can read your mind." Rowan taps his forehead. "And don't worry, I'll send them some money."

"If you ever make it back," I snark with a huff.

"Won't know till after the party. How do we get there?"

I'm on the edge of bragging about having the foresight to actually grab my phone before making an escape. Then I see the notification. "Oh no."

Rowan pauses and sets a hand on his belt. "What's 'oh no'?"

I flash the screen for him to read, the critical bits blinking in red. *Low Battery. 10%.*

"It's a miracle it made it this long." I shrug. "Now what?"

He ponders for a moment, pacing the same four sidewalk squares till he finally throws his hands in the air and gives up.

"Just get us walking directions to the party and screenshot

them. Get directions to my hotel from there too. Between the two of us, we can memorize them."

I don't expect the words 'my hotel' to come out of his mouth.

"You're leaving after?" My voice sounds like a kid asking their mom to stay home from work and play.

"I have to eventually." He darts his eyes to the ground. "That way, Aaron can take you home."

I don't want Aaron to take me home, the selfish voice in me cries. *I want YOU to.*

Rather than play off the bubbling volcano feeling above my organs that best be left dormant, I give my hair a wild shake and move fast to load the app, smiling nervously.

"Are we really doing this?"

Rowan looks down at his ankles and groans. "I look like I defend a Canadian underwear store. There's no 'really' about it. Let's go."

I'VE GROWN accustomed to a certain setting when I hear the word party. They typically involve alcohol, lots of it, and the occasional use of hard recreational drugs. Meanwhile, I'll sit on the couch of whoever millionaire producer's house we're at and sip a Perrier while people twice my age scurry by and dance like any of the music they've selected is relevant. It's like the senior prom I'll never get, only way worse, and I'd rather be in bed or doing just about anything else by the time everyone swears they're getting good.

Needless to say, my social standards are skewed. To me, a block party sounds like the equivalent of a Costco-sized children's birthday party. There are likely a few fun games, some mass-produced cake, cheap trinkets for everyone to take home, and if you're really bougie, dance music that makes the adults question the other adults' parenting choices.

That was all before I stepped foot into Boroughween.

There's no questioning where the party is happening. Once Josie and I have walked for roughly a mile, we could feel the sidewalk start to vibrate underneath our feet from a set of speakers blasting "Monster Mash" nearby.

"How far?"

"Still three blocks," Josie answers. "I guess the Boys & Girls Club doesn't screw around."

The swell of music isn't the only thing getting louder. Before anything is within viewing distance, you can hear the heard of people on the block cheering and clamoring. This isn't a rinky-dink block party. It's a full-blown street festival. Police barricades pop up at the end of the road.

An officer keeping an eye on the back end stops us and instructs us to go back and make a left in order to get in through the main entrance. At this point, my feet are screaming. If I hadn't just tested my luck at the thrift store, I would've limboed under the barrier and ran in anyway.

"Look at you following the rules," Josie teases, nudging my side with her elbow.

In my defense, I don't steal things regularly. I don't necessarily have a need to, but desperate times call for desperate measures. Josie wasn't leaving without that dress. Seeing her walk out of that bathroom was like watching someone realize they were alive for the first time. I couldn't let her miss out on that feeling. Selfishly, I didn't want to either.

After we've gone another quarter mile up the next block, we round a sharp corner and make it to the front, guarded by several more police and shiny garland-wrapped barricades. The Boys & Girls Club *absolutely* wasn't screwing around. We're greeted by a twenty-foot banner with the words *7th Annual Boroughween Festival* swaying high overhead. A scroll of sponsors is listed underneath. It explained how there was clearly so much money poured into this event.

The entrance was designed to be Instagrammed. Bales of straw are stacked high enough to climb with an assorted variety of pumpkins scattered throughout, both orange and plain, and carved with spooky faces. A long rope of orange twinkle lights is sewn between the layers and dimly lights the picturesque scene.

As you move past that, you're immersed in a small, carnival-like atmosphere, minus the overpriced deathtraps. Red and white striped tents line one side of the street, each with hand-painted signed for street games like Soda Toss and Cornhole. Kids in costumes make up most of the lines, while nerve-stricken adults toss handfuls of candy into their bags regardless of if they've actually won the games.

Food trucks are parked on the opposing side of the road. They smell like actual meat-scented heaven to someone like me who has spent the entire day living off sugar and caffeine.

"What should we do first?" Josie shouts above the noise.

"Wanna text Aaron?" I ask.

Her face falls. She seems offended I'd bring up the idea of meeting her date. Had stealing the dress really bothered her that much?

"Sure," Josie finally replies, moving quickly to make contact. Her phone had gone down to eight percent, and if hers was anything like mine, there was no five percent. You'd move down to six and then hear it make a *The Price is Right* whomp-whomp sound effect. Then you were screwed.

The event is crowded, but it's not overwhelming. Those who've stumbled upon it while trick-or-treating walk around and do everything once before getting bored and leaving. Only those waiting for food and music seem to be the ones camped out.

"There's the stage!" I point to the end of the road, back where we'd try to come in before.

We walk further down past several more booths, mostly radio stations handing out free swag and more candy. The stage is nothing on the level of a Springsteen show, it's barely big enough to house a handful of instruments and a few large amps on both sides. Think school auditorium on a DIY budget. There is a huge open space for people to gather near the front, with a sign directly in the center with a schedule of events. We'd already missed the costume contest. Up next was the live music.

"Fate's Bitch," Josie announces. "That's Izzy Ezra's band."

I point to where the word *Bitch* has been scratched out with a black sharpie and replaced with the word Fish.

"Fate's Fish," I correct. "Probably because there are kids here."

"Because that's the worst thing a child could see." Josie points to the little boy walking past in a Michael Meyers costume, complete with a severed head.

"Should we wait for him here?"

"Who?"

"Aaron!" I shout again.

Her mouth cracks open as if she's about to say something, just as a guy dressed in full Heath Ledger Joker garb comes up and taps her shoulder from behind.

"What's up, pussycat?"

It's the jerk from King Kone, putting an emphasis on *pussy*. My eyes nearly roll back into my skull. He *would* be the Joker. Josie's face goes pale. You can almost hear what she's thinking. *'Not here, why here?'*

"Julian!" She shouts. "Have you seen Aaron?"

Julian taps his lipstick smeared cheek. "Yeah, he's around here somewhere, probably trying to cop a kid out of their candy."

Why would he need to steal children's candy? Everyone here was handing out candy. That was sort of the point.

"Can you tell him I'm here?" Josie asks. She tugs at the skirt of her gown like it's regenerating more tulle as time goes on.

Julian squints as he gets a load of me standing next to her, pulling the rubber pencil out of his pocket and giving it a toss in the air. "Are you her bodyguard or something?"

"Or something," my voice goes icy.

Josie refuses to let it escalate. "Julian, this is my cousin. Cousin, this is Julian."

"You look really familiar." Julian chuckles. "Are you at Bedford?"

My heart speeds up. Maybe ditching the hoodie and sunglasses was a premature decision.

"He's from Montana," Josie lies effortlessly. "He and his aunt are here to visit my mom."

Yeah, she was much better at making up a convincing story than I was. Stealing the teen marriage b-plot from season two back at Save Rite wasn't my smartest decision.

Julian snaps his fingers and stomps one foot. "The guy from TV with the huge nose! The one in that movie about the stupid mute people with the deaf kid! Jim from *The Office!*"

There were at least four horrible things in that one sentence alone, but as long as he wasn't about to say 'you're Rowan Adler,' I'd happily take Jim Halpert.

"I get that a lot." I sound dubious.

Julian crosses his arms and gives a bypassing Wonder Woman elevator eyes. "I'll let him know you're here, Flosie."

"It's *Josie*," I correct.

Yikes. It was this exact chivalrous, overprotective nature that got me in trouble with Michael Brewer. Ashanti may have appreciated it, but I wasn't about to go down that path again. I was risking things enough as it was by being here.

"Whatever, Mr. Incredible." Julian knocks my shoulder hard before creeping away to find where Wonder Woman wandered off—try saying that five times fast.

"Thanks." Josie's head hangs to the skirt-laden pavement underneath her feet. "Told you he was the worst."

Anger continues to course up inside me. "You know, you're allowed to be an introvert. That's not a bad thing," I state above the noise, "but that doesn't make you a doormat."

The hollows beneath her eyes sink, slowly nodding in agreement.

A group of frazzled stagehands appears behind the drum kit to prepare the stage for the band, hurriedly twisting at chords and strumming guitars to see if any noise bleeds through the amplifiers. I had no clue what time it was, but if they were prepping for showtime, it must've been close to eight.

"JOSIE!" A deep voice calls out.

Her face glows as she spots Aaron running towards her with a wave. He's dressed as... a basketball player. Hot AND not original. What a catch.

"Hey!" She smiles. "Did you get my text?"

"I saw it right as Julian told me you were here. Hi, cousin!" He awkwardly waves to me and closely studies my outfit, trying to figure out who I'm supposed to be.

"I don't know who I am either." I shake my head.

Aaron passes me over and grabs Josie's fingers. It causes my chest to grip so tightly, I wanted to scream. I barely knew her. Why was this bothering me so much?

"There's free face painting over there." Aaron points to the small booth near the Ameritrade table. "Wanna do it?"

She nods her head with a giggle and bounces over with him, looking back at me to collect her train with a half-smirk.

My lungs feel like they're being wrung out of oxygen. No way this was it. I refused to allow the last image of Josie I saw to be running off with some guy who probably wanted to get a dragon painted onto his face.

Instead of enjoying my last several hours of freedom by stuffing my face with peanut butter cups and owning every single five-year-old at Disk Drop in order to win a Boys & Girls

Club rubber bracelet, I stand in front of the stage and sulk. It didn't matter how I felt, this had been the plan all afternoon. For once, I'd be a decent human and help someone I cared about instead of making things worse. I guess I didn't realize how much I cared or even how much those feelings mattered.

This was worse than anything on *Dawn Heights* because it was real. I liked Josie, and I'd just thrown away the one chance I had to tell her in order to help her land some guy who didn't even know her favorite movie, even if I hated it.

Near the side stage, I quickly spot a familiar yellow crop top holding an oversized panda mask while searching for in-ear monitors. It had to be Izzy Ezra.

If Izzy and Indio had come together, he couldn't have been too far away. Lo and behold, I quickly spot him next to the face painting booth. He and Josie are immersed in conversation as Aaron mindlessly stares at his phone several feet away. Weird.

That's not the only thing that feels off. A moment later, I see Julian with his spray-painted green hair walking by and carefully observing the situation, smiling deviously.

I might not have much of an intuition—Lexi says I trust people too easily—but I'm smart enough to pick up on something suspicious. I would know. I've been stalking Josie for the last ten minutes by standing in line at The Wobblin' Gobbler for a turkey leg I couldn't afford.

I continue monitoring Julian closely. He hops in line a few food trucks down at some empanada wagon, quickly firing off a text and yawning. My attention bounces back to the face painting station, watching Aaron as he replies to a message almost immediately. There was no way this was a coincidence. They were up to something, and my fear was that Josie was at the center of it. If there was ever a time to play the devil's advocate, it was now.

Julian does a double take as I march over and give him the

traditional Bro Nod of Mutual Respect, a gesture that isn't reciprocated.

"'Sup?" He confusedly barks.

"Ehh, you know." I make a zany face. "Just had to get away from the cuz."

The cuz? I could feel my dialogue coach falling victim to a brain aneurism two thousand miles away.

"Are you and Josie close?" Julian fiddles with his pockets.

I quickly think up a lie. "We were as kids, but not so much now. My aunt is forcing me to hang out with her while I'm here. She's really weird."

Julian smugly turns up his nose. "Yeah, I kinda thought she was hot at first, but she acts like she's above everyone else because she's smart."

I almost respond with *'because she is, especially you,'* but quickly remember I'm supposed to be her jerk cousin from Montana, not her knight-in-shining-long underwear.

"Did she piss you off or something?" I ask. "She mentioned she wasn't one of your favorite people."

Julian makes a face. "Not really. Some people are just annoying and deserve it."

You're one to talk, jackass. "How so?"

He points to Aaron. "She thinks that's a date."

Funny. I'd spent the second half of my day under the assumption that's exactly what this was and feeling sorry for myself about missing out on the chance to spend more time together. If this wasn't a date, then what the fuck was it?

"It's not?" My voice squeaks like I've hit puberty all over again.

Julian's Joker smile curls towards his ears. "I bet Aaron twenty dollars he couldn't get her number last night. She's too stuck up. Then he ran into her this morning and got it and it pissed me off, so now we've upped the stakes to fifty dollars."

I gulp. "Upped them how?"

"HOW ARE YOU DOING, HALLOW-PARTIERS?!"

A voice echoes from the speakers, followed by a burst of eardrum-shattering reverb. It's an older, heavy-set man dressed as a giant baby, complete with a sky-blue bonnet. He's the game show host type who says things like Hallow-Partiers and thinks he sounds super cool. The crowd cheers weakly, several preteens in the audience are booing for no apparent reason.

"GREAT!" The man shouts again. He's forgotten he's holding a microphone. "THE LIVE MUSIC IS ABOUT TO BEGIN! LET'S GET SOME MORE OF YOU CRAZY KIDS UP FRONT!"

As the screaming baby's tirade continues, I creep in towards Julian and cunningly raise an eyebrow, getting a whiff of his hot corn dog breath. Gross.

"Care to let me in on it?"

I TURN BACK to look at Rowan as Aaron leads me off to get our faces painted, and it was a huge mistake. Seeing him standing there in front of the stage with his lonely puppy dog face destroyed me. Why did I feel so awful? This was his plan, *our* plan, for me to face my fears and actually give Aaron a chance. A real guy was better than something fake I could watch on TV and get nothing from.

Except it sort of sucks, and the more Aaron talks my ear off about the basketball team, the more I want to run back to Rowan and ask if there is anywhere else I can help take him before the night is over. Is this how Stockholm Syndrome starts?

"Having fun with your cousin?" Aaron finally asks. It's the first thing he's said that wasn't about himself.

I nod. "We've been going around the city today. It's been fun."

"That's cool! I went over to Julian's after practice. We're trying to focus up before this game next Wednesday because..."

UGH. Did he ever shut up about basketball? Was this how I sounded whenever I ranted to Mom or Pru about why *The Shop Around the Corner* is superior to *You've Got Mail* in every possible way? Because I was starting to think I owed them a formal apology. As in, hire a skywriter formal.

An impressive Romy and Michele duo man the face painting booth in their pink and blue holographic dresses. Each of them wears a name tag that reads Mary and Rhoda, a joke that's lost on fifty percent of the crowd.

"Are you much of a face painting person?" Aaron's question breaks through my tunneled focus. Is anyone much of a face painting person on a typical day?

"Maybe when I was five," I chuckle. The last time anyone painted my face was at a schoolmate's ninth birthday party. I asked for a tiger and ended up looking like a sunburnt Avatar.

Romy waves me over and tugs at her blonde wig as I take a seat in one of the folding chairs. She asks me in a thick Ukrainian accent what type of painting I'd like, pointing to a battered display board behind her that looks like it was printed back in 1990.

I bypass all the cheesy kid designs and rule out anything too creepy, like the marionette and zombie lips. I settle on a star design that frames the eyes with spiraled white stars and a few blobs of silver body glitter. It would match the aesthetic of my dress, even if I had no idea what I was supposed to be. Princess bride?

"Are you getting anything?" I ask Aaron. His phone chimes. He quickly looks down to send a reply.

"Nah, I don't fuck with that chick stuff."

Like clockwork, Indio approaches the booth and waves to Michele, asking her in Korean if she's almost finished with the first-grader she's working on. At least, I think that's what he asks. I'm interpreting based on a lot of pointing. He sarcastically begins clapping as he sees my overflowing dress spilling out the sides of the tent.

"That's cute." Indio looks me up and down. "What are you, *The Runaway's Bride?*"

"Very funny."

"Having a good time?" He smiles. Indio never smiles.

A sneaky grin explodes onto my face. "You hooked up with Izzy Ezra, didn't you?"

He looks stunned I'd even bring up such an allegation, even though it's not an allegation. It totally happened. He didn't have two visible hickeys an hour ago.

"That happened fast," I laugh.

"We'd been flirting for weeks. It's not that fast."

"What happened to the natural flow?"

Indio looks to Aaron, who has wandered off into a corner, completely ignoring me. "I could ask the same thing."

I lower my head, earning a shout of protest from Romy. She grabs my cheeks and moves my face back up, adding more delicate brush strokes.

"This was Rowan's idea," I explain. "He wanted to see me open up and go on a date."

Indio exchanges more words in Korean with Michele as she opens a paint palate. He takes a seat in the chair next to me. "So, he likes you then?"

My body freezes. Some people are naturally flirtatious, I deduced that's merely how Rowan was. The notion of him being serious about any of it hadn't once crossed my mind. Obviously, I liked him. He was thoughtful and funny and yes, as attractive as everyone had been trying to convince me he was for years. What on earth did he possibly see in me to cause him to return the feelings?

"That doesn't make sense," I chuckle with an uncertain edge. "He wanted to see me with Aaron. Why would he like me?"

"Because what your old movies fail to show you are how

stupid men are," Indio touts, Michele shouting an 'amen.' "We do stuff like root for the girl to get with the guy who's all wrong for her because we want to see the person we love happy."

"He doesn't love me."

"Probably not. You just met." He relaxes. "But he doesn't feel nothing either."

My muscles suddenly grow tense, my teeth chattering in the mild wind. I wish I had my dad's old hoodie to throw on so I wouldn't feel so exposed.

"How do you know?" I ask solemnly.

"Josephine." Michele turns Indio's head to face mine. "I saw him at that coffee shop. That boy looks at you like he's ten seconds from jumping you at any moment. I'd say I hate you, but I suddenly have other interests."

I look and see Izzy off to the side of the stage as Fate's 'Fish' prepares to go on. Izzy is holding a creepy, helmet-like panda head that makes it look like he's performing in the animatronic band at Chuck E. Cheese.

Was it really that easy? Could you go from shy flirting a few times a week to having almost-sex in a Prius that fast? I'm not sure that was my style. In fact, I know it's not. That still doesn't make the possibility of Rowan's interest any less likely.

Romy starts dabbing the body glitter onto my eyelids with slow, rubbing motions.

"I think you forget," I tell Indio. "We have other interests too. The pictures, remember?"

He goes quiet. "Are you having second thoughts again? I brought my camera, by the way." He tugs at the camo print messenger bag wrapped tightly over his shoulder.

Second? More like third, fourth, fifth, possibly even thir-tieth thoughts. A disgusting, slimy feeling fell over me when-ever I thought about what we were planning on doing to Rowan. This would've been so much easier twelve hours ago if nothing else had happened or if he hadn't turned out to be such a normal human being.

"It's not like I have many other options now," I laugh in spite of everything. "Scholarships aren't enough. I just quit my job, and my mom is practically begging for college money."

"Not everything is as black and white as it seems, Josie. There's a rainbow in this somewhere." For once, Indio's snide demeanor sounds earnest, almost encouraging. He needed to make out with Izzy Ezra more often.

"What are you getting anyway?" I point to his dull makeup. Michele has made him look slightly paler thanks to a thin coat of white paint, but the real questionable choice was the smeared glitter all over his face.

"I'm Asian Edward Cullen," he explains. "Izzy likes Twilight."

Aaron finally meanders back toward the booth with his phone still gripped tightly in his hand. As tempted as I was to check mine for any messages from Pru, or god forbid Mom, I was trying hard to keep the small percentage of battery I had left.

From the stage, an adult-sized baby appears and starts screaming at the audience through his microphone. Either he'd eaten a dangerous amount of candy, or the man had taken too much Adderall.

"Izzy's band is about to go on." Indio jumps out of the chair and opens his camera bag. "You don't mind if I go be all cute and supportive, do you?"

I smile. "We'll reconvene, I'm sure."

"Because that worked out so well the last time," he remarks coolly.

Indio's eyelashes blink remnants of loose, shimmering dust. He pauses just shy of Aaron and presses two black fingernails against his chest.

"Word of advice? She loves old movies. Might be a good talking point."

He squints. "So, like, *Bridgerton* shit?"

Indio shoots me the side-eye and runs over to the stage, where a handful of costumed attendees are all gathering near the front, mainly those of the child-sized variety. I sure hoped those six-year-olds were ready for Fate's Bitch.

An aggressive electric guitar begins shredding through the cute carnival noise and garners the attention of several more in attendance. Izzy Ezra isn't the only one wearing an animal mask. The drummer is a frog, the bassist is a penguin, and the keyboard player is a monkey. I mostly want to know where on god's green earth they found four nightmare-inducing fluffy animal heads.

The bass kicks in along with the drums, and honestly, I'm still not sure one minute into their first song what type of music they play, other than they had to be breaking at least four noise violations. A group of teenagers dressed as The Beatles (plus a Yoko) begin aggressively moshing against one another and creating an audience of their own. That is if you consider stomach bumps and a bunch of bad, sober dancing a mosh pit.

Romy shouts an expressive 'STARS DONE' and holds a mirror up to my face to examine her work. It's definitely cheap face paint, but as I lightly tap at one of the wet points covered in glitter, it fills me with a confidence I didn't know I was missing. I can practically hear Rowan's voice in my head saying something like, '*It's your war paint.*'

Aaron bends over to tie his shoelaces as I continue to study my face in the mirror. "That's really cool!" He chimes. "I should've gotten one!"

Something about the way he says it rubs me the wrong way. It's way too enthusiastic for someone who couldn't care less about face painting ten minutes earlier.

The band's first song ends, and the small crowd loses their minds. My final verdict is that Izzy Ezra's band is what Limp Bizkit would sound like if they did EDM covers of David Guetta songs. It's the musical equivalent of cocaine.

"Wanna go watch?" Aaron grabs my hand and lifts me to my feet. It doesn't ignite the same spark in my chest as it did earlier that day. His hand mostly feels sweaty and calloused. I'd rather be holding a wet tuna.

"Sure." I nod. Where had Rowan wandered off to? Would I be able to find him in the growing crowd?

"JOSIE!!!"

Nevermind. I'd found Rowan.

The caped crusader comes running up to us out of breath, nearly knocking Aaron to the ground in his pursuit of justice.

"Are you okay, Row—Hunter?!" I catch myself, flashing him a guilty expression.

Rowan quickly undoes the checkered scarf from around his waist and hands it to me. "Don't walk into the crowd!"

"Why?"

Before he can answer, Julian speeds over to join the conversation with his hands tossed in the air, shouting, "WHAT THE HELL, DUDE?!"

Rowan's eyes meet mine. A bag of bricks abruptly drops into my gut. It's an instinctive feeling that requires no explanation. I reach behind to the back of my dress and feel the layers of tulle just beneath the bottom, right at the spot where Aaron had bent to tie his shoes. A streak of red paint bleeds across my fingers, poured entirely down the back of the skirt.

They were going to pull a *Carrie* on me. A prank. A genuinely awful prank.

"You ruined the plan, dumbass!" Julian shoves Rowan's shoulder. "She wasn't supposed to notice!"

"Yeah, and when she did." Rowan yanks into Julian's

pocket and pulls out a lime green sanitary pad. "This moron was gonna hand you this."

"Hey!" Julian shoves Rowan again, harder this time. I can see the smoke practically billowing out of his ears. It's taking every ounce of willpower for Rowan not to shove him back.

The band's next song concludes with applause, only to have the scene we've created draw about as much of an audience. I'm not sure which is redder, my face or my ass. I tie the scarf around my waist, unsure how good it does to cover anything. Now I just look like a rejected bride whose fashion sense closely resembles a punk artist.

"Chill out!" Aaron fans Julian. "It was supposed to be a joke, man! Don't get butthurt!"

Rowan faces me with a livid expression. His jaw is clenched tight. I know without a word what he's asking, but I don't want him to do it. Rowan doesn't need to defend me because this isn't his fight to have. It's mine.

Izzy tries to recapture the crowd's attention by giving an impassioned sermon on the band's next song (something about outdated gender norms and abolishing the patriarchy), but there's a growing circle forming around the four of us. Indio digs his way back from the stage and watches on in stunned shock. He quickly switches his camera into position, ducking behind an onlooker to grab a few steady shots of Rowan.

That's my breaking point.

"Are you guys seven or something?!" I shout. "Why is this funny to you? News flash: Girls get periods! Or were you both raised by unstable father figures who never loved you enough to teach you that?"

The crowd oohs at the comment, a zombie scarecrow off to the side of the audience shouting a "PREACH!" and filling my meek self-assurance with a strange surge of righteous arrogance.

I keep going. "You two are assholes! And Julian." I turn to him with a finger pointed at his nose. "You can make my life a living hell every day till graduation. You're an entitled little shit and I don't care what you think! So why don't you just step off?!"

Boom.

As fast as a CGI semi-truck can sideswipe a teenager's Honda Accord on *Dawn Heights*, it happens. Vengeful tears sting my eyes and my fists curl up. I inch closer to Julian with my dress dragging behind me and throw a punch so hard, I think I may have broken my wrist along with his nasal cavity. That's not the worst part (it's actually the best part.) As Aaron sees me dive to attack Julian, he jumps in to try and stop me.

The whole thing happens in slow motion. One second, I'm decking Julian and feel fantastic about my life, then the next, Rowan is on the ground lying on top of Aaron... and his mask is gone, fallen in the line of duty.

The crowd screams in unison as Izzy Ezra shouts a very un-Fate's Fish-friendly "HOLY FUCK" into the microphone.

The shock of the whole thing takes a moment to set in for everyone. What are they supposed to look at? The girl with the paint-soaked rear end who just threw the first punch of her life, the Joker with the nose whose gushing blood, or the exposed A-list celebrity lying on the ground wearing a ridiculous Halloween costume? It goes without saying that within seconds, Julian and I are old news.

Rowan gasps as he realizes his mask is lying on the ground next to him, still mostly undamaged. Only by then, there are at hundreds of cell phones out and snapping pictures. And everyone is screaming because it's ROWAN ADLER.

If the last bit took place in slow motion, the next happens on fast forward. Rowan whips the mask off the ground and tosses it over his face, blinking wildly through the tiny slits and turning to me while rattling his head and backing away. Several folks from the crowd immediately try to jump him and get self-ies, while I use my skirt as a makeshift weapon to swat them away like flies.

"JOSEPHINE!!!"

Indio's voice rises above the clamor. I look up to see him toss me a set of Prius keys. I hold them in my hands, looking confused, only to have his blank white expression—literally—preface his instructions.

"I'm parked on Walter Matthews. GO!!!"

I grab Rowan's hand tight, similar to how he'd grabbed mine on the way to the subway earlier that morning. I drag him along and tell him to run. *Fast.*

It's all-out pandemonium at this juncture. The band is evacuating the stage, and the small corner where the fight occurred is growing with more and more people upon hearing shouts of *IS THAT ROWAN ADLER*?! It's like watching the GIF of Donald Glover on *Community* reappear with pizzas in the Darkest Timeline come to life. The writers of *Dawn Heights* wish they could write scenarios this insane. Police sirens begin whaling as throngs of people shout frantically, scat-tering every which way.

All this makes for a reasonably smooth getaway for Rowan and me, who are running like our lives depend on it, mainly because they actually might. With every bounding leap, I lose a little more of my tulle in the crowd, shedding the bottom of the dress like a snake shedding its skin. Flashes of illuminated pumpkins pass my vision amidst muffled screams like we're in a scene from a horror movie.

I might have girlbossed a little too close to the sun.

Rowan looks back every half second to make sure nobody is following us. We had one or two stragglers but quickly lost them when we ducked behind the straw display and kept moving back towards the open street.

Walter Matthews Boulevard is a block down the road. I grab Indio's keys and begin pressing the panic button in order to find the car.

Rowan finally breaks his stunned silence. "Where are we going?!"

I point to Indio's car, a shining silver ray of hope, as I wheeze painfully. "Keep going!"

I'm sure the car alarm blaring isn't a great look when we're already on the run from an angry, slightly horny mob. I quickly disable the confounded beeping and stand next to the driver's side door, gripping the handle tightly and failing at catching my breath.

"Get in!" Rowan demands.

I shake my head. "I can't drive!"

"What?!"

"I barely had my permit when we moved! I walk everywhere!"

"Oh my god," Rowan mutters under his breath. He slides over the hood of the car with an unbecoming flatulence noise and loops the keys off my fingers. "I can drive. Get in!"

Everything sensible in me knows I should be worried sick. I just caused a miniature riot, and because of it, Rowan's cover was blown. I should be focused on the only important thing: getting us both where we needed to be.

I look over at Rowan, who is still inhaling furiously after our sprint and trying to figure out how to use all the various buttons and gear shifts. As much as my ears were buzzing and my brain was burning, having him here somehow made all of it feel so normal.

He throws the car into drive and pulls up the automated navigation system, going quiet for several seconds too long.

"Do you have a plan?" I ask. "We should probably move quick!"

More deafening silence. Rowan has the glean in his eye, the same one he had earlier when he jumped onto the train and got the tattoo and, well, basically all day. Something inside told me we weren't about to go to The Four Seasons.

He inhales sharply and finally turns to face me. "Have you ever had a trash plate?"

CHAPTER 22

ROWAN

TO BE FAIR, I panicked.

I panicked when Julian told me what Aaron was planning on doing, panicked when I ran over and tried to stop it from happening, panicked when Josie punched the asshole in the nose, and panicked when the mask fell off and a teenage girl in the audience saw my face and fainted. By all accounts, my reactions to everything tonight were completely valid. Whether or not this decision was had yet to be seen.

When I tell Josie I'm driving us Rochester, she thinks I'm kidding and asks where we're really going. Once we're on the road for an hour, it's pretty clear I'm not.

"Do we even have enough gas for that?" Josie worries. It's the Josieiest concern possible.

"I think so." I tap at the gas gauge. "You still have your ten bucks, right? That could buy us some more gas if we need it. I had an old friend whose parents drove one. These things can go hundreds of miles without filling up!"

The annoying robotic female voice on Indio's GPS continues to spout out information. I shift over a lane and zoom past a grandma going ten miles under the speed limit. Josie gulps and grabs the passenger side door.

"Why aren't you going back, Rowan?" Her question sounds more like the start of an interrogation.

There are at least ten appropriate responses. Guilt, fear, anger, frustration. All of the above? I throw the mask off my face and toss it into the cup holder next to us like a haunting relic of the hell behind us, trying to come up with exactly what I want to say.

"Everyone is going to know I'm okay, and I'm probably going to be sacrificed on the freaking altar when I get back," I sigh. "There's something I want to do before that happens."

She nods pensively, a far cry from the argumentative, apprehensive Josie from earlier. I was a worse influence than I thought.

"What about you? Do you need to get home?" I ask. "I don't want Pru to wonder where you are. I should've asked before assuming..."

"She's sleeping over with a friend," Josie explains. "Plus, my phone is down to two percent. The moment I call or try to send a text, it's dead." Her expression twists into something unstable. She squints, the painted stars on her cheeks cracking at the tips. "Are you worried?"

"Constantly." I smile.

She sighs and leans back in her seat. "How far is where we're headed."

I grit my teeth, expecting a big reaction. "Another four hours."

Nothing. Not even a flinch. My recklessness had become as jaded to her as it had to me.

I take one hand off the wheel and massage the bruised shoulder Aaron had collided with when we both dove onto the concrete. The chaos of the moment had taken so much freedom away from me, I hadn't been able to stop once and tell Josie how proud I was of her for sticking up for herself.

"Does it hurt?" She studies my shoulder.

I run my arm in forward circles till I hear a satisfying click. "I've had worse. On-screen fight training mishaps."

"And off-screen."

"Michael Brewer was my first." I cheerily raise my fingers off the wheel. "I guess you and I aren't fight virgins anymore."

"Why is that somehow more and less impressive at the same time?"

We both chuckle for the first time since Boroughween. The shining city twinkles in the background as the dark, nearly November sky trails our way onto slower, emptier highways with fewer skyscrapers and more dense woods. I have no clue if what I'm doing is the right thing. It seemed like I was always trying to make right and necessary one and the same.

"I get why you did it now," Josie states. "The whole punching your co-star thing."

"Liberating, isn't it?"

She makes a high-pitched squeal. "I wouldn't say that. It's nice to stick up for yourself. Or others."

"I don't think he'll be bothering you anymore. I'm pretty sure you broke his nose."

Her satisfied smile morphs into typical Josie existentialism. "I can't get sued for that, can I?"

The question lingers in the air for a moment too long. We both start belly laughing as it settles, unable to contain the frenzied tears from falling down our faces as our cheeks turn warm and rosy. Delirium had already set in, and we still had hours of driving to go before reaching our destination.

After we manage to compose ourselves as well as two teenage felons can, I notice Josie staring at me. Her sideways smirk causes a hollow pit to form where my stomach should be.

"What?" I ask.

"This is the first time I've really stopped to see your face all day."

My foot goes heavy as I accelerate. Is she checking me out? "Did you forget about those twenty gloriously awkward minutes at your house this morning?"

"That feels like a lifetime ago. They don't count."

It's true. We were closing in fast on midnight. My hapless walk to King Kone in Brooklyn while looking for food was eons ago.

"You know," Josie adds. "It's lucky for you I came along."

"Why is that?"

"Because if I know you, you left your MetroCard in the clothes you ditched." Josie holds up her cell phone, her wallet stuck onto the back. She confidently wags it over her face with her transit card peeking out like a prairie dog. "Good thing I have mine, or you'd be walking back."

"It's not like I can go back wearing this anyway." I tug at the obvious getup. "We'll have to figure something out."

Josie half-smiles. "We always do." She opens the center console of the Prius and begins digging around, giggling to herself as she holds up a pair of dark purple cat-eyed sunglasses. "This is a good start!"

"This too!" I whip out a ball of crumpled one-dollar bills buried beneath a stack of used Garbage CDs and a Stillwater Coffee tote bag. I bounce my eyes between the road and the money to count out just over twenty bucks in singles. Either this was tip money from King Kone, or Indio had a side gig Josie knew nothing about.

Josie's face falls. "We're really going to steal more money, Rowan?"

"It's not stealing if we have the intent to return it, which I do." I hold a finger. "Plus, I'm starving. We're getting a trash plate."

"What is a trash plate? You still haven't told me!"

I take Indio's flamboyant purple sunglasses and place them over my eyes for a test run. They're the worst things I've ever seen, and that's probably why Indio wears them. Either this will stop everyone from looking too hard at me or the complete opposite.

"Josie." I turn to her, not able to take myself seriously in the rear-view mirror. "We're going to the best place in the world. Just take it in."

Josie smushes her forehead into a tightly wrinkled washboard. "But I mean, you were in New York. You had the whole city at your disposal and..."

I wait for it. "And what?"

"You wanted to take me to a block party." She half smiles. "Is that really how you wanted to spend your one free day?"

I shrug, tapping the wheel with a shaky sigh. "Not really, but I'd say it was worth it. You were kind of incredible back there."

Josie's gaze is still locked onto the side of my face, causing me to sweat profusely. Her jaw quivers like she has something else to add. After a pause, she swallows her words and sinks into her seat with a weary yawn.

The next few hours are primarily quiet as Josie toggles back and forth between radio stations and ends up settling for one of the Garbage albums, somehow falling asleep to the bridge of "I Think I'm Paranoid." I, on the other hand, feel completely wired. Those pills knocked me out hard enough that I may not sleep for another week. It explained how Aunt Lexi was able to do so much all the time. One thirteen-hour power jaunt, and she was good to go for days.

As we pull up to Mark's Texas Hots a few hours later, I stare into the windows and realize my 'best place in the world' comment may have been premature. Six-year-old me had biased thoughts on the world.

The outdated interior gives King Kone a run for its money with its Tiffany lamps and teal booths that smell like broken dreams. I enjoy my fair share of hole-in-the-wall restaurants in LA, but this place looks like it was pulled from an alternate dimension.

"Are we here?" Josie stirs with a stretch. She rubs her eyes, smearing glitter all over her face like it's fairy blood. I don't have the heart to tell her.

I grab the cash and sunglasses from inside the console and nod. "Let's go."

The line is out the door as the hungover Halloween crowd hits. I was tempting fate by hoping nobody would recognize me in their incapacitated state. Gossip tends to travel slower in the middle of the night. Once we're inside and away from the shivering cold, I snag us a booth and order the same thing I always ordered as a kid. The display of food that arrives at our table a few minutes later can only be described as a godless atrocity.

A mountain of macaroni salad, a double portion of home fries, a cheeseburger, and a local white-hot dog. All topped with a spicy chili-like sauce, ketchup, mustard, and bits of chopped raw onion for either presentation or straight up giving up on life. Josie apprehensively pokes it with her plastic fork.

"You've seriously never had one of these before?" My face contorts in satisfied delight with the first bite. I'm about to recreate that one scene from *When Harry Met Sally*. It's salty, spicy, sweet, and every disgustingly wretched thing I always remembered.

Josie stabs around the plate and takes a bite with a little of everything. Her nose scrunches high onto her head. "This is awful."

"Right?!"

She shakes her head, going in for more untouched potatoes. "I get the 'trash' part now. How often did you come here and eat these growing up?"

"At least once a month."

"And you're still alive?"

I snort and nearly choke on a bite. "Touché."

Josie settles into her seat with a yawn. Her dirtied, shredded skirt flows into the aisle for everyone to step on. "Was it another Grandma Rose thing?"

I bite down hard on my cheek, a chilling sensation running down my spine. "My mom, actually."

She sets her fork down carefully and nods her head. I'm used to this reaction. It's the *I'm sorry your parents sucked* face everyone gave me growing up whenever they asked what my mom and dad were like. My usual answer: frequently absent or nonexistent. It was the best worst icebreaker. I'd rather make people feel uncomfortable than accept their sympathy.

That's not the case with Josie. Nothing about the way she perceives me comes off as fake or judgmental. She listens to what I have to say like it's worth knowing. It's exactly why I wanted to tell her about Grandma, then Ashanti, and now this.

"She left when I was eight." I wipe a glob of sauce off my chin. "I still don't know where she went. I had this sick thought after I signed on to do the show that I'd get super famous. She'd come looking for me to beg for forgiveness or bum some drug money, and I would tell her to fuck off."

"Let me guess. She didn't?"

"Not even once. Grandma never heard from her again. My aunt hasn't either. Worst case scenario, she's dead." I shake my head, feeling the weight of the world falling at my feet. "She had her positive moments, but they were few and far between. Whenever she was in a good spot, we'd come here. It was the one thing she knew I liked to do."

Josie draws an extended breath. I think it's her way of not having to eat any more of the plate. Good thing I'd nearly demolished the entire thing.

"What about your aunt?" Josie wonders. "What's she like? She's your manager, right?"

"Slash agent. Slash pain in my ass," I joke. "She's the polar opposite of my mom. She's almost too involved."

Grandma used to call Lexi a mama bear with zero maternal instincts. She'd fight to the death for her clients to get them what they deserved, but she had no clue how to deal with them on a personal level. Unfortunately, that was true of me as her nephew as well.

"I'd been living with her for a while when she suggested I try out for the drama team. She said I was always causing a scene, might as well have an audience."

Josie laughs. "She's not wrong."

"I tried out for basketball and didn't make the cut, so I figured why not give it a go. I got in, and the first production of the season was *Little Shop of Horrors*. I was determined to get the role of Seymour and rehearsed like a mad man to nail the audition."

Mad man might be an over-simplification. I once stayed up through the night to watch the movie adaptation with Rick Moranis four times just so I could observe the way he played the character and see what made him so likable in the role.

"Did you get it?" Josie asks.

"Yup. I totally nailed it, and the show too. It... helped," my voice drags. "It gave me something to focus on that wasn't my family or how unhappy I was to be living in LA. She started encouraging me to go out for real auditions and stuff and—"

"You decided you wanted to be famous?" Josie assumes.

I twist at my paper napkin. "Do any normal people ever really want to become famous?"

Josie raises her upper lip in disgust. "I don't know. I have a feeling Julian will find a way to ride this high till kingdom come."

Fresh regret swells up and burns like indigestion. Every bite of food in my stomach crashes like a tidal wave at the thought of how he'd try to exploit this.

I shake it off. "I never wanted to be famous. I wanted to do something I enjoyed and hoped other people did too. *Dawn Heights* fell into our laps and it just kind of blew up."

"Kind of?" Josie defiantly slaps a hand on the table. "There are thirteen-year-old girls who sleep with your face above their bed."

"Keywords being 'blew up.'" I reluctantly shovel a final bite into my mouth.

Josie shrugs her shoulders. "What now? *Dawn Heights* isn't what you want anymore?"

I wipe my mouth with the same twisted napkin and drop my fork at the end of the table, looking satisfied and conflicted.

"I like the security of it. I like having money. It's nice to have a cushion."

"You like the attention too," she teases, "admit it."

Guiltily, I rock my head. "It doesn't always suck. Fans can be awesome, but when it *does* suck, it's like you're not a person anymore. You're just some headline that's allowed to be picked apart and left to rot. None of the good bits matter anymore."

Josie's hair bounces as she shakes her head. "I'm not sure I could live like that."

"Says the wannabe screenwriter."

"Keyword there being 'wannabe,'" she mocks.

"What's stopping you?"

Josie's nose darts down to the floor. I was starting to notice she had a habit of looking at her feet and hunching her posture when she got nervous. It was better than my habit of straight-up running away.

"Other than the fact that my family is in enormous debt because of my dad?" She sighs after a beat. "The plan was to leave New York, right?"

"Was?"

Her eyes bounce up quickly. "Still is."

"You sound unsure."

Josie leans an elbow on the table and lies her head flat on her palm, wearing her exhaustion like a badge of honor. "I wanted to move back to Ohio and get an apartment with my best friend. We planned to go to the same school together. She doesn't talk to me anymore since she started dating some guy, and I'm pretty sure she's applying to schools he's apply to just so they can stay together."

"I'm sure that will work out great," I say sarcastically. "Where does that leave your plans then?"

"My mom says I should look into schools in the city. She says it's a dream location for someone who wants to write and go into filmmaking."

I smirk. "Is it weird if I say I like your mom?"

The comment brightens her spirits enough to sit upright. "She's pretty great. I know she's right, and if the money thing isn't an issue anymore after she meets with my grandparents, I'm just not sure."

"It sounds like you know what you're supposed to do, but you're scared of it." I squirm at my comment once it settles in the air. "Was that too honest? My filter shuts off after midnight."

"I'd argue your filter is never on."

"I deserve that." I raise guilty hands.

"We're in the same boat." she stabs the remaining bite of

plain mac salad and offers an approving nod. At least she liked one thing on the plate.

"How so?" I ask.

Josie wets her lips and folds her hands together, weighing her next words wisely. "With the show. You said they want you to renew for another eighty seasons, right?"

"More like eighty-five. We're out to beat *Riverdale*'s attempted record."

She giggles. "If you don't want to, don't do it. You're almost eighteen. You're free to make your own choices."

I trace a thin trail through scattered black pepper flakes on the table. "I'm not sure what I'd do. The show has been the only success I've known. It was everything everyone says will never happen to you. It's like I was spoon-fed everything I wanted to work for. What if I've already peaked?"

"Personally, I think you peaked with the lady who had a crotch tattoo of your face."

"Hilarious."

Her dark eyes sparkle in the lighting. "Rowan, if acting is something you don't want to resent, start doing things you love instead. Fuck them if they won't give you the chance to prove yourself."

I dramatically throw myself back in the seat. "Did you just say the f-word?"

The muscles in her face twinge proudly. "I'm a city kid, remember? It comes as naturally as breathing."

"Then you need to learn to curse. You suck at it."

The two of us snort obnoxiously. Two half-naked pirates in the booth behind us look over to see why we're acting so annoying.

"I'll make you a deal." I extend a hand. "I'll stop being a little bitch about my future if you will too."

Josie is reluctant to grab my hand, like shaking it is some sort of death sentence she isn't ready to accept. The scales tip in her head: Will it be the master plan, or something else—something brave?

Josie slips her short fingers into mine, giving them a firm grip. "Deal. But? No guarantees."

"Good thing I'm not much of a guarantees guy."

Josie flops back in the booth and rests her eyes for a moment. Either she's about to fall asleep again or throw up, maybe both.

"You didn't just come here for food, did you?" She guesses.

I fidget for a moment. She's right, but I still hadn't found a way to tell her what I wanted to do without making it weird. As if the rest of our day had been normal.

"I want to go see something," I explain. "You'll probably think it's dumb, but it's important to me."

She leans in and stares into my sunglasses without a grain of hesitation.

"I'm in."

I ALREADY KNOW exactly where Rowan wants to go, well before he can work up the courage to tell me: His old house. What else could there possibly be for him in Rochester? (Outside of questionable taste in food and aggressive heartburn.)

He seems surprised by my enthusiasm at the idea. "You don't think that's too weird?"

"Not at all." I shake my head.

I would do anything to drive past our old house exactly as it was one more time. According to our old neighbors, the people who'd bought it after we moved painted it split pea green and begun adding an oblong studio tower in our massive backyard to rent as an Airbnb. It sounded utterly unrecognizable.

"How far is it?" I ask Rowan.

"Not far." He turns a sharp right onto a small residential street, a few blocks from where we'd stopped to eat.

It's little after four in the morning and still pitch-black outside. Streetlights illuminate the neighborhoods in soft amber hues. It's a humble little neighborhood, each of the houses looks like an old, tiny cottage pulled from the pages of a storybook and left to decay. None of them are well maintained, boasting overgrown vines and broken fences. Somehow, it works as part of their charm.

"Just up ahead." Rowan points to a cozy, white farm-style home on the left side of a dead-end street. He pulls up on it quickly and sets the Prius into park, his face pressed up against the window in awe.

"How long has it been since you've seen it?" I poke his seatbelt to get his attention. He goes right back to staring like it's the eighth wonder of the world.

"Since the day I moved," Rowan says quietly. "It was leased when we lived there. Grandma took over when Mom... you know."

"Yeah." I reverently bow my head.

"There wasn't a chance in hell Lexi would keep it, let alone leave Los Angeles. She stayed long enough after Grandma's funeral to box everything up and make sure all the paperwork was completed."

"And get you."

"Reluctantly." There's a hint of seriousness to his tone that makes me uncomfortable. Rowan may be a lot of things, but the last thing anyone would think to call him is unwanted.

Rowan shuts off the car and opens his door, unfastening his belt and jumping out to jog across the eerily quiet street and stand on the sidewalk out front. I follow suit, feeling the cold air blast against my bare arms. A thunder of crickets chirps a peaceful harmony as my dress scratches against the road.

The house resembles most of the other homes, perhaps smaller and with a fresher coat of paint. A wide concrete porch wraps around the front, with a rusted metal rail trailing up the steps. There's a dying rose bush and a plastic children's playset in the yard that's seen better days. It isn't much to look at, unless you are Rowan. Then, you're at a loss for words.

I stand beside the boxy brick mailbox with my arms crossed for at least ten minutes, allowing him to take it all in and process. After an eternity, he turns to me with wet eyes that melt every silent judgment formed in our long silence.

"They got rid of the tire swing." He points to the large maple tree out front with a protruding branch. Rowan half-smiles with a sniff. "It had a really cool tire swing."

Silently, Rowan walks back to the car. He searches for pockets in his long johns to shove his hands into, coming up empty. I take one last look at the house, not sure what I should be feeling. Sadness? Relief?

I follow suit and silently hop back into the passenger seat, shoving my skirt inside and closing the door behind me with a thud that wakes the neighborhood. Rowan grips the wheel for a moment, leaning forward and gazing mindlessly out the windshield like Dad's ancient Grandma Opal did once when she came to visit and nearly got us killed on the highway.

He goes to turn the key into the ignition but stops just short. Instead, he looks to me, continuing to say nothing.

I force a smirk, softening my tired gaze. "What does it feel like?"

Rowan reaches for the mask in the cupholder, wanting to cover the pain written all over his face. He wipes away a fat tear and slams back against the cold plastic seat, breathing steadily.

"Like it's not mine anymore," he whispers. Content, yet dripping with disappointment.

I look out his window and take it all in a final time. The longer you stared at the house, the plainer it appeared. Either I was missing its charm entirely, or everything Rowan was feeling had more to do with what happened inside than out.

"Hey." He blinks back more tears as he scratches his chin. "One more place? Last one, I promise."

I fasten my seatbelt and lean against the window. "It's your vacation."

It takes Rowan another minute to finally get going and silently roll us on our way. He drives out of the residential pockets and back onto the main highway, tapping buttons on the GPS and zooming quickly along as a handful of other cars lag behind us, going a reasonable speed.

"Just curious," I interrupt his self-imposed quiet, "do you actually have your driver's license?"

"If you're asking if I'm legally allowed to be behind the wheel of a moving vehicle, yes," Rowan assures. "The state of California only made me take the driving portion of the test twice."

The horizon comes into view as he pulls off the highway. The coast beside us stretches on without end, fading into total black as it bleeds into the haunting crystal sky. Several jerking turns later, he drives us into a sandy parking lot lit by a single bell-shaped lantern. The vibes feel just as sketchy as they look.

The wind coming from the water is intense and bitter. Rowan and I remove our shoes and start walking barefoot in the freezing sand, planting ourselves off the ocean enough to avoid the current. My dress was going to drag an actual gallon of sand back into Indio's Prius. Between this and the dried paint on my seat, we didn't just owe him stolen tip money, we owed him a new car.

Rowan leans back and props himself up with his hands, listening to the crashing waves and watching as the bubbling whitecaps melt back into the darkness. I whip his thin scarf from around my waist and cloak it across my shoulders like the world's worst shawl. A smear of dried red paint scrapes against my shoulder like a terrible reminder of everything that's behind me. Literally.

"Why here?" I ask Rowan, my teeth chattering.

Rowan stares up at the softening blue sky, his face unmoving and somber.

"This is where my grandma took me right after she found out her heart was failing. She had a minor heart attack and it was all downhill. She told me things didn't look good but that I didn't need to be afraid. Lexi would take care of me after she was gone and not to be too sad about all of it."

My heart aches for him. The way he spoke about his grandmother made her seem like the most perfect human to ever grace the planet.

"I know that's heavy," he adds. "I'm sorry to keep going all Lifetime Original Movie on you."

I dig my fingers in the sand behind me. It had been years since I'd set foot on a beach. I inhaled deeply through my nose, breathing in every second of salty air.

"Don't apologize. I think we all have a tragic backstory to tell," I reply.

Rowan adjusts his posture, leaning forward and picking at tiny grains of sand. He grows quiet again as we both take in the stillness of the atmosphere around us, watching as the sky turns from pale blue to a murky lavender yellow, seagulls squawking in the distance.

"My dad told us over pizza," I laugh to myself. "Pizza is how my family handles bad news. He and Mom came home from their meeting with the oncologist with a box of this insanely expensive thin crust that Pru hated because she's a sauce snob. That's when he told us about the diagnosis. He was admitted the next day."

Rowan's attention is pulled away from the sky. "Did they think he could beat it?"

"I'm pretty sure only he did. He kept telling us all about the things he would do once it was over." My whole body stiffens, my words pouring out thick like honey. "It happened fast. He was sick, and then he was gone. There was nothing we could do but watch."

Rowan pinches his mouth together, grabbing handfuls of sand to run through his hands. "Do you have the weird days too?"

"What weird days?"

"The ones where it's like they were never even here at all?"

The question comes at me like a sucker punch, knocking the wind right out of my lungs. I'd had more of those days in the last several months than I cared to admit. Until now, I didn't know anyone else could feel the same way.

"Yeah. Some days, I don't feel anything. Then other days, I miss him so much, I can't breathe." I sop up my tears with the scarf without any shame.

The two of us sit in total silence as the scope continues to soften around us. I try my hardest to sob quietly, but the tears start to stream hot and harrowing onto everything in their path —my cheeks, my dress, the sand. Rowan shifts on occasion to make sure I'm alright, allowing me to feel whatever it is I'm feeling. It's a cocktail of every ugly, horrible thing to ever exist mixed with each happy memory, all swirled together and spurting up and down like a lava lamp inside my throat.

"Shoot," I finally sniff and wipe my eyes, "as far as tragic backstories go, we're pretty pathetic. When did we become an episode of your stupid TV show?"

"I think we're worse."

We slowly erupt into cringeworthy giggles, throwing our heads back like two kids on a sugar rush. None of it makes sense, but that's what makes it real. It's pain and irony and every bizarrely beautiful thing the day has held, culminating into this one moment where the sun explodes into the distance with the weight of so many complicated things lifted.

A pair of morning joggers appear from the corner of the

beach, forcing us to compose ourselves. I continue to wipe melted paint and glitter from my eyes, scared of what my reflection would look like if I were to see it in a mirror. I catch a quick glance at Rowan as he studies the waves, looking like he wants to go run straight into the icy water. The dark bags under his eyes look like bruises, but the levity in his stare tells a much different story.

Rowan loosens his posture by pulling his knees to his chin. "We have to go back, you know."

I raise an eyebrow. "You're telling this to me?"

"We made a deal." He pauses. "No more running."

He was right. No more avoiding it. No more avoiding all the realities we'd been running away from for far longer than the last twenty-four hours. The more it settled into my gut, the more it hurt. We'd have a few more hours in a car together, and then we'd say goodbye.

What would happen after that? Would we go our separate ways, and life inevitably stay the same for both of us? Bravery is easy in theory, but in practice, it's riding a bull through a China shop while wearing a blindfold.

The original plan still burns in the back of my brain like a rotting tumor. The one where I went behind Rowan's back and told some clout chasing wannabe journalist all the personal information he'd shared with me in confidence. The more I think about how easily I went along with it, the queasier I feel. Was my future worth losing the trust of someone I cared for, someone I liked?

Rowan presses his arms deeper into the sand behind him and accidentally brushes my hand with his, causing all my concerns to evaporate like mist. He instantly flinches back and offers a nervous apology, lowering his head down towards the sand.

Gathering every ounce of courage I have left, I inch my

fingers closer to his till our fingertips are awkwardly inter-twined. Our eyes lock briefly before quickly looking away from one another with sideways smiles as we sit in stillness and enjoy the most unromantic gesture ever recorded. Every second of it is perfect.

WITH OUR COMBINED FUNDS—MY ten dollars and whatever we're 'borrowing' from Indio—we have just enough left after dinner (nay breakfast) to afford half a tank of gas and an oversized clearance gas station hoodie for Rowan. It reads: *If Jesus Had a Gun, He'd Still Be Alive Today.* I can't imagine why it would be on sale...

"Please don't wear that beyond the hotel," I urge him as he pulls it on over his costume. "Or ever again."

"Wearing this in New York, I'll be lucky if I make it that far," Rowan says.

Between it and Indio's sunglasses, both of us pray it's a passible enough disguise that people don't recognize him from the night before. No doubt photos from Boroughween had made the rounds online by now.

I'd rifled through Indio's glove compartment and every place a phone charger could possibly be hiding to potentially see for myself, coming up empty. The last text I see before my phone goes dark is from Pru, sent moments before we'd escaped from Boroughween. She tells me she had fun with Emma and asks if I'd be there when she got home in the morning. If she had seen the news at all, she likely assumed I was dead in a gutter somewhere.

I fall asleep for the second time halfway through the five-hour drive back. This time, I'm in a comatose state for the entire ride, not stirring until the GPS reads our destination as five minutes away.

"Hey." I yawn, stretching my arms wide across the back of the seats. I notice a string of saliva dragging from where my face was pressed against the window. Way to be charming.

"Welcome back." Rowan smiles warmly. He looks simultaneously exhausted and fully alert. Those sleeping pills must have done a number on his circadian rhythm.

I cover a second yawn and reach down to my toes. "Sorry I crashed."

"Better you crashing than me," he jokes.

"Where are you routing us?"

He points to a tiny red blip on the faded screen, abruptly slowing for oncoming traffic. "Your neighborhood."

A fizzy, soda pop sensation shoots down my arms. "Oh."

"Technically, King Kone. I'm going to drop you off and park this across the street. You can tell Indio where it is once you have access again."

"I'll leave the key in the shop's mailbox and text him," I say. "Hopefully he made it home alright."

"Something tells me he didn't go home." Rowan suggestively raises an eyebrow at the sight of the Stillwater bag beneath my feet. It had to be Izzy's. I fight a smirk. He holds up a single finger. "Also, please get your license."

"Oh sure, for the next time something like this happens."

There's an uncomfortable quiet lingering between us as the car slugs through Sunday morning traffic. I open my mouth several times to say something that would make the heavy, unspoken tension less painful to endure. Things like 'thanks for everything' or 'that was fun.' None of it feels right. As the distance on the GPS becomes shorter and shorter, the more it feels like saying goodbye to my best friend all over again.

Approaching my street corner causes my heart to ache more than all the times I swore it did before. I don't want Rowan to leave. Being around him felt so natural. Who else was going to encourage me to extend my reclusive boundaries by stealing things and punching holes in my body (and the occasional jerk's nose?)

Rowan pulls up to the first vacant spot on the curb down the road, throwing the car into park and jerking his head back into his seat.

"Home."

"Home," I repeat, meaning it for the first time ever.

We sit inside the car for an agonizing length of time, neither of us wanting to make the first move. Rowan cracks eventually and undoes his seatbelt, opening his door slowly like he's apprehensively about to rip a band-aid off his leg hair. He walks around the car and taps on my window for me to unlock the door, opening it with a modest bow.

"After you, your highness." He gestures to my skirt.

I roll my eyes. "I don't recall any of the Disney princesses looking this ratchet."

"Yeah well, they could never pull it off like you."

The alleyway next to our building is empty compared to nightfall. There are a few lifeless bodies covered with filthy blankets and newspapers against the dark red bricks, too far to see or hear anything from where we're standing. There are wet puddles of rancid mystery water and reflective gasoline pooled up in concrete potholes near the blackened dumpsters. We dip inside a dark corner to avoid being seen by neighbors walking their dogs.

I pull the MetroCard from behind my cell phone and slip it between Rowan's fingers. "Please don't lose this one."

"If I do, I'm not even going to try to get back to the hotel. I'll come back here and live out the remainder of my days in this dumpster."

"They light it on fire every night."

"Exactly." He lowers his sunglasses.

We nervously chuckle like a bunch of morons who are too busy ineptly fidgeting than to adequately convey our emotions like the budding adults we claim we are. Hard to believe that yesterday morning, I couldn't wait for Rowan to get out of my hair. When had I become one of those girls I'd spent years making fun of? And why did I like it so much?

Rowan breaks the ice, shoving his hands in his hoodie pockets and handing me Indio's car key to pass on. He unsteadily rocks on his feet.

"Big gulps, huh?"

I laugh into my wrist, finishing the quote from *Dumb & Dumber.* "Welp, see you later."

There's a solemn beat between us. Quickly, Rowan leans in for a hug, wrapping his arms around my sides and giving them a friendly tap that reads like *Well done, partner.*

It was ludicrous to expect him to feel the same way I did. Just because I'd fallen for his charm didn't mean he'd fallen for me. Who the hell was I compared to half the actresses on his level?

"Thank you," I offer, all the happiness sucked out of my voice. "For everything."

'Thank *you,* Josie." The way he says my name sends a chill down my spine. For the first time in my life, I don't resent being named after a guitar-wielding cartoon cat lady.

We separate at the sound of a blasting car horn coming down the road. Rowan waves gingerly as he turns down the sidewalk and begins walking towards the subway station a few blocks away. I turn to face the brick wall and take a deep breath, pinching back oncoming tears.

What if he forgot the directions? I think to myself. *Maybe I could catch up and go tell him to take the local train, not the express.*

It's futile thinking. I needed to let go of this schoolgirl crush I'd developed on Rowan Adler before it consumed my every waking thought. He was a rising celebrity with an award-winning future ahead of him—I was a broke senior without a MetroCard and glitter permanently lodged in my pores. All the looks, the hand holding on the beach, everything I'd interpreted in my head as him showing any signs of mutual affection were merely delusions conjured by a lonely girl who dreamed of having a fairy tale. It was never going to happen.

I start the walk-of-shame back to my apartment when abruptly, there's a frantic tug on my shoulder. I go into fight or flight mode, ready to win my second scuffle against any mugger in this alley who dare take me down when I'm feeling so despairing.

To my surprise, it's Rowan.

"Oh my god! Is everything okay?" I ask, watching as he lowers his hood and removes his sunglasses. He breathes heavily like he's on the edge of a full-blown panic attack.

"Yeah," he finally murmurs. "I just, umm..."

Rowan doesn't finish the sentence. Instead, he delicately places his hands on mine to keep them steady, then quickly ties something around my left wrist. It's Pru's friendship bracelet, still warm from sitting on Rowan's skin. The ends are fraying from wear, but the braids are still wound tight, the yellow threads resting across my hand like intricate strands of gold. Forget diamonds. I'd take this over expensive jewelry any day.

The scope around me begins to narrow, and my mouth goes

dry, a chorus of violins playing a frantic melody in my head. Instinctively, I want to thank him, but that's not what happens. Instead, I lean in close and run a hand through the back of his hair, hoping he wants this as much as I do. It's a question he answers without any hesitancy by moving the rest of the way and closing the gap, our lips meeting as his body presses firmly against mine.

What races through my mind aren't the countless number of girls who daydream about this scenario, all of whom would gladly kill me to be here. It's the way our noses don't quite fit with one another and the unlawful combination of onions and city sewer smell coming off his clothes. We're kissing like it's the first time and the thousandth time all at once. It's nothing like any of those Audrey Hepburn kisses I grew up idolizing, or even a sultry, sexy kiss like you'd see on *Dawn Heights*. It's intensely clumsy, and we're both trying way too hard to make it seem like it's effortless, but that's what makes it ours. One-hundred percent awkward, unscripted bliss.

Rowan leans in a final time to brush his mouth softly against mine before finally pulling himself away with a warm sigh and cheeky smile. He spins on his heels to continue on his way, hurriedly making himself incognito again as I stand there dizzy and breathless, wondering if people six states away could hear how loudly my heart is beating.

I bite down on one cheek to keep my smile from bursting right off my face and impaling the two apartment buildings between the alley, a faint giggle escaping like an automatic reflex. I brush a hand against my mouth to make sure it's still there.

That just happened.

I just kissed Rowan Adler.

The next few moments are a complete blur. I exit the alley at some point because I've mindlessly dropped Indio's keys at the King Kone hiding spot and eventually find myself walking into the main door of our building. Excitably, I greet Ms. Ramada from the third floor, who is downstairs gathering her mail. She judgmentally raises a thin eyebrow as she gives my outfit a once over and offers a coy smile.

My legs wobble like Jell-o as I do a giddy spin down the hallway and smile at the familiar unkempt wallpaper. The euphoria is enough to make me forget how physically and emotionally drained I am. The endless list of things I needed to worry about was nonexistent for one shining moment. To kiss someone is one thing, but to kiss someone who treats it like it's the most significant moment of their life is a unique kind of high.

If only I knew how short-lived that high would be. As I glide towards our front door and punch in the first two numbers of our key code with trembling fingers, it abruptly swings open and slams back with a thud that no doubt puts a hole in the back wall.

My mother stands in the doorway, which need I remind you, is NOT in Washington DC. Her arms are crossed tightly against her chest, a face filled with pure indignation as her hair practically singes from heated rage. If there were ever an instance in my life that required an aptly timed record scratch, it would be now.

The moment her nostrils flair is the exact moment I stop breathing.

"JOSEPHINE RILEY BRADFORD! WHERE THE HELL HAVE YOU BEEN?!"

SNEAKING into my hotel at little after noon while wearing an outfit that screams 'republican hipster raided a homeless man's suitcase' isn't how I pictured my micro vacation ending. Then again, neither was that kiss.

The moment replayed over and over in my head while on the train ride, a welcomed distraction from what would await me with my aunt. So much in fact, I nearly missed my stop and started the whole damn process of getting lost all over again.

One of the annoying questions I'm repeatedly asked in press junkets is if I ever feel anything while kissing Ashanti, or anyone else on the show the writers have me dating on a given week. For starters, how is that journalism? It's up there with asking every male actor with toned abs what their workout routine looks like. Secondly, of course I did, but that 'feeling' was always the repulsive weirdness of Frenching someone who looks at you like you are their kid brother. Nothing kills a moment more than kissing someone who secretly wishes she were kissing her girlfriend instead.

With Josie, it was different. It had been nearly an hour, and my whole body was still buzzing. I'm pretty sure it doomed me for life. No number of acting classes would get me to pretend anything was half as real as that.

Pushing the kiss to the back of my mind seems impossible at first, but as I press the button up to the twenty-ninth floor of The Four Seasons, the warmth permeating my bones and soaking through my clothes turns into ice, cold fear. I'm wildly shaking, barely able to ball a fist to knock on the hotel room door.

I take a deep breath, exhaling sharply before beating on the wood for a total of four seconds. It doesn't take longer than that for Alex to leap into the doorframe, his build blocking any sunlight inside from peeking out. His bright blue eyes water at the sight of me. He hangs his head with a breathy laugh that lifts every weight off his massive chest.

"Holy shit." He pulls me into a hug. "You're alive!"

My body hangs like a lifeless pencil in his suffocating grip. "Was there ever any doubt?"

I close the door behind me and glance around every corner, expecting Aunt Lexi to pop out and start smacking me with a hot pink stiletto. Alex locks the door behind me and stuffs his face against the viewfinder to assure nobody has followed me upstairs.

"I'm good," I assure him. "Nobody noticed me come up. I told the guy at the desk I was staying with my parents on this floor."

Alex doesn't say anything. His vision becomes mistier with every passing second. The weathered look on his face is two-parts relief mixed with one-part imminent vomit. Worried sick might be an understatement.

"Where's Lexi?" I finally ask.

"In her room," Alex's voice cracks. "Waiting."

"Waiting?"

"*Waiting*." Lexi's high-pitched voice stabs me like a knife in the neck. She slides the doors to her loft open and approaches me slowly.

My aunt looks like she hadn't slept in days, which was true most of the time, but never like this. Her hair hangs wet and limp in a low ponytail like she'd just taken her tenth hour-long shower in days. It soaks the back of her striped pajama shirt. There wasn't a trace of makeup to be found on her face, minus a thick application of under-eye cream that made her nose look glossy.

I'd only ever seen her this way once before, right after Grandma died and she knew I was about to become her responsibility. The same sense of objective disappointment that floods me then fills me up again now, making me wish I was never born at all.

The three of us stand frozen in place like chess pawns for far too long. I'm tempted to crack a joke in order to make the air in the room feel thinner. *Wow, the front desk guy wasn't lying when he said the nearest bathroom was far away, huh?*

Lexi pulls into one of the pockets of her saggy black sweats and pulls out my cell phone, tossing it at me like she's launching a grenade. I duck low just in time to get smacked hard in the same shoulder Aaron had pummeled earlier. I groan as I reach to pull it up off the floor.

"You'd better have one fucking good explanation, Rowan!" Lexi foams through clenched teeth. Her once disturbing expression is changing into a furnace of something I know all too well. The mother of all discourse is about to be unleashed.

"Lexi, I'm—"

"If you're about to say you're sorry, try harder!"

A selfish sort of anti-guilt swells up inside me. I know I'm not blameless here. Leaving was wrong, not coming back was wrong, scaring them by not making any contact for nearly two days was wrong. Regardless of how wrong I know I am, there are zero regrets.

My feet begin to bob back and forth, my chin poking outwards as my lips curl in tightly on themselves. "I'm not sorry for leaving."

Alex prudently moves behind Lexi, intensely mouthing *Quit while you're ahead* and giving me the throat-slashing motion. Too late for that.

"You're not?" Lexi scoffs, setting her manicured hands on her hips. "Do enlighten me, Rowan. I've spent the last twenty-four hours on the phone with every living soul at Webstream telling them you were sick in bed with the flu and had to miss the meeting. Then, newsflash! Pictures of you at some party last night show up all over social media!"

Her words slice through my bones like a chainsaw. That was it? In the whole time I'd been gone, that was all she'd been worried about? Me missing that goddamn Webstream meeting? My head throbs with every rapid heartbeat. There wasn't any concern for Rowan, her nephew. It was all for Rowan, her most significant career asset.

Every fiber in my body goes rigid, my tongue locked up so tight, it feels like it might permanently stick to the roof of my mouth. I toss the sunglasses and hoodie onto the couch and march my way past Lexi into mine and Alex's room.

"EXCUSE ME!" Lexi's clamoring rattles off the walls. "WE'RE NOT FINISHED!"

Her pushiness goes in one ear and out the other. I bend down and reach for my untouched suitcase, digging for a pair of clean clothes. The anger practically radiates off me, red and hot.

"I'm taking a shower," I reply over my shoulder, slamming a t-shirt and sweats into the crook of my elbow.

"No, you're not!" Lexi hovers over me.

"Yes, I am!"

"ROWAN ADLER!" She shouts, catching my attention. She sounds like Mom and Grandma all rolled into one, and for a brief second, it's petrifying.

I stand to my feet and shrug, going completely numb. "What?!"

Lexi's hardened demeanor abruptly crumbles like a Jenga tower. A soft moan creeps out as she covers her mouth with one hand. A literal flood of tears spills out of her eyes, drenching her shirt. It's definitely not what I would expect from Alexis Adler. This is the woman who never cried once at her own mother's funeral.

My stiffened posture goes limp, feeling weakened but on edge. I'm not sure if this is her way of getting me to let my guard down so she can lash out or if she's really having as big of a meltdown as she seems to be. Alex backs up slowly towards the doors and holds up a finger, either excusing himself for a moment or subtly resigning and requesting his final paycheck.

Lexi gasps for air, finally collapsing at the edge of my bed and wiping a trail of snot off her nasal depression.

"Rowan," she gulps, "*please.*"

Her *please* is drenched in desperation. Bile pools in the back my throat like resentful barf. Every emotion rises to the surface at once, breaking through my silence and apathy till I'm pacing in front of her and waving my hands in the air like I'm on an acid trip.

"I said I'm not sorry for leaving, and I'm not! Because I never get to leave! Not here, not anywhere! Every single aspect of my life—my decisions, my finances, my career, my damn free time—it's decided for me, and I'm sick of it!"

I pause, waiting for her to retaliate in some way. If there was anyone in the world who could win a debate they were on the losing side of, it was Lexi. My delay proves to be in vain.

Her puffy hazel eyes shoot up with all the laser focused attention of someone being read their last rites.

I fold my hands together in a praying position, continuing to move back and forth. "Lexi, I'm grateful for everything you've done for me. You took me in and dealt with my bullshit and helped with everything regarding this job ever since. I owe you more than I could ever repay, but I'm almost eighteen. I need to start making decisions for myself before I lose my mind! And yes, leaving was royally fucked up, and I'm sorry. You shouldn't have been forced to lie for me, but I didn't feel like I had a choice!"

More silence. The only noise in the room comes from Alex's distant heavy breathing from behind the door. Nosy bastard.

"I want to be more than just another client or some guy on a TV show. I'm also your family!" My voice cracks. "Is it too much to be treated like that?"

Another set of whimpering sobs explodes from Lexi. She hangs her head low and wipes her eyes with a heavy sigh, delicately massaging the comforter with small circular motions.

"I lied for you because I knew you ran away." Her tone gets raspy. "I told Alex we weren't going to report you missing because I knew you'd come back."

I ring the shirt in my hands like a sweat towel. "How?"

"Because your mom did. Jen pulled this crap all the time when we were kids."

"She did?" My words come out squeaky like a cartoon character. Lexi's statement hits me like an atomic bomb.

My aunt nods. "She'd run off and return days later. Your grandma and I never knew what she did, just that she'd always come back."

"Till she didn't," I scowl.

Lexi licks her lips and pats at the bedding she's smoothed

wrinkleless, inviting me to take a seat next to her. I'm still apprehensive. This could be one massive red herring and I'm about to be strangled to death. I meet her halfway by taking a seat on the opposite corner of the mattress, bouncing my legs like crazy to keep my adrenaline from shooting me thru the roof.

"You're not your mother, Rowan." Lexi sniffs. "You care about other people too much."

I blow a raspberry. "Yeah, I sure proved that by scaring the shit out of you."

Lexi turns to face me. "When Alex realized you were gone, he wanted to call 911. I said to wait it out. When morning rolled around, and you still weren't here, I knew you weren't coming back anytime soon. I called everyone and explained that you were sick, so there wouldn't be any cause for concern. They said they'd reschedule if they had to—*assholes*."

"Nice to know a potentially life-threatening illness is considered such an inconvenience," I joke.

"I told Alex if you weren't back by last night, we'd file a report and deal with the consequences. Then pictures started showing up online. I received several angry voicemails, as you can imagine."

I tip to the edge of my seat. "To which you said...?"

"It wasn't you." Lexi rolls her eyes. "I said you were still in bed with a fever, how it was a coincidence that some doppelganger would be at a party getting everyone's attention."

"I doubt the internet believes that."

"I don't care what the internet thinks." The abrupt edge in her tone makes her sound much more like the Lexi I know. "I saw the photos and knew you were safe. That's all that mattered."

I sink low into the sheets. Her confession erodes my anger and replaces it with unexpected compassion. Was my aunt actually being a positive parental figure for once? Complete with all the cliches I'd seen on *Full House* reruns?

"Rowan." Her shoulders sink. "I'm sorry."

"For what? I'm the one who—"

"Left? Made me check the room for cheerleaders hiding under your bed? Caused me to smoke my first cigarette in over a year? Yeah, you are." She nods with a soft sigh. "But you're also my nephew, and I know I don't always treat you like you are."

I snicker. "Grandma made taking care of me look easy."

"Your grandma was tougher than me. She'd be proud of you. Rebellious streak aside, you're a really good kid."

"At least until recently," I huff, thinking of the fight and everything that had happened ever since. Even by Reckless Rowan standards, I was a human disaster.

Lexi pinches her lips. "I might have something to do with that."

"You don't make *all* my decisions for me."

"No, but I don't always help you through all of them either."

I unfold my arms and hunch over my knees like a wet noodle. "You fix every mess I create. I'm not sure how that counts as not helping."

Lexi's usual stick-up-ass posture relaxes. She cocks her head to one side and stares ahead at the shrunken marble statue of Michelangelo on the oblong coffee table across the room.

"When you fell into my lap, I had no idea what to do with you."

I chip away at a hangnail on my thumb. "You said I was challenging."

"You still are." Lexi playfully swats my arm. "This job entails thick skin. You learn to live life without much of an emotional barometer to gauge things with. Then you walked into the picture and felt things harder than anyone I'd ever known." She stumbles over her words. "That was hard for me."

That's the understatement of the century. She barely knew how to speak to me for the first several months I lived in her house. You'd think she'd never seen a child before in her life.

Lexi fiddles with her damp hair. "When you got into drama, and I saw it was a healthy outlet for you, I thought maybe it would be the one thing we'd have in common, the one thing I could understand."

"Not every actor is blessed with a guardian agent."

She ignores my sarcasm. "That's why I pushed you. I knew how to push people, and I saw that you had passion. Not everyone I push does. What other teenage boy watches *Little Shop of Horrors* four times in one night to land a part in a school play?"

"Still my finest work," I boast proudly.

"You have better work in you." Lexi's eyes meet mine for a brief second before darting back to her hands. It's the sincerest I've heard her speak of my career in... *ever*.

I finally rip the hangnail off my thumb and suck at the blood on my finger like a vampire. "I want to think I do."

"Rowan, *Dawn Heights* was a once-in-a-lifetime miracle," she laughs half-heartedly. "It's a phenomenon every studio tries to create in a petri dish. That doesn't make you any less talented because you didn't have to fight for it. Sometimes it just happens."

"Are you about to go all Uncle Ben on me and say something like it's not about how I got famous, but what I do with my fame?"

"I was before you were a smartass about it." She smiles.

My ears start ringing loudly. "Is this the part where you apologize for pushing me too hard and giving me no choice but to run away?"

"Not even close."

"Apology accepted."

Lexi snorts. "I promise to push less and communicate more if you promise to stop acting without thinking so much."

I lower my head. "That's fair."

There's an atypical levity to the moment I hate to ruin by saying the next thing on my mind, but if I don't, it'll only come out later in a way that feels scripted. I think about Josie, about our deal, feeling like for once, my opinions mattered.

"I don't want to renew my contract," I state, confidently rolling up my oversized sleeves and not thinking too hard about how dumb I look trying to be taken seriously in this costume.

Lexi raises her eyebrows, her gaze going glossy. "You don't?"

"You seem surprised."

"I'm actually not. It's just strange to hear you say it."

"I'M SURPRISED!" Alex's voice booms from behind the door. "CAN I STILL KEEP MY JOB?"

Fatigue settles in for the first time since I took the sleeping pills, resulting in drooping eyelids and a pounding headache. I run my hands through my grease-slicked hair with a forced smile. "Are you mad?"

Lexi turns up her nose. "Mad? No. Inconvenienced? Extremely, but we'll work it out. Worst case scenario, they'll reboot the show in twenty years, and you have a guaranteed fallback."

"Thanks," I guff at her attempt to comfort me.

Lexi bounces her butt over to the edge of the bed and mildly rubs the small of my back the way Grandma used to when she wanted to cheer me up.

"Rowan, you're gonna fall on your ass a few times on your way to better work." I'm about to tell her to quit while she's ahead, right before she adds, "but you'll get there, and I'll help you up every time it happens. That's my job."

"As an aunt or a manager?"

Tiny crow's feet appear at the folds of her eyes. "Aunt. I just happen to make a fairly decent cut off of it."

It might not be conventional encouragement, but it's the first heart-to-heart I've ever had with Lexi that hasn't resulted in one of us slamming a series of doors or absentmindedly running off into the night. She was right. If moving on was the choice I was making, it wouldn't be an easy one. I'd need to prove myself before anyone trusted me with a role I could sink my teeth into, but if it meant doing something I loved and finally having it matter to me in the way I'd wanted it to, I'd face as many rejections as necessary to get there.

"So." Lexi squints. "Are you going to tell me where you were and what you did?"

Where would I even begin? The train? Falling asleep at King Kone? Waking up at Josie's and the chaos that followed? All the big things felt so small compared to the reality of what happened: I met a girl who made my life a little better for a day.

"Wandered." I shrug. She's not amused by my answer.

"I tipped off the press that we were staying at The St. Regis in Midtown. Hopefully this puts us in the clear till our flight leaves tonight."

"Smart." I nod. It explained why there weren't hordes of paparazzi waiting for me as soon as I approached The Four Seasons. I'm sure they were having a field day waiting for no one several miles away.

A banging knock rattles the room and forces Lexi and me to jump back with a gasp. It's Alex again. "SERIOUSLY," he inquires, "AM I FIRED?"

Lexi sends me a sideways glance and raises a hand for me to shake, her bony wrists protruding with gnarly green veins. "I'll order us food while you shower, and you come out and tell me all the things we potentially need to fix. Deal?"

I squeeze her hand in mine with a pump. "Deal."

Lexi yanks my arm with an angry jerk and holds it up like a proud poacher with their kill. She stares at my new tattoo and the disgusting bandage swaddled around it.

"You can start by telling me what the hell this is."

POP QUIZ! When your mother, who is supposed to be on a personal trip for several more days, surprises you by coming home early, and catches you coming in from an all-nighter with a random boy you just met (who also happens to be famous), do you:

1. Tell her the truth
2. Lie as if your life depends on it
3. Run back out the door and hope it's not too late to hop a turnstile and catch the next train.

If you're me, the answer is none of the above. Luckily, and I do use the word ironically, Pru had walked in the door ten minutes before me and was already sitting on the couch getting an earful when I arrived. Mom banishes me to my bedroom while she finishes pumping my sister for information, giving me time to collect my thoughts and wallow in fresh sadness.

I refrain from slamming the door shut behind me, instantly digging through my closet to grab the baggiest clothes I own and escape the 'blood' stained dress. I lean in front of my standing mirror, taking baby wipes to my face to remove every last trace of star paint and glitter, tossing my hair into a messy bun. I take a good look at myself before wanting to crawl into bed and sleep for the rest of the day. Snuggling deep into my blankets and closing my eyes, I breathe deep to find any trace of Rowan from the night before.

I wondered if he had made it back to the hotel and if his body would need to be identified by his dental records after being ripped to shreds by his aunt. That same cruel fate was awaiting me with Mom, my only solace coming in the form of reflections from our alleyway kiss. Forty minutes suddenly felt like ten lifetimes ago. Between then and now, the mighty had fallen hard and then landed on the pavement without a parachute.

My trite self-loathing is interrupted by a soft knock on my door. Mom's concerned voice floods the cracks in the door-frame. "Jojo, can we talk?"

She opens the door and presents herself with hands raised in surrender. I sit up with a thin smile and wave her in. The conversation was inevitable. Why prolong any punishments that awaited me?

Mom rubs the legs of her jeans, taking a seat at the edge of my bed. "You know, I thought maybe when I sent you a text saying 'I'm on my way home, we'll talk about it once I'm back,' I might get a little more from you than radio silence."

Talk about my luck. I typically received five texts a week, none of them ever important enough to warrant a fast response. Why is it on the one day everyone needed to reach me, I decided to drain my battery loading subway routes?

I leap to my feet and pull my phone off the corner of my desk, plugging it into the wall charger and feeling it buzz as a red bar flashes onto the screen. It was so dead, it needed to be defibrillated before it would even power on again.

"My phone died while I was out," I explain. "I'm so sorry, Mom."

"It's not the unanswered text I'm concerned about, Josie," Mom observes the obvious. "It's that you were out all night."

There it is. The Tess Bradford Look of Contempt, tight-lipped and snarling. It's enough to drag me to my knees and force me to confess the entire situation while begging for mercy.

As I muster up the courage to say something, Mom interjects again. "Pru tells me she was at Emma's house, and you gave her permission to go."

I nod. "That's true."

"I know it is. I had her call Emma's mom. She says they had a great time at her dad's, and Pru was a perfect guest."

I wait for the zinger. "And?"

"Where were *you*?" Mom's 'you' oozes with rage. It's concern and wrath all wrapped into one tight package that makes me feel lower than low.

The longer I sit there and contemplate what I want to say, the more I realize there's no version of the truth I can offer that would sound real. 'I spent all day with Rowan Adler' was either the world's worst Wattpad or the laziest alibi ever.

I clear my voice, grabbing a pillow and holding it tight as both a comfort and a potential shield. "I was with a friend."

"A friend," Mom curiously repeats. "Have I met her?"

I cross my legs, embarrassed as ever. "Him."

Mom forces her eyebrows to stay in a scowling position, lest they shoot through her skull. This was a newsflash if she'd ever heard one.

"Oh." Her voice goes high-pitched. "Is he... nice? Have you known him very long?"

A day, I think to myself. Unless you count those five thousand instances where I'd seen his face on magazine covers.

"Not long." I shrug, thinking up another clever work-around. "He's from New York." *Sort of.*

Mom eyes the lifeless wedding dress sitting in the corner, the tulle bunched up against the wall like a smushed insect. She studies the scarf and red paint like she's trying to make sense of it all.

"And that?" She points as if it's a piece of incriminating evidence.

"There wasn't a sexual awakening." I cock my head.

The color drains from her cheeks. "I never said that!"

"It was heavily implied."

"Josie, I've had to worry about you for a lot of reasons. Running off with a boy has never been one of them."

I twist at one of the ends of my pillowcase. "Not sure if that's a compliment or not."

Mom nervously chuckles, giving my bun a kittenish flop. "Because you've always been the dependable one, no other reason. I'm thrilled you were with a friend, but my god, did you have to scare the daylights out of me? I came in after not hearing a word from you or your sister all night and neither one of you were home. Can you imagine how that felt?"

I reluctantly nod my head, feeling an imminent well of tears about to spring forth. I bite down on my lip with force to stop them from unleashing. Restlessness overtakes me like a bad Syfy channel movie tsunami. The weight of everything—school, college, Dad, the last twenty-four hours—leaves me in a tailspin. I gulp for air as the pressure takes me under.

Spending time with Rowan forced me into being myself for the first time since coming here and losing everything I cared about. I missed him, of course, but more than that, I missed how I felt when I was with him. Brave and badass and like my future wasn't silly or uncertain. Things my dad would always tell me, but had stopped believing once he was gone.

Mom instinctively dives like a ninja at the sight of my quivering lip and wraps me in a hug that causes me to melt into her chest and weep.

"It's okay, sweetheart." Mom strokes my hair and kisses my forehead, rocking me back and forth like a child in need of a lullaby.

"This is so ridiculous!" I muffle into her plain white t-shirt. It smells like sweat and airplane pretzels. "I'm the one who ran off like some stupid teenager!"

Mom pulls me off of her and looks straight into my eyes, gripping my arms tight. "I hate to break it to you, but you are a stupid teenager. This is my job, and frankly, it could be much worse." She side-eyes the dress again. "Unless it is."

I chuckle, snuffling up a wad of thick mucus. "No, it's not."

She wipes away the teardrops as they continue splashing across my cheeks like fat water balloons. "You know I was kidding about the whole finding trouble thing, right? I'm not against fun but please, never do this to me again. At least send me a text? Or bring an extra charger?"

I gasp for cool air between sobs. "Am I going to be punished?"

"You and Pru are sharing your location on your phones with me for the foreseeable future," she remarks, "but let's consider this a first strike. Let's not go for the other two, hmm?"

I allow the strained gravity of the room to dissipate briefly before speaking again, not wanting to seem the accusatory one when I'd just gotten away with sneaking out. That failing to include all the lying, stealing, and plotting along the way. Had she really not noticed the earrings either?

"Mom." I sigh heavily. "What are you doing home?"

Now it's her turn to look like she wants to cry. Mom balls up her blonde hair and flops it onto the top of her head, falling limp onto her shoulders.

"They were even more awful than I remembered as a kid."

"I could've told you that." Yikes. *A little harsh, Josephine.*

She leans comfortably into my bed, bracing to tell me the story. "They picked me up from the airport, and we went to dinner. It was awful."

"How awful?"

"Had my old college boyfriend accidentally run into me at the next table so we could 'reconnect' awful."

I practically curse my grandparents for attempting something so callous. Dad hadn't even been gone a year, and they were already determined to make their eighteen years of marriage seem like a distant memory.

"Let me guess." I wipe my nose with my sleeve. "It got worse from there?"

Mom tucks a strand of hair behind her ear, the lines on her face growing deep. "I sat down with them yesterday afternoon and explained what we needed. I told them that you and your sister deserved to get a proper education and shouldn't be punished for my mistakes. That's when I realized something."

"What?"

"That loving your dad wasn't a mistake, and I shouldn't have to say I was wrong for it." Salty tears stream into the corners of Mom's mouth. "The second my parents reminded me how I'd run my future into the ground by marrying him, I grabbed my bag and rebooked my flight. After that, it wasn't worth it anymore."

I knit my eyebrows together, bracing for my next confession. "It's probably not the time to tell you I quit my job, is it?"

Mom squirms, pinching her eyes shut like she's just been hit with a BB gun pellet. "I can't say I'm surprised."

I rub my eyes. "I'm sorry."

"Why?"

"Because I know how much the money helped us."

"Josephine." Mom grabs me by the shoulders again, giving me a slight shimmy. "I'm the mother, remember? You chose to help support us. I'm grateful, but we'll live without it. If anything, you are the one I should be apologizing to."

I draw back sharply. "For what?"

"For not being a better grown-up." Her gaze is stern, yet as fragile as I've ever seen it. "That you'd ever feel the need to put your goals aside for Pru and me. I know how much UC means to you."

I reach over and pull one of her hands into mine, giving it a slight squeeze. Rowan's friendship bracelet lies twisted on my wrist, forcing the corners of my mouth to turn into a mum smile. His confident voice burns in my subconscious with fiery enthusiasm.

"Mom," I whisper, "I have no idea what my future is supposed to look like, but I know college isn't going anywhere. And for the record? This single parent thing sucks, but you're doing a really good job."

That about does my mother in. Thank god Pru was in her room. Two Bradford women in a sea of pajamas and dirty hair drowning in their own sorrow was enough.

As harrowing as it felt to know we were just as on our own as we were before, there's a newfound steadiness to Mom's demeanor. She's not putting on her brave face and hoping I don't see through the charade, as she had been for so long. Her shoulders are pinched back with resilience, unshaken in this strange new reality we've been forced to accept.

Dad wasn't coming back, but that didn't mean we weren't going to be okay. Accepting his absence wouldn't remove the pain, but perhaps one day, the thought of him missing birthdays and Christmases and Sunday afternoons wouldn't hurt as badly as it did today. He wouldn't want us to miss out on our lives just because his was cut short.

Mom wipes her chin with her wrist, mopping up the tears and tugging at the thread around my wrist. "Your sister caved and gave one to you?"

I give it a spin. "My friend did, actually."

"The boy?" Mom's earnest expression turns fresh, playfully lifting her forehead. "Do I get to meet him?"

If you ever attend a DawnCon, I inwardly groan.

My insides ball into a giant knot as I realize in that instant, there was a slim chance I'd ever see Rowan again. At least, outside of a screen. I'd be watching Webstream one day seventy years from now and flip across *Dawn Heights*. I would point to the image of his face and tell my grandkids all about the time we made out near a dumpster and how great it felt.

"Sure, Grandma," they'll say. "Let's get you to bed."

The bracelet was all I had left of our time together. The longer I look at it and remembered the way he smiled at me as he walked away, the more my heart shatters into a sharp, disfigured mosaic of scattered fragments.

I shake my head, a loose curl escaping from my bun and bouncing into my eyeball. "I'm not sure I'll be seeing him again," I explain. "I don't know how it would work out."

Mom chews her upper lip and nods. Confused, I'm sure.

"His loss then." She winks. "I'm going to go make food. You want food?"

I blot away at the last of my tears and force a smile. "Yes, I'd love food."

Mom lovingly pats my thigh and gives me another kiss on the head, excusing herself and heading for the kitchen, where nothing good is bound to become of all the slamming pots and pans in the background.

Pru promptly whips her head into my open doorframe, shielding her eyes from the bright sunlight filtering through my window.

"You're still alive?!" She howls in a hushed tone.

"Yes." I roll my eyes, waving her inside and silently motioning for her to close the door so Mom won't hear us.

Pru skips over to my bed and flops onto her stomach next to me, rolling like a log and tipping her glasses down her nose.

"How was the date?" She sings.

"It wasn't a date," I retort. "It was an unintentional, personal kidnapping with benefits."

"A date then." She rises and folds her legs to match mine, sprawling her ruffled pink skirt like a doily across the sheets.

"You didn't tell Mom," I state.

Pru blinks. "You sound surprised."

"Because you tell Mom everything."

Pru points a finger at my nose with a threatening flair. An armful of colorful bracelets lines her arm. "I might be a tattle-tale, but I'm not a snitch. Besides, I owe your boyfriend. Also, did you pierce your ears?!"

I aggressively shush her. "He's not my boyfriend!" I retaliate with a sour taste in my mouth. "And why do you owe him?"

Pru holds up her phone and reveals Rowan's verified Instagram page, @itsradler. Seeing his face pop up on the small photo grids causes my heart to thud in a way I wish it didn't. I nearly pass out when I notice his thirty-six million followers at the top of the page. To list a few: Kim Kardashian and Taylor Swift. Who was I kidding by thinking I was magically The One?

"He gave me a shoutout!" Pru announces, tapping on his story.

I rip the phone out of her hands, watching my expression explode in the phone's reflection. Rowan had posted it moments ago, meaning he'd made it back to the hotel safely. I breathe a burdened sigh of relief.

The story was a screenshot of an account called @pruslooms, with a small tag underneath that read: *Help support small business and give her a follow!*

"No way!" I beam. "You have an Instagram account?"

Pru takes her phone back with an aggressive shove. "That's so not the point! And I'm actually offended. I've had a secret personal account for years."

My sister adjusts her glasses and taps around her screen several times till she's showing me a flood of incoming direct messages. Most of them asking how much the bracelets are, where they can buy them, and if she ships internationally. She was already up to eight thousand followers.

"I told him all the money I made for them was going towards your college tuition." She lifts my arm and tugs at the bracelet on my wrist. "Not your boyfriend, ehh?"

My jaw lands just shy of the shag rug beneath my bed. Few things in life have rendered me completely speechless, that including the discovery I was accidentally harboring a celebrity in my bedroom. Of all the things Rowan could have done once he was back at the hotel, he decided to promote my sister's Instagram. If I wasn't falling for him before this, I certainly was now. Why did love have to feel so wonderfully awful?

Pru looks over her shoulder, making sure Mom's painted toes aren't sneakily trying to hide underneath the crack outside my door.

"Are you going to tell me what happened?" She rubs her hands together with a hungry smack of her lips. "Please?"

I blink back another round of tears and flop back onto my pillows with a relaxed sigh. Closing my eyes, I smile cunningly.

"Yes, I did get my ears pierced."

CHAPTER 27

JOSIE

IN THE WEEK that follows the Halloween weekend from Hell —Hell-o-ween, as Pru has affectionately started to call it—her Instagram receives twelve thousand new orders in the United States alone. To reflect the sudden spike in supply and demand, Pru raises the price of the bracelets from five dollars to twenty-five, raising, no joke, over two-hundred thousand dollars after the cost of supplies and shipping.

"Don't forget about taxes!" I remind her as I walk with her to school on Friday morning. "They'll bite you in the butt if you don't account for them on the front end."

Pru waves me off, pulling her mesh scarf tight around her neck. "I've already talked to my financial advisor about it. It's being worked out."

I pause mid-walk. "Financial advisor?!"

She makes a noise in the back of her throat. "You're not the only one who knows people, Josie."

Every night that week after homework is spent helping Pru make the bracelets at a breakneck pace. She studies each order meticulously to assure the proper colors have been chosen and that each bracelet is being made according to her perfectionist standards. Mom even spends the few nights she's not working getting in on the action and braiding till her fingers are numb.

"I still don't understand how that *Dawn Heights* guy found you!" Mom tilts her reading glasses and holds two blue-colored balls of yarn under a desk lamp. "Do you have a classmate whose dad is in the movie business or something?!"

My sister and I look at one another across the living room with suspicious glances. I press my lips together to keep myself from laughing. Pru plays it off significantly better than me.

"I guess it's just one of those once-in-a-lifetime things, Mom!"

With continued sales and the help of Pru's mysterious financial adviser (Emma's CPA dad), she and Mom agree to open trust accounts for us with a portion of the money. The rest of it, with Pru and I's blessing, will go towards paying off the remainder of Dad's hospital debt, taking a massive burden off of Mom for the foreseeable future.

Once Sunday rolls around, and we're caught up enough to catch our breath, I reach out to Indio and ask if he'd be willing to meet at Stillwater to discuss our plan. I'd been using bracelet-making as an excuse to put it off. He'd sent me at least thirty texts over the last week asking when we could connect so I could see his pictures.

I wasn't ready to face the reality of what we were planning to do. I'd sat in front of my computer for hours the night before with a blinking cursor and a blank document meant to be filled with juicy Rowan Adler revelations. Instead, I wound up on Webstream to cringe my way through the entire first season of *Dawn Heights* so I had an excuse to see his face. Josie from a week ago would have been appalled.

I shiver the entire walk to Stillwater, both from the brisk impending winter and the sheer terror of what I'm about to tell Indio. I spot him at a corner booth making sex eyes at Izzy Ezra, who makes me a latte in a mug with a foam heart on top and asks me to show it to Indio. As if I needed yet another reminder of how alone I was.

Indio smirks as I approach the table, his black fingernails tapping across a large, yellow manilla envelope.

"Let me guess," he wheezes, "you don't wanna sell the story?"

I set the cup on the table and shake my heavy down jacket off my shoulders, swinging it over my chair. "How did you know?"

"Babe, I knew the night of the show you weren't going to go through with it. You don't have what it takes to be a Martin Bashir. You haven't sold your soul yet."

I thud into the chair, sprawling my legs wide onto the floor and blowing my hair off my face. "Are you pissed at me?"

"Surprisingly, no. He ended up helping me out too." Indio blows a kiss over to Izzy, who catches it and stuffs it into their apron pocket. *Ugh.*

I shrug. "So, what's the point of us meeting then?"

"Two reasons. One, I thought you might like to know that Izzy is being promoted to assistant manager, and they're looking for someone to work the bar. Want a job?"

My mouth forms a perfect O, nearly falling out of my seat. Wide-eyed, I turn towards Izzy, who nonchalantly shrugs and mouths, "I'll put in a good word!"

"Yes!" I laugh, "I'll totally put in an application!"

"Great!" Indio slides the envelope over to my side of the table, knocking the latte and destroying the heart. "Second, I thought since we're both too chicken shit to go through with it, you might like to have these as a souvenir."

Slowly, I unclasp the envelope and pull out a thin stack of 8x10 photos, some in color and several in black and white—only Indio would try to make paparazzi photos artistic. They're of Rowan and I wandering around the city, all from a distance and some taken at various hilarious angles.

I pause when I get to one of the photos taken of us inside the tattoo parlor. Indio must've shot it from the small portion of the front window that wasn't tinted. Rowan lies on the chair as the woman injects him with ink. I look at him with an adoring smile I can only look back on now as me fawning over him and not even realizing it. It's simultaneously embarrassing and devastating.

My mouth goes dry. "Wow."

Indio points to the photo in my hands. "About this one. Once I saw those photos of him at the block party making the rounds online, you know, the block party where you kicked someone's ass and ruined Izzy's show..."

I facepalm. Luckily for me, the face paint I was sporting that night made me virtually unrecognizable in any of the photos that went viral. That still didn't stop Julian and his idiot friends from being too intimidated to make eye contact with me at school over the last week. My red wedding days were all but over.

"Yes, I remember."

Indio nods. "I ended up paying this tattoo lady a visit and asked if she'd double-down on that whole, 'he wasn't there, he was sick in his hotel room' bullshit his people were spewing to cover his ass when the pictures got out. She told The Fizz her daughter had met him in the hotel while he looked for ice to bring his fever down. That's how she got an autograph. They interviewed her and everything."

"You're kidding," I laugh.

Indio glances up at Izzy with a goofy smile. "I owed the kid. And you."

I point to my chest. "Why me?"

"I might be an 'art school asshole,'" he uses finger quotes

around my description, "but I'm not stupid. You really like him, don't you?"

I sip the latte and allow the warmth to slide down my throat, melting my frigid bones. "Does it matter now?"

"Maybe not." He tilts his head and taps the photo. "But you look happy here."

Pru encouraged me to log into my Instagram for the first time in ages and send Rowan a message a few days after we went our separate ways. I'd almost garnered enough courage to write something long-winded and sappy, but when I went to his account, I quickly learned he had DM's disabled for users he wasn't following. And he followed no one. The crushing weight of his celebrity once again reminded me just how out of his league I was.

"Speaking of school." Indio sips the last of his iced matcha latte. "What are your plans now that you're loaded?"

"Hardly loaded." I drink. "Right now, I can afford about two semesters at NYU."

"You're applying to NYU?!" His pink eyeliner bends out towards his ears.

I smirk. "Just an option. A friend challenged me to expand my horizons."

I'd yet to tell Mom, but I was considering the possibility of a gap year to continue saving money and potentially look into some local filmmaking workshops. Rowan had been right. I hadn't completely given up on applying to University of Cincinnati, but Ohio was the only pocket of the world I'd ever felt safe in. It was time to see what else it had to offer, especially New York.

My fingers dance across the glossy prints tucked underneath the envelope, a lump rising in my throat each time I looked down. It was starting to seem like my inability to reach Rowan was karma getting back at me for the mere idea of selling him out. Each time one of our conversations replayed in my head, be it serious or stupid, the harder it was for me to reckon with my own willingness to hurt him so carelessly.

Indio must be reading my thoughts as I stare down at the photos with a misty, desolate look. "You didn't do it, Josie."

I clutch the handle of my mug. "I know."

He smiles at me softly. "Like I said, you have a soul, and that's rare. I think that's why he liked you too."

. . .

I blink, and two weeks later, it's already Thanksgiving break. The bracelet orders have slowly trickled to far more manageable numbers. Pru recruits a handful of classmates to come over on weekends and help braid in exchange for a cut of the money and free hot chocolate. It gives Mom a much-needed break and allows me to start barista training at Stillwater.

In my free time, I make a list of places in the city I want to go and see. So far, I'd ventured to Central Park for some after school reading, and joined Mom and Pru during one of their many trips to The Met to recreate iconic scenes from *Gossip Girl*. Rowan would be proud, but deep down, I wasn't doing it for him. I was doing it to prove to myself that I could. Perhaps a little for Dad too.

Several days after the holiday, Mom asks if I can get home early from Stillwater to watch Pru while she heads to an interview. It's with a local art gallery that would pay more than two of her current jobs combined. She'd be perfect for it. Thankfully, one of my friends is dating the assistant manager and allows me to slip out during a lull in the Black Friday weekend crowd.

It's not quite winter yet, but apparently, Brooklyn hasn't gotten that memo. The air feels downright arctic and hard to inhale on the walk home. Every warm breath causes me to look like a fire breathing dragon.

I pass a rolling newsstand on the street corner near our apartment and spot the front cover of this week's Word on the Street. It displays a shiny recent *Dawn Heights* cast photo with a big red X over Rowan's face. The headline reads: **ADLER IS OUT: What's next for the young star?! Is a Michael Brewer/Ashanti Nath love triangle to blame?!**

Sparklers ignite in my chest. Rowan was finally free from *Dawn Heights*. More than anything, I wished I could tell him how proud of him I was over a plate of cannoli. I hoped he would sit there and share similar thoughts about me.

Something catches my attention as I get closer to our apartment. The sky is a dull shade of dark gray, making the glistening bright red car parked in front of our building all the more noticeable. I jog towards the vehicle to see it up close, ripping the cheap wool mittens off my hands and stuffing my fingers underneath my armpits for instant warmth. There's no way this is a coincidence.

I know this car. It's my *dad's* car. The same 1970 Mustang Mom had sold months prior. Cherry red, custom interior, now sporting a New York State license plate.

"No way," I slowly mutter under my breath, a trail of hot smoke following.

I yank open the silver driver's side door handle. To my surprise, it gives. Whoever's doing this was, they clearly underestimated the questionable morality of leaving an unlocked car in the middle of Brooklyn.

The four-seated interior is a refurbished sable leather, a

custom wooden steering wheel the size of a giant serving plate sitting atop the driver's seat alongside matching dashboard trimmings. I toss my weight into the seat and run a hand along the wheel. I can almost hear my dad in the background, his deep, ever-cheerful voice telling my mom, "I told you the work would be worth it one day!"

I search the back seat and cupholders for any evidence that this was indeed his car, finally popping open the glove compartment and finding a keyring inside with a small, green Post-it note attached.

You needed this back. He worked too hard on it.

P.S. Please get your lisense, Josie.

—R

I nearly choke on my own spit, completely overlooking the egregious misspelling of the word license. I'm a split second away from crying when I look back in the glove box and see a small, white envelope tucked between the registration form and a pine-scented air freshener.

Hands shaking, I turn the envelope over and run my hand over the gold-dusted wax seal. I carefully lift the top portion and remove the contents inside. A second small Post-it slips onto the floorboard. I reach for it and read quickly. It lists a return mailing address over in California. My heart begins to beat so aggressively, I'm afraid my ribs might break.

The envelope contains several neatly folded pieces of paper containing a handwritten letter—the best way to get to know someone. I laugh like a giddy, lovesick teenager as I read the opening line and hold the letter tightly against my chest, soaking in a moment I thought would never come again.

Dearest Josephine...

ACKNOWLEDGMENTS

HOLY FREAKING CRAP. YOU GUYS, I DID THE THING! And it only took three years, twelve rewrites, a pandemic, two New York trips, so. many. tears, and at least nine-bajillion cups of coffee.

To Anna Stileski and the BTS team at Bow's Bookshelf—I can't thank you enough for taking a chance on an idiot who sends an entire manuscript instead of the first three chapters. The way you have continuously championed and believed in this story has meant the world to me. Josie and Rowan couldn't have found a better home with you. And I'm forever grateful they did.

Amber Liu—You artistic and magical unicorn of a human being! You took several random, nonconnected ideas for a cover design and made something so far beyond what I could have imagined. It takes my breath away every time I look at it. Thank you for your dedication to this project and the long, late hours it took to make the artwork perfect!

My OG beta readers, Maddy, Tiffany, Olivia, and Isabella —You saw this story in its first (and frankly, ugliest) forms. Your feedback back helped turn it into what it is. Thanks for never pulling your punches. I'm sorry the video store didn't make it. And the bookshop. And the texts. And...

The Jensen Family—Caring for your family is a treasure. Thank you for the sacrifices you've made with your time in allowing me to pursue this new adventure. MM, A, and C, I can't wait for you to grow up and read this someday. Hopefully, you'll still think I'm cool then.

Mary and Jordan Nikkel—You've not only held a torch for this story, but you also carried me in the process. I've become the human I am today because of how well you both have and will continue to love me. I pray every single character I ever create is a small reflection of that. (This is where I'd put our bananas. IF WE HAD THEM.)

Sarah Lara—For being the Ann Perkins to my Leslie Knope. Thank you for always being my loudest cheerleader. Till the end of the line, pal. And I really hope you like the book. It would be awkward if you didn't after all this.

Lauren Hickman, Hannah Roddy, Katie Milhorn, and Caitlin Lassiter—GROUP CHAT STANS FOR LIFE! Thank you for always putting up with my random celebrity rantings in the middle of a serious conversation. It paid off. I'm so glad you all still like me.

The members of the Twitter #WritingCommunity—I'll never forget how nervous I was to put myself and my work out there for the world to see, and the instant love and support you showed me in return. You believed in these characters long before you ever knew who they were. I hope they were worth the wait.

Every YA author who inspired me to write the angsty, fluffy, imperfect dream teens of my heart—You paved the road for so many of us to chase our dreams. Thank you for the stories that got me through the hard times (and by that, I mean yesterday.) May we never stop finding out who we want to be when we grow up.

Thanks to all the coffee shops in Nashville who have allowed me to sit and patronize their establishments over the years as I've sat and worked on this till my eyes burned. And simultaneously, the Nashville bakeries where I'd go immediately after to sit and cry about it.

New York City—From the subway rats to the street art, the sewer smells, and all the crowded streets in-between. This is as much a love letter to you as any of the other love letters in the story. You have my heart.

Greg and Audrey—The OG Joe and Ann. I can only hope I gave this story an ounce of the romance and charisma you gave it originally. (You're also both very much not alive and will never see this. Oh well. It's the thought that counts.)

To my family—Thank you for driving me to Borders as a kid on rainy days and leaving me there for hours so I could exist among the page smells and hot chocolate. You never understood why I did it. Does it make sense now?

Thank you, India. Thank you, providence. Thank you, disillusionment. (Someone please laugh at this.)

God—I hope my stories never stop making You smile.

To the person holding this book in their hands—Thank you for taking a chance on my words and allowing my silly little idea to become a reality. Some of you have been by my side since I was blogging my feelings on Tumblr (I'm sorry), others have been around since my fanfic days (so, so sorry). Thank you for never giving up on me, even when it sucked. You're the reason I got better.

Last, but never least... to anyone who has ever lost something. A family member, a friend, or even just yourself. I hope you find permission in these pages to dream again.

ABOUT THE AUTHOR

Sarah Ainslee has worn many hats. Nanny, barista, social media manager, and occasional band wrangler (don't ask). Through it all, "writer" is the only title that has ever stuck. Telling stories is what she always comes back to.

She's a YA contemporary author with a penchant for awkward encounters and whimsical adventures—a dash of romance never hurts either. She writes stories for the teenager inside all of us who still doesn't know what they want to be when they grow up.

Sarah currently resides in Nashville, Tennessee. When she's not writing, you can catch her hunkered down at a coffee shop, sharing every in-depth thought about her love of superheroes and romcoms over on her Instagram.

twitter.com/sarahisawriter

instagram.com/sarahisawriter

CPSIA information can be obtained
at www.ICGtesting.com
Printed in the USA
JSHW020148080423
40104JS00002B/98